LOISAIDA

A Novel

Dan Chodorkoff

Fomite
Burlington, Vermont

ISBN-13: 978-0-9832063-2-3

Fomite
58 Peru Street
Burlington, VT 05401
www.fomitepress.com
Cover photo copyright © 2011 by Dan Chodorkoff
Cover design by Uli Belenky
Author photograph by Andrew Kline

For Betsy, her love and support made this book possible.

Chapter 1

The East River is not really a river at all. It is a tidal strait, part of the larger Hudson River estuary, a wash that runs from Upper New York Bay to Long Island Sound. The estuary is where life emerged out of the ancient ocean, where species mutate and change is born; the womb, mother of all, bearer, maker; container of boundless life burrowing in her mud, birth and death endlessly cycling through her depths, expressing the powers of sun, earth, stone, water, and ice. It is fecund beyond measure, the edge, where the Laurentide glacier ended and salt water and fresh water merge, the margin between land and ocean.

Silver shadows shine just below the dark surface, teeming by the billions, reaching for the sea, newly hatched and defenseless against gulls, terns, and cormorants, but trusting to the beneficent, mindless rhythm, answering only to the moon drawing them inexorably outward and upward, east to even greater mysteries and vastness beyond knowing.

The one means nothing here, caught in the midst of the many. The small flicker for survival; a reflex, an instinct, their greatest hope anonymity. And the big devour the small in an ancient choreography; a cycle, a meditation, a moment without despair or malice. All part of the whole and connected, indelibly marked by a web of discourse beyond language.

On the shore stands a city full of people, born of the estuary, but distinct; remaking the world in its image yet still connected to the larger cycles that make everything possible: Nitrogen, oxygen, carbon dioxide; still bound to the tides, the sun, the moon, and the soil by the ancient web, growing ever more fragile. Here, too, change is born, but here the one matters, struggling for solace, recognition, connection; redemption their highest aspiration.

"The garden! Damn it Mike, they can't take the garden!" The wind off the river rattled the window of Catherine's small room. "I don't believe it." She threw down the Metro section of the *Times*. "Fifty million dollars! Five hundred units, all for the yuppies!"

Mike, his voice heavy with sleep, poked his head over the edge of the loft. "What?"

"The garden! They're going to tear up the garden and build apartments! Where do they expect us to go?"

"They don't care. They'd just as soon we ended up in the East River."

"That doesn't help, Michael." She glared at him. "I'm serious." She fussed with a strand of hair that had escaped from under her beret.

"Money talks, bullshit walks"

"Mike! Come on."

"Well, what are you gonna do? Write graffiti? Oh yeah, that'll stop them for sure."

"Michael!"

"Don't be pissed at me. It's not my fault."

"I'm not pissed at you, but if you don't start taking this seriously... I mean, Dude, it's the garden! Doesn't that matter to you? All the great times we had? I mean, like, how can you be so laid back? What does it take to get you going?"

"Why are you so uptight about it?"

"Uptight? I'm not uptight, I'm angry. There's a big difference."

"Oh yeah, what's the difference?"

"Duh! The difference is, uptight is you; just uncomfortable, but not enough to do anything. Angry means I'm ready to do something. I'm gonna do something…"

"What? You're going to stop the City? Come on Cathy, get real."

She was on her feet now, pacing back and forth beneath the bare light bulb that swung gently in the draft from the window. "Mike! High rise towers? We need the garden. Why not fix up the abandoned buildings? I'm not just gonna sit back and let them take it away. We'll organize. We can use the paper to get the word out. I've been working on a story about the garden anyway."

"Great." Mike rolled his eyes.

"Now you are starting to piss me off. What, you think we should just let them have it? Oh, that's right, you're Mr. Mellow. 'Don't worry, it'll be cool.' Well I don't think so, Dude. They can't just take the garden!"

"Oh, you're gonna fight the city?"

"Yeah, and I'll stop 'em!"

"You, and who else?"

"Me, myself, and I, and I bet there are lots of other people in the neighborhood who feel the same, if you won't get off your ass to help."

"You really are the patron saint of lost causes."

"Fuck you Michael!" The article in the paper was the last straw. Everything was falling apart; Con Ed was hassling them, her job sucked, and now this. She pulled on her leather jacket.

"Where you goin'?"

"Out!" She scowled at him over her shoulder as she walked toward the front room.

"Obviously. Out where?"

"To the *Avalanche!*" She slammed the door behind her and took the dilapidated stairs two at a time.

Catherine shivered, pummeled by a blast of cold air when she stepped out onto Avenue D. She turned up the collar on her jacket and walked toward the park, a gust of wind at her back hurried her on her way. She walked down 9ᵗʰ Street, a gray ribbon that unfurled straight before her for two blocks to its brown terminus at Tompkins Square Park. Why was Mike being such an asshole?

There was a crew of dealers who worked out of the corner bodega with empty shelves, trolling the block for customers. They wore down parkas, North Face, with wool caps pulled over their ears against the cold. She walked through them with her head down and her eyes focused on the sidewalk, ignoring their muttered offers of "rocks" and "the really good shit."

She strode toward a vacant lot where a building stood just a few days before. It had collapsed; another neighborhood victim of neglect and abuse, and its death had filled the lot with a small mountain of bricks. People's lives were still visible in the rubble. A high-heeled shoe, red satin peeling, stuck out of the pile; a baby doll with a crushed head lay on the ground next to pieces of an old kitchen range.

She stopped for a moment to stare. Three men swaddled in tattered layers were in the lot poking around for anything of value that had survived the building's collapse. Their shopping cart held a few dented pots and pans, some old books and a broken lamp. The lot seemed to be oozing cold, and she shivered again as she walked by. Sometimes she really hated Mike. What did he mean, "patron saint of lost causes"? How could he just write off the garden like that?

Despite the weather, two young Latino men lingered outside the graffiti-filled storefront of a social club, smoking cigarettes and drinking from cans of Budweiser. Sounds of salsa exploded when the door of the club opened onto the street and for a moment the rhythm made her want to dance, until the sullen stares of the young men brought her back down to earth.

She was used to being stared at. Beneath her battered old motorcycle jacket with the turned-up collar a shapeless black sweater hung almost to her knees, purple tights and a pair of black paratrooper boots completed her outfit. Her hair, cut to frame her thin face and today the same shade of purple as her tights, stuck out from under a black beret that sat at a jaunty angle, drawing attention to high cheekbones, large gray eyes, and full lips. A gold ring pierced her nose and another, her eyebrow.

Catherine ignored the men's looks and kept walking. She passed a *botánica*, its window full of reds, blues and yellows -- religious statuary, bright bottles of herbal tinctures, and hanging bundles of dried herbs. Scented candles burned behind the glass, and Catherine could smell their perfume. She had always wanted to go into the little shop, walked by it nearly every day. But she never did, fearful of violating some unspoken Puerto Rican taboo. She and Mike had been fighting for weeks. Why was everything so hard?

The wind rattled the lids on the trashcans that lined the street. On a tenement, its windows and doors sealed by plywood sheets bearing the stenciled message "Keep

Out", a remnant of yellow tape, "Police Line: Do Not Cross", hung from the cast iron banister of the buildings entry, flapping in the breeze freshening off the river. Outlined on the steps in yellow chalk was the shape of a person, a grim reminder that, as the fresh graffiti on the plywood proclaimed, "Crack Rules."

A player ran out of time last week -- Willy, a member of the street corner crew Catherine had just passed. She could only guess who put the 9mm slug into his head, splattering his brains on the steps of the abandoned building. An irate customer perhaps; a distributor who thought he was holding out; maybe a runner or a lookout who wanted to move up in the organization; or it might have been a rip-off by another dealer, or a turf battle. She would never know.

The cops had stopped looking by now. They would just as soon let the crack dealers kill each other off. Catherine averted her eyes as she walked by the reddish-brown stain on the bluestone stair treads. Why was Mike always putting her down, making her feel like a little girl? She was fucking seventeen.

A man came toward her, looking crazy, and shouting at her in Spanish. She recoiled momentarily and then stepped around him. What did he want? He was an old man, with three or four day's growth of beard covering his blotchy face. She had noticed him before, shuffling through the streets of the neighborhood day after day. It looked like there was a pint of Old Duke riding in the pocket of his dirty khaki trousers. A common wino at first glance, one of many who slept on the stoops and dozed in the sun on Tompkins Square Park's wrought iron benches. But his eyes set him apart. Instead of being dull and yellowed, they were dark and shining, and drew her into his grizzled face. And in his back pocket, flush against his sagging buttocks, rode not a bottle, but a notebook.

He wore a metal helmet, maybe surplus from some war. He had painted it blue, the color of the sky on a clear day, and in white lettering had written, "*El Árbol Que Habla*," His name was Enrique Langdon, and whenever he could engage the interest of a passerby, like Catherine, even for a moment, he recited a poem.

Catherine didn't get it. What did he want? What was he shouting? Those bright eyes staring at her, and all that passion in his voice. Kind of spooky.

She passed by the next storefront down, a gallery, one of several that had opened on the block early in the eighties, a few years before Catherine had moved to the neighborhood. One night in the fall when she had passed by, an opening had been in full swing there. A limo disgorged guests, a jazz quartet played in the gallery, and the party spilled out onto the sidewalk, the guests sipping wine from plastic goblets, laughing among the tenements and the abandoned buildings. A group of them sat on the stairway where the yellow chalk outline now served as a memorial to the murdered crack dealer.

Neon constructions exploded in the gallery window; pinks, greens, and oranges mocking the grayness of the day and the neighborhood.

"Too commercial", Mike had sneered when they had first strolled together along 9ᵗʰ Street, on a warm Saturday afternoon last spring. "It's already just like Soho or 57ᵗʰ St. down here." He was an artist, but she watched the shows come and go herself, made up her own mind, and sure enough, found little that appealed to her.

Catherine stopped and glanced at the window. She questioned almost everything she experienced. She was always on the outside, observing, and never liking what she saw enough to become a part of it, at least not until she had started hanging out on the Lower East Side. In eighth grade she had decided that the life of a suburban princess was not for her. Drugs, sex and rock and roll: they all led straight to the Lower East Side. It was dangerous, it was erotic, and it was not Scarsdale. She started coming down on weekends, and on days when she and her friends cut school. They poked around the shops on St. Marks Place and Avenue A, and on nice days, they would hang out in Tompkins Square.

She was bored by MTV and in constant battles with her parents. She shut herself in her room and spent hours listening to the tapes she searched out on her forays into the Lower East Side. The music spoke to her; feelings and ideas that she could never explain to them. She wrote it all in her 'zine, but she never let them see it. She was cynical, angry, and fed up with the hypocrisy she saw all around her.

The Lower East Side was a magnet for her and others like her, the place to be. It promised adventure and excitement; a romantic bohemia where she could escape the boredom and hopelessness of her life in the suburbs; it was a place to find something essential that was missing in Scarsdale.

In the Park and on the Avenue she found kids she liked: kids who felt the way she did, were into the same bands, and had a kind of "fuck you" attitude toward the world. They called themselves anarchists, but it was more of a feeling than anything else. At first, it just meant freedom to her: freedom not to be who she was expected to be, but to define herself on her own terms. Her parents didn't get it; they freaked out and sent her to a shrink. ODD, Oppositional Defiance Disorder, he told her parents. She had laughed.

The garden -- the cause of her current anger, the spot where they hung out in the warmer weather -- was just ahead. A sign, done in graffiti style, read "*El Jardin*," but they just called it the garden. The large vacant lot had been turned into a vest-pocket park years earlier, long before she had moved to the neighborhood, with a few cast iron benches and an amphitheater built into a hill made of rubble. Willow trees shaded a small lawn in the summer. The sides of the surrounding buildings, some occupied and some abandoned, were covered with brightly colored murals.

It was their patch of green in the gray of the city. When it was warm enough there was always something happening there. It was where she and Mike first hooked up, sharing a joint in a circle with Raven and the others while some Billy Idol wanna-be strummed his guitar. Didn't any of that matter to Mike?

El Jardin was empty today, except for a young Puerto Rican couple pushing a blue baby stroller and an older child riding around on a plastic tricycle with a giant front wheel. The baby was crying; the kid on the bike was screaming with excitement. They looked cold.

It was the heart of the scene for her and her friends; their spot in an often hostile neighborhood. No way the City was going to take it away from them. No fucking way!

Catherine paused in front of the gate to the garden for a moment, then she swallowed hard and crossed Avenue C, walking faster. The paper must be off the press by now, waiting in the basement office, where the glow of the computer screen would hypnotize her as she entered words, where she might lose all track of time, and some nights, without knowing it, would work past dawn, coming out of the basement into the shock of daylight.

Catherine gazed over her shoulder for a last, lingering look at the garden as she approached a four-story town house. It had a fresh coat of tan paint and eggplant trim that highlighted the building's marble columns topped with gargoyles. The massive oak door had shiny brass hardware. Window boxes with minia-ture boxwood hedges hung from the second floor. The house looked like it belonged in a fancier neigh-borhood, Greenwich Village or Gramercy Park. "Yup-pie scum," muttered Catherine under her breath as she walked past.

A church stood next to a tenement that seemed to overflow with crying children and their screaming mothers. Outside the church was a hand-painted sign that read, "Free lunch-Mon.-Sat. 12P.M." Though not quite eleven, there was a line that extended down the block, and around the corner opposite Tompkins Square; all kinds of people, all standing quietly.

It was hard for her to walk by them, to see their faces. A black man stood there staring at the ground, a troubled crease in his forehead. A skinny white girl Catherine had seen turning tricks over on Third Ave-nue also waited patiently. Her right leg was encrusted in a grimy cast, and a quietly sobbing three year old boy dangled from one of the girl's crutches. Catherine pulled down her beret and crossed the street to the north side. Tears welled up in her eyes. She still hadn't learned to selectively inattend to the suffering around her, an urban survival skill too easily acquired by most. Her back stiffened when she thought about the injus-tice of it all.

She saw the storefront offices of Action for Hous-ing and stopped to look in the window at a artist's glossy rendering of the three high-rise towers they planned to build in the garden. Catherine imagined a bulldozer tearing up the grass and uprooting the willows, the amphitheater crushed by its treads. She flushed, tightened her fist, and blood pounded in her temple. The interior of the office was dark, no sign of life. She looked up and down the block. No one was watching her, there was no one around except the people on line for the church soup kitchen, and they wouldn't care. Catherine unsnapped the top pocket of her motorcycle jacket, pulled out a black felt marker, and wrote "Poverty Pimps Out" in bold script under the storefront's window. She would show them, and Mike too.

She stormed away from the office, cruising by a large, dingy building that was once the neighborhood's elementary school, and now housed *La Cabaña* Community Center. She and Mike had gone to some events there; an exhibit of work by some local artists, a performance by the Lower East Side Puppet Theater in the basement auditorium, and once or twice to the films that they showed last summer. But she really didn't know what else went on there. It was a huge building and there were always lots of people going in and out. Most of them were Puerto Ricans. She wished that she spoke Spanish or something; their lives were a mystery to her. She saw them coming and going at the community center, and they looked like they belonged there. She envied them that sense of belonging. It was as though they lived in a parallel universe, not really touching her own.

On the corner of Avenue B, directly across from Tompkins Square Park, she stood in front of the Christadora House, waiting for an opening in the traffic. She watched as a husky black guy wearing a blue uniform and hat trimmed with gold braid, swung open the entrance for a young woman in a fur coat. Catherine glared at her, and the fur-clad woman got the message, averting her eyes and walking a little faster toward the waiting B.M.W. Catherine laughed to herself. But she was bothered by some vague memory of the woman's face and, after a moment, thought that maybe they had gone to the same high school, though the girl in the fur would have had to have been a few years ahead of her. She turned a scornful eye toward the departing car.

A triplex apartment with a rooftop garden in the Christadora had been featured in the *Sunday Times* style section a few months earlier. It was rumored in the neighborhood that the apartment had sold for over a million and a half dollars. A million and a half bucks, and they looked out their window at the church soup kitchen, the crackheads and junkies, and the abandoned buildings that still lined the block. Catherine shook her head.

At the eastern entrance to Tompkins Square a group of black and Hispanic men huddled around a fifty-five-gallon drum that held a blazing fire, listening to someone rapping out of a boom box. Catherine wanted to stop and warm herself there, but she knew it was a bad idea, instead she walked across the almost deserted park, rubbing her gloveless hands together to ward off the cold. A police car cruised slowly past the restrooms and entrance to the kiddy pool, closed for the season. Bare trees blended with brown grass and the bleakness of the city. The wind whipped a discarded newspaper around her feet. The scene was very different from her memory of the same promenade in the summer under a canopy of green leaves, the walkway dappled with sunlight.

A cold gust of wind brought her back to reality as she watched two bearded men pass a bottle encased in a brown paper bag between them. Not great weather to be homeless. She was thankful for her squat, as funky as it might be. At least it was warm and dry.

Catherine exited through the gates on the park's West side and waited for the light to change. Horns were honking, and an ambulance was trying to make its way across the intersection with its siren shrieking at the indifferent drivers. It seemed like an eternity before the traffic signal turned green and she flew across the avenue, heading for the basement office of *The Avalanche*. She could read the huge headline posted on the door all the way from the corner of 9th Street; "Lower East Side Shining Path Declares Class War!"

Chapter 2

She bolted down the steps and entered the narrow basement room. The office held three green metal desks, each covered with piles of paper and littered with the accumulated detritus of a hundred late nights; paper cups, empty pizza boxes, crumpled candy wrappers, and an ashtray full of cigarette butts and half-smoked joints. The floor was carpeted with the overflow from the desks. Against the far wall stood a folding table that held a computer, a laser printer, and the offset press,. The room smelled of fresh ink and newsprint. She pulled off her jacket and took a deep breath.

"Hey Cathy, what's up? What do you think? You like it?" Raven asked, leaning back in an office chair with his black cowboy boots propped up on a desk, a cigarette dangling from his right hand. In his forties, he had a long thin face with a prominent nose, dark eyes, and a mop of black curly hair that was turning gray and thinning on top. "It's our best issue ever," he enthused, without giving her a chance to reply. "Hardest hitting yet. They can't ignore us now. "Shining Path Declares Class War!" They'll see it painted on every wall from 14th Street to Houston before the week's over. Brilliant, if I do say so myself." He flashed a smile and flicked his ashes onto the floor.

"It looks good, Raven, pretty good." She thumbed through a copy of the tabloid. All of her work -- the late nights captive to the glow of the computer screen; the office waiting like a silent lover to embrace her, calling to her every night after the restaurant closed -- it was all worth it. The tabloid, with its screaming headlines and wild graphics, gave them a voice, told their side of the story. The paper had some problems, but despite them she felt a part of something important, maybe for the first time.

"Yea, we're really getin' to them," Raven, still beaming, took another drag from his cigarette.

"Oh yea, we're really getting to them," she shook her head. "Haven't you heard about the garden?"

"What about it?" He took his feet off the desk and leaned forward in his chair.

"Dude, they're gonna build high-rise apartments there."

He exhaled a cloud of smoke. "Who is?"

"The City, and those developers over at Action for Housing." Catherine brushed a strand of hair out of her eyes.

"The hell they are!" Raven wrinkled his brow and crushed out his cigarette on the cluttered desktop.

"It was in the paper, Dude, an article on the front page of the metro section."

"No shit?" Raven, on his feet now, prowled back and forth between two desks. "Those fuckers. They better watch their backs. The Shining Path..."

"Oh, come on Raven; don't start believing your own headlines. There's no Lower East Side Shining Path."

"Fuck you, Cathy. Who says there isn't? Anyway, there will be."

They'd had this argument before, when Raven came up with the Shining Path headline. She was against it; too violent. But Raven had insisted, and bullied her and the others to see things his way, as he usually did. His headline referred to the neighborhood's battle over gentrification, a very real struggle. But despite Raven's wishful thinking, there really was no Shining Path. While he claimed to be an anarchist, Catherine remained unconvinced about the political wisdom of his strategy, though she had to admit that it really did make for an attention-getting front page.

Raven was off on a tirade now, all things she had heard from him at least a hundred times before. She barely listened. "I'm telling you, Cathy, it's class war. The Shining Path is the vanguard of the mass struggle, an agent of the people's revenge. I mean it, after the revolution we'll line 'em up against the wall and..." The rhetoric spewed forth; she blocked out his words and focused on his face. He was flushed bright red, his eyes practically popping out of their sockets, and a

18

vein in his forehead pounded out a heavy metal beat, while his voice rose until he was shouting at her. In the beginning she had been impressed by Raven's rage. But now she almost felt sorry for him.

"Yo, Cathy." Raven broke through her reverie. "I got an idea. Let's go out and write some graffiti tonight. See if we can't get something started. It'll be fun. Like the old days. Come on. I'll buy you an egg cream afterwards."

Despite herself, she smiled at his offer, but then shook her head. "I'm working, and if I blow them off again, they'll fire me for sure." She looked down at her nails and began to chip away at the remnants of her black polish. "Sorry, but we've got to eat."

"Why you stick with that dumb-ass job is a mystery to me," Raven was still prowling the room. "How come you don't just dumpster-dive like everybody else?"

Catherine shuddered. Scarsdale wasn't that far behind her yet. Who was Raven to lay a guilt trip on her anyhow? Judging by the debris on his desk, he lived on pizza, candy bars, beer, and coffee. She was the one who was there every night typing and laying out the paper. He just hung around the office drinking coffee and smoking pot. Super militant at demonstrations, he would grab his black flag and run to the front of any march so that it looked like he was leading it, and he was always the loudest one at Community Board meetings. But he really didn't do too much else.

Raven's apocalyptic revolutionary vision was expressed primarily with a can of spray paint. His graffiti covered the neighborhood, mostly the letter A in a circle. He also claimed to have introduced some popular slogans, including "Die Yuppie Scum," but Catherine doubted it. He considered himself something of a literary figure and was sure that his inspired "Lower East Side Shining Path Declares Class War" would raise his stature to new heights. Raven had already begun his campaign on the walls and storefronts along Avenue C. And he had noted with satisfaction just the night before that someone else had written it on the door of the men's room at ABC's, a local club that he frequented.

He was there in the *Avalanche* office because he owned the building. Raven, listed on the paper's masthead as publisher, bankrolled the purchase of the computer equipment and the old press with money that came from dealing pot in the park. He had created a little kingdom where he was lord and master, and kept it afloat with the profits from his dime bag business. The street urchins who crashed in his building were his sales force. He suggested an occasional idea for a story and liked to write headlines. Beyond that, he generally just hung around the office. The rest of the collective had come to view him as a pain in the ass, but a necessary pain; he had money and connections.

"Well, I'm goin' out tonight. We gotta keep the pressure on, keep them out of the neighborhood, save the garden, or it's all over. Class war. That's what it's all about. Why the fuck don't people see it? I'll trash the Community Board meeting if they try to vote on it. I can get a dozen people there with one phone call. This shit ain't gonna fly."

At least Raven is ready to fight, thought Catherine. She looked up from her nails. "Right, keep the pressure on, if they'll even let you into the meeting, after last time."

She was sorry that she had brought it up when Raven snapped back "Oh yeah. Let 'em try to keep me out. They can't fuck with me, I know my rights. I'll get my lawyer down there before they can turn around. Oh, I'll be at the meeting, don't worry about that! They can't censor the press. It's in the Bill of Rights." Raven, no matter what else he was, was an ardent defender of his civil liberties.

He had been a celebrity in the movement briefly in the late sixties when he had thrown a pie in the face of the Secretary of State, who was giving a speech at Columbia. Raven had argued that his pie attack was an expression of his First Amendment rights. Catherine had been impressed when she first met him; he was practically a legend.

He had bought the run-down building that housed the paper's office years ago for almost nothing. His living quarters were upstairs, a multi-floor rabbit warren, cluttered with the debris of decades of hard living; stacks of old newspapers lined the walls of the living room, where parts from two or three ten-speed bikes had been scattered on a filthy shag carpet. The kitchen sink was piled high with dirt-encrusted pots and pans. On the upper floors, a series of cramped bedrooms off central hallways held stained mattresses on their floors. The outside world was only a dim shadow when viewed through the grimy windows that should have served to bring daylight into the front rooms, and the whole house smelled of cat piss. It served as a crash pad for kids who hung out in the park and the garden.

Catherine had stayed there when she first touched down in the neighborhood. But she was no poser, no weekend warrior, like some of the kids she'd met there. She had been cutting school and hanging around in the park for a while. By the time she was sixteen, it had become a regular routine with her. And that summer she stopped going home for days at a time, crashing at Raven's place. It drove her parents crazy, and she liked that.

In fact, she liked what it did to her parents even more than she liked the reality of crashing on Raven's floor. It was filthy there. Once, a rat ran across her face while she was sleeping. Maybe it was only a mouse, but it freaked her out anyway. And Raven was a pig. He kept hitting on her even though he was almost three times her age. But that didn't bother her. At least not enough to send her scurrying back to the 'burbs like some of the other kids, whom she viewed with contempt. She was no suburban princess and would prove it to them all.

Eventually, after Raven tried to crawl into her sleeping bag one night, she had moved out. He was disgusting. She later learned that it was his practice with every woman who stayed there. He left her alone now, concentrating his energies on more willing victims. It seemed to her, though, that he was always particularly quick to condemn one of her ideas or to dis her. Still, it was a small price to pay to be part of something as important as *The Avalanche*.

She smiled as she thumbed through the paper. Twelve pages, printed on newsprint, a jumble of text, photos, and drawings. The paper was a visual assault; it got your attention. They planned to bring it out every month, but this was only their third issue in almost a year. They sold it on street corners and at neighborhood bookshops and newsstands, printing around 2000 copies. Last time, they had ended up with almost half of them baled up, still sitting in a corner of the office.

The work was done by a core group of four; Catherine, her boyfriend Mike, Paula, and Josh. They knew each other from the garden, ABC's, and the park. The paper had been their idea, and Raven had ponyed up.

He was in fine form now, strutting back and forth with clenched fists. "We gotta stop 'em. You know, we ought to start shootin' landlords and developers! At least beat a few of 'em up, make 'em think twice about coming down here. Propaganda by the deed." The threat of violence always bubbled just beneath the surface with Raven. Catherine had seen him in several fistfights, always with kids a lot younger than he was; the type of people he surrounded himself with. Raven never worried about other people's feelings, which gave him a certain kind of power.

They did have to do something, but she doubted that violence would help. Catherine felt her stomach start to do flip-flops. She wanted to run away. Raven intimidated her, even though she realized that he was a jerk.

When he finally stopped Catherine tried to change the subject. "I have an idea for an article. Did you know the garden was started by the guys who run *La Cabaña*, that community center?"

"Those guys?" The vein in his forehead started pounding again as his face turned red. "That's Chico Santiago, that sellout. We're not printing anything that gives him credit for shit."

"But Raven! That's the history. I just wanna give some background. Like, they started out as squatters, you know."

"Fuck that!" he screamed, pounding a fist into his open palm. "I'm the publisher! What I say goes! If you don't like it, get the fuck off my paper!"

Catherine recoiled and stared at him, wide-eyed, but he turned away and lit another cigarette. They always made editorial decisions collectively. While Raven bullied them, and usually got his way, she had never heard him invoke his authority before. He was publisher in name only; they had let him take the title to satisfy his ego.

She knew him well enough to realize that it was pointless to try to argue when he was so enraged. Still, she was shaken. First the garden and now this! Everything was turning to shit. She tried to think of a snappy rejoinder, but in the end, she simply pulled on her jacket, grabbed a couple of copies of the paper, and, with a sinking feeling in the pit of her stomach, walked out of the office and headed uptown.

Chapter 3

A Puerto Rican man stood in front of the door of *La Cabaña* Community Center. He glanced around, then entered the old elementary school. He was a big man, tall and solid. His black hair was pulled back tightly into a ponytail, and dark eyes flashed beneath heavy brows and a broad forehead; the sharp, chiseled features of his Taino Indian ancestors. While not handsome in a conventional way, his was a face people did not soon forget. His name was Carlos Santiago, but he was known in the neighborhood as Chico.

He walked into the open lobby. White walls were hung with large canvasses; tropical hues; pastel greens, blues and pinks, the work of a neighborhood artist. The building had come a long way in fifteen years, no more graffiti-painted walls, peeling plaster, or mounds of garbage. Everyone had said that it was too big a job for them, everyone but Chico.

At first the city fought them, sending in cops. The housing department put a padlock on the door of the abandoned school; that night he and the others returned, and clipped the lock. The Housing Police came back the next day. It went on like that for a week or so. Then one day the cops were met by a crowd of about 300 people carrying signs and raising clenched fists in the air. They backed off after that. Chico's group had squatted in the school building ever since, fixing it up little by little; using whatever they could to keep things going.

They did a lot there now; after-school programs and tutoring; basketball in the old gym; and their cultural and arts programs - poetry, folkloric dancing, theater, music, art exhibits, and a film series.

Chico and a crew of young bloods had plastered the neighborhood with xeroxed posters calling for the meeting tonight. The first few folks came into the lobby, from the block association. "Hey, *cómo estas?* Thanks for coming." People trickled into the basement auditorium in ones and twos. When 7:30 came around the hall held almost a hundred; mostly people he knew, but a few others.

Down front was a guy with a shaved head and a black leather jacket who hung around in *El Jardín*. A tall young girl with purple hair who he had noticed walking on the block just yesterday was sitting in the fifth row, near the neatly dressed man who bought the town house across the street.

Chico walked to the lectern. The room had a musty smell, and with the lights on, he could see the green paint starting to peel from the walls. His family had come to the Lower East Side when he was eight years old, speaking no English. He remembered the kosher butchers and delicatessens giving way to *bodegas* and *botánicas* along Avenue C. His father had pushed a hand truck in the garment district and his mother worked in a plastic factory in Brooklyn. He was terrified, humiliated, and later bored almost to death, in this very auditorium. He left school in the ninth grade without knowing how to read or write.

Chico half expected to hear a bell ring, calling the assembly to order. The seats, bolted to the floor in tidy rows, were small, and the adults who filled them sat with their knees close to their chins, chattering among themselves, like anxious children.

"Listen up!" Chico banged an empty water glass on the lectern to get their attention. "Let's get started. Thanks for coming. You know why we're here; to talk about the housing project they want to build in *El Jardín*. We got to make a decision before the city decides for us. Tonight we can speak our minds. Everybody will have a chance to talk, ask questions. If we don't have answers, we'll find them out. Then we figure out what we want to do next. This isn't the Community Board, no 'official members', everybody here gets to vote. Doesn't mean the City's gonna listen, probably not. Any questions?"

No one spoke at first. Finally, a young Puerto Rican man with a pencil mustache stood up in the second row. "What's the deal, Chico? I mean what's the problem, man? We been waiting a long time for housing down here. They're finally gonna build it and some of you people want to stop them? I can't see that. We need the housing. It's for poor people and that's that. Anyway, that's how I see it."

A dozen voices suddenly filled the auditorium. "Hold it! Hold it!" Chico boomed out over the hubbub. "Raise your hands. Talk one at a time. Don't worry, everybody will have a turn." He pointed to a middle-aged woman with curly hair in the first row waving a white handkerchief, Luce Guerra; he knew her from the block association.

She stood "Sure, it's true, we need housing, but we also need gardens. Why can't they build on another lot, one filled with garbage, and leave *El Jardin* for the community? That's what I want to know."

"What community?" A women in back rose. "I can't even let my kids play over there no more. It's all full of people with green hair and winos. They always takin' pot and actin' crazy over there. I think we do much better with the housing." The crowd applauded and the women who had spoken sat back down.

"Wait a minute!" The guy with a shaved head, rings through his eyebrow, and a gold stud in his tongue jumped up. "We live in the neighborhood too. We got a right to hang out. It's a people's park. We don't do no hard drugs in there, and everybody needs some place they can party. Don't dis us. We got a stake here too!"

"Sit down!" "Fuck you, asshole!" "Get out of our

neighborhood!" "Go home!" The cries rang out from all corners of the auditorium. The guy sank back into his seat.

"Listen up! Listen up! People got to be respectful, let everybody speak, and don't get loud. Take turns or this isn't gonna to work." Chico waited while the crowd calmed down. "I think it would be a good idea also if everybody said their name and where they live before they talk. That way we get to know each other a little, Okay?" People listened to Chico. He was respected; he always had been, even when he was a kid.

He had been a big boy, fearless and smart in every way but book learning. He rose through the ranks of his gang, the Dragons, fast, until at age sixteen, he became warlord; a leader, defending his neighborhood and his honor against enemies from cross-town or other sections of the Lower East Side. The gang was the only chance he had to prove that he was somebody.

"You next." He pointed to a Hispanic woman with gray hair poking out from beneath a colorful scarf.

"Yo hablo solamente en español,"

"That's okay, You go ahead and talk. I'll translate for you. *Yo voy a traducir.*"

"Her name is Maria. She says she's old and maybe what she wants isn't so important as the young people. But she remembers when we started *El Jardin*, and it was a beautiful garden, a real community place built by the people themselves. Now it's filling up with garbage again. She wonders why that is. Don't people have any pride? If we can't take care of it, maybe the city should take it away. Of course we need housing, but there are many other places to build. *El Jardin* used to be special. Why can't we make it special again? She remembers the first year when it was a garden. She grew tomatoes and peppers there. They reminded her of her own garden, in Puerto Rico, and that was so nice."

"She watched while the young bloods painted the murals one summer. She loves the murals. What will happen to the murals if they build there? She wonders why they have to build there when there are so many other lots. She doesn't want more houses there. She wants grass and trees. What will happen to the willow trees she helped plant? They're big enough to give shade, to sit under now. Will she have to start over again somewhere else? She's too old to start over. She wants to stay here." When Chico finished translating, the applause was loud and long, broken by cries of "*Vaya*" and "Speak on it, sister." She blushed crimson and sat down.

Chico remembered the start of *El Jardin* too; a crisp fall day eighteen years ago. He woke before dawn with a knot in his stomach. They had announced a workday to clean up a vacant lot on 9th Street where a kid was bitten by rats the week before. He worried that no one would come. The posters they put up promised food and entertainment, but they had been too busy trying to chill out some static between a couple of local gangs to get anything together.

He pulled on a pair of denim overalls while it was still dark and drove a battered old Volkswagen van he had borrowed down to the Fulton Street Fish Market. The market was bustling as the vendors were getting ready to close up shop for the day. "You got any damaged fish, or stock that you're going to throw away?" He managed to collect enough fish, clams, oysters and even some lobsters with broken shells to fill a large waxed cardboard box. He covered it with ice and hoisted it into the van, then headed back up the F.D.R. Drive. The sun rose over the East River, a huge red ball hanging over the spires and spider-like cables of the Brooklyn Bridge backlighting the Brooklyn skyline with a blood-red glow. He exited at Houston and drove up Avenue C to 9th Street.

His crew arrived early, too. By 7:00, there were a half a dozen of them, four men and two young women, standing in the lot near a stack of shovels and rakes and a contractor's wheelbarrow they had borrowed from the Green Guerrillas, a gardening group. Chico wondered if their plan was going to work as he stared at the pile of brick, old bedsprings mingled with discarded television sets, last year's Christmas trees, and ten years worth of trash, torn apart and spread all over by the rats that made the lot their home.

There was nothing to do but get started. So they picked up rakes and shovels and began filling the garbage bags Chico had convinced the owner of a local *bodega* to donate. Chico knew that they felt like it was hopeless. "Hey, listen up. You do good with this lot and I'll get you all jobs with sanitation, $35,000 a year and you can move to Westchester." They laughed. "Jorge, you been looking all over for this, haven't you?" He held up a tattered Raggedy Ann doll. "You know the dogs stay out of this lot. They're scared, 'cause the rats are bigger than they are." The work found a rhythm punctuated by his jokes.

He was convinced that the environment was a key to rebuilding the community. If they could make some physical order out of the mess of the decaying neighborhood, give people some space where they could relax and meet together, if they could build something that people could see, feel, and touch, it would show them that they could do for themselves. He saw it as a way to take a problem, the garbage-strewn lot, and turn it into a resource for the neighborhood.

Chico had talked a lot about his ideas with Jack Hoffman, an older white guy who lived on Fifth Street, so he was pleased when he saw him arrive and pick up a shovel, their first volunteer. Chico had heard Hoffman talk about the neighborhood as an eco-system years before.

After his time in prison, Chico was hungry for new ideas and radical alternatives. One day he picked up a book by Hoffman, *Discourse on the Ecological City*, and when Chico found out that the author lived in the neighborhood, had tracked him down. They became friends.

"Brother Jack, good to see you. Thanks for coming." Chico clapped him on the back. "Man, I was getting worried nobody would show up."

"It's only eight, Chico, still early. Give it a while. It takes time."

A few kids came over to watch what was going on, but they stayed outside the lot. A wino observed the work crew from a stoop across the street, sipping regularly from a bottle in a brown paper bag. Finally, a young family - mother, father and their ten-year-old boy - came out of a building down the block. Chico went over to greet them. "*Hola!* Welcome. Believe it or not, this is going to be a beautiful park when we're done. A place where we can all relax and your son can come to play." They picked up rakes and started working.

A few others joined them as the day warmed up. The garbage bags started to fill, but there was no other sign of progress. The pile of rubble still loomed.

At around noon Chico started a fire in a fifty-five-gallon drum. "Anybody hungry? You ready for lunch yet?" He took a few chunks of halibut from the top of the box of fish and started to grill them on an old refrigerator shelf he had placed over the fire. Chico pulled a pocketknife from his overalls and used it to turn the fish. The smell of the grilling halibut brought a few more people to the lot. Some, who had merely been onlookers, including a growing group of curious children, joined in the work. They piled bricks in one corner of the lot, scrap wood in the center, and kept

34

filling trash bags and stacking them on the sidewalk in a growing heap.

A young man with a bandanna wrapped around his head arrived with a conga drum. "*Vaya!* , Pedro." Chico shot a fist in the air from behind the grill. "You made it, comrade. Thank you, thank you." Pedro began to play. His drumming drew other *congeros* who layered their rhythms on top of his, sending a pulsing beat up and down the block. A crowd gathered, and most joined the work crew. The lot, so grim just a few hours before, began to feel festive. The block was coming to life. Chico allowed himself to smile.

The contours of the collapsed building's foundation were being slowly revealed, like an archeological dig, as patches of earth were liberated from the tons of debris that had concealed them for almost a decade. A group of teenage girls began to dance an impromptu *bomba* in one of the cleared areas. Chico stepped out from behind the grill and danced a few steps with them. By now there were dozens of people congregating in and around the lot, most of them working, at least a little.

Chico cooked and kept up his banter through the afternoon. Somebody took up a collection and returned with a keg of beer as the shadows lengthened. By sunset the lot was basically cleaned up. The brick was stacked to one side and a mountain of bagged garbage filled the sidewalk. When darkness fell the scrap wood piled in the middle of the lot fed a fire in the 55 gallon drum. The block's residents ate fish, drank beer, talked, laughed, and danced by the light of the flames, their shadows enlarged on the sides of the abandoned buildings around the lot. Chico stood before the fire, his back to the growing chill of the night.

Chico sighed and pointed to a thin white man wearing gold-rimmed glasses and a dark blue suit. "My name is John and I live here on the block. I appreciate what this woman just said, but we've got to be realistic. That lot is an eyesore. I'm sure it was very nice once, but it's a mess now, and the city is in no position to restore it. Believe me, I'm a financial analyst, and the city is broke. So, if it's a question of housing or garbage, I'm all for housing.

"Let the market decide what the best use is for the property. There's room for everybody here in Alphabet City, that's what makes it such an exciting place to live. If a developer is willing to risk his capital investing in the neighborhood, he should have a right to make a profit. If people can't afford the rents here, let them move somewhere else. That's the way the world works -- the era of socialism is over on the Lower East Side. We have a prime location here, let's make the most of it. Let's attract a better class of people to the neighborhood. That can only help all of us."

Boos and hisses punctuated his remarks, but John persisted in a closing comment. "I don't appreciate this rudeness, either. I happen to be a homeowner in this neighborhood and I have as much right to be heard as anyone else." Then he sat down.

"Die yuppie scum!" "Gentry get out!"

"Cool it people, Chill out!" Eventually the crowd calmed down, and Chico pointed to Catherine, sitting in the middle of the fifth row. She had seen a poster on a lamppost on 9th Street.

She stood. "My name is Catherine and I live in a squat down on Avenue D. Like, I'm really sick of hearing who can and who can't live in this neighborhood. Dudes, we've got to save the garden! My grandpa was born here, and my great grandma still lives here, so I am as much a part of this community as anybody in this room. Save the garden! Save the squats!"

Someone from the rear of the hall called out, "Go back to the suburbs!"

Catherine returned to her seat, shaking. She had come to the meeting to try to do something. First they'll take the garden, then they'll come after the squats, then the gentrifiers will take over the whole neighborhood. People need to help each other, hang together, otherwise it's all over. Why couldn't they see it?

Catherine was not one of those suburban mall rats who hung around Sam Goody's waiting for the latest releases to show up on the shelves. She had never felt comfortable confining herself to the tepid little world that her parents and friends from school expected her to live in. Perfect lawns and screwing the captain of the football team in the back seat of his Camero just didn't excite her. They could not stop her from doing what she wanted. And what she wanted more than anything was to not be a part of their world. Strangely enough, she did feel like she belonged on the Lower East Side, as much as she belonged anywhere.

Chico pointed to a man with flowing black hair and a full beard. "My name is Pedro and I live in Loisaida, not Alphabet City," he nodded toward the yuppie. "I am a poet and I have this to say to the young lady who just spoke. I will support the squatters. I will support them when I see Puerto Ricans living in their buildings. I will support them when I see evidence of real commitment to this community. I will support them when I see them respect my culture and support our struggles.

"It's a two- way street, you know, young lady. When you show disrespect for us by the way you abuse *El Jardin*, it is hard for us to respect you. At the same time, I think we have a common interest in keeping *El Jardin* as an artistic and cultural resource for our community. While we desperately need housing, we also need poetry -- and that is what *El Jardin* should be about. Don't ask me to choose. We need both and we must have both.

"Poetry demands decent housing. Poetry eases our hunger and increases our thirst for life, but we also need roofs that don't leak and places to warm our bodies, not just our souls. *Viva Loisaida!*" He tossed his dark mane and sat down to thunderous applause.

Viva Loisaida! It was a balmy August night, Chico

was eighteen. He and Santo, the President of the Dragons, were robbing an elderly Jewish man in the hallway of one of the co-ops on Grand Street. The man grabbed at Santo's arm, a feeble effort to resist, and Santo lunged at him with his eight-inch stiletto. Chico shouted "No!"

They were both arrested; Chico sentenced to ten years as an accessory. He served three in the state prison at Attica, where he was haunted by the vision of the old man lying in the hall with his blood draining into a growing pool on the floor.

He never wanted to hurt the man; if he had been able to, he would have stopped it. But it was too late and he kept seeing the vision. He knew something was wrong and it had to change. He had to change.

"You mean to tell me you can't read, chump? How the hell you ever gonna learn anything?" Joe Williams was a Black Panther and Chico's cellmate. "You better get serious, get some discipline. Use this time to get yourself ready. We got important work to do on the outside, but you got to be able to read. Damn, the man really fucked you around, didn't he?"

Joe taught Chico to read and write. He held political education classes in Attica with Panthers, Weathermen and Puerto Rican nationalists. "The enemy is the system, the racist, capitalist system. Brother Malcolm, Mao, Ho Chi Min, Che, they got it right. Don't be wasting your time on bullshit, on fighting your brothers. The man wants you to do that. The enemy is the system. Don't forget it!" If there was any chance Chico might forget, it ended after the riot, and the murder of Joe and fifty others by Rockefeller and the state police. No, Chico couldn't forget, and by the time he came out, he was changed.

He got off the bus from Attica and walked out of the terminal into midtown. The city looked different to him. Concrete, granite, bricks, and mortar; the system was everywhere choking out or paving over any trace of life. The streets were full of people, except they seemed like robots.

But as he walked south and east, out of midtown through Union Square and past Stuyvesant Village, he discovered pockets where lives still touched each other, where grass grew; simple things breathed life back into people, and they connected with each other and the larger, all-but-forgotten cycles that make everything possible.

He crossed 14th Street, and the vacuum was filled; the droning and emptiness gave way. Chico blinked in astonishment as the gray streets lined with gray buildings merged into the hot pinks and blues hanging from Loisaida's clotheslines. "Free space" the graffiti proclaimed. The sharp angles, the rigid geometry of the rest of the city, seemed to crumble into rubble and decay, soft edges revealed. A small tree grew through the remains of an old tenement. A white goat tethered in a building's back yard contentedly chewed the grass. Starlings chattered in an abandoned building. The neighborhood looked like it was transmuting. Like when he helped his mother in her garden back in Puerto Rico, compost overripe for turning and hot with the odor of decay; rich soil for cultivation.

He knew he had returned to his place; the margins, where change happens, where energy is transformed and new species emerge; the edge, the source, the estuary where the river meets the sea.

He felt it as he walked the streets late at night, with his hands shoved deep into the pockets of his jeans; he saw it. He had always lived as much in the what-could-be as he did in the here and now, a dreamer. But his dreams had power. They were what sustained him and they were what attracted others. People knew that Chico was there for them, because his dreams included them. Loisaida was his place, his natural habitat. He felt alive there. He could not walk through midtown or Wall Street without feeling cold and numb. He had to return to Loisaida to find the warmth.

Angela Lopez, a young woman who worked with him at the center, spoke next. "Pedro is right. We need bread and roses, art and housing. The deal is this, though. This ain't no low-income housing project. It's a smoke screen for the gentrifiers. Brother nailed it on the head when he said we need both, but we ain't gettin' neither with this deal. I bet our fuckin' councilman's makin' out like a bandit, though. Turns out he's the developer." A grumble rose from the crowd. "Everybody get it now? It's a scam, big time. What you

41

want to do about it, people? What are we gonna do about it? We got to get together, can't be fightin' each other. Got to focus on the enemy, there's lots of other places to build housing, can't let them take *El Jardin*."

"Right on!" "*Vaya!*", and "Talk about it, girlfriend!" rang through the auditorium. Chico sensed a spirit in the crowd that hadn't been there before.

Chapter 4

The doors at the rear of the hall suddenly swung open, framing Councilman José Rolón and his entourage. Rolón, clean shaven, with dark hair slicked back, was large, running to fat, but dressed in a dark blue designer suit that made him look almost svelte. His white shirt was crisp and his yellow tie held in place by a large diamond tie tack. A camel-colored overcoat draped on his shoulders, he walked into the hall as if he owned it. "I saw your poster. I thought you might like to hear from somebody who has the facts about the situation." He strutted to the front of the auditorium trailed by his camp-followers, a short black guy and a woman with curly red hair, wearing a trench coat. The councilman claimed the podium, forcing Chico to one side. Chico furrowed his brow.

"This project will be of the utmost benefit to the community." The black guy unfurled an artist's rendering. "Garden Towers will provide 500 units of new housing when completed. These state of the art residential units will be a source of pride for this community. The land is city owned, and we already have a signed agreement. Our financing is in place and we plan to begin construction in April. Any questions?" He stared out into a sea of blank, silent faces.

"Why build in the garden? There's lots of other places," Catherine finally shouted.

"Are you against low-income housing?" Rolón's eyes narrowed, staring at her. "People here have waited a long time for this, and we don't want your kind to screw it up. We're taking back our neighborhood from people like you. What gives you the right to deprive poor and working people of new housing? You have no place here. This is a neighborhood for decent, law-abiding folks. We don't need little girls with purple hair telling us what to do. The will of the people cannot be thwarted. *Viva* Garden Towers!" The hall was silent.

Catherine swallowed hard and stood. "The Garden is for the people. We're people, too. We've been pushed out of Tompkins Square, Dude. Where else can we go? We've got as much right to be here as anybody! You say you're for the people, but you're really just a poverty pimp. It's a scam, and you can't get away with it."

Rolón was seething, someone had just tagged the Action for Housing office "Poverty Pimps Out". He turned red, glaring at Catherine "A Poverty Pimp! Who the hell do you think you are? I was elected to represent the people of this neighborhood and I do! Action for Housing is undertaking this project as a public service. We need housing in our neighborhood. Why do you people think you can stand in the way? You can't stop progress! The neighborhood is changing! Anarchy is no longer acceptable on the Lower East Side! We will not be intimidated by a handful of middle-class juvenile delinquents!" He was shouting at her.

Then he turned to the crowd. "The bulldozers are coming in April. A new era of progress on the Lower East Side. I guarantee it. The project is in the pipeline. We will get Community Board approval at the next meeting. And we will not let anyone stop us from moving forward."

"If anybody has any legitimate concerns, bring them to the Community Board; that's the place to talk about this, not here. You've got no authority to make any decisions. The board has the power. Don't listen to them." He looked in Catherine's direction. "We've got enough homeless and bums without that trash coming in here and screwing things up. We refuse to be a dumping ground for the city. We've got a chance to make something of this neighborhood. We are living in the real world. Money talks! Do these people have any money? Can they build housing or get you better police protection? I don't think so." He swept his arm over the audience "Back me up on this. I can deliver. If this project doesn't go through, there will be a lot of angry people down here."

A balding, round-faced priest, identifiable by the

collar he wore under a sweater, rose. "Father Bob, St. Brigids, right across the street from Tompkins Square. The homeless need apartments, too, Mr. Rolón. They've been driven out of the park, and the police have been pushing them out of the abandoned buildings. Will your housing project help them?"

"This is housing for low and middle-income working people. This neighborhood is tired of being a dumping ground. Let the bums go somewhere else. Don't you care about your parishioners, Father? Take care of your flock; let the city worry about the bums and winos. You've been bringing them in here with your free meals and your AIDS clinic. We want to see an end to that. We're trying to clean up this neighborhood, to make it a decent place to live."

"I just wrote a letter to my good friend the Cardinal about you, and I'm sure you'll be hearing from him soon," Rolón smiled at the priest. "We want to take this neighborhood back for the decent people. You're not helping us, father. You're part of the problem."

"Jesus said to help the downtrodden and feed the hungry. That's my flock and those are the people I care for. We'll see what the Cardinal says. Meanwhile, I'll serve my parish as I see fit, and God will be my judge, not you, Councilman."

"Yea, I guess we will see, but I'd watch my back if I were you. There are wolves among the lambs. You're making a lot of enemies down here."

"Is that a threat?"

"Oh no. Just an observation, Father. Render unto Caesar and all that. You know what I mean?"

"No, you'd better tell me".

"It's better to leave politics to the politicians, Father. Now Father Brenner, who was here before you, he understood that. We got along just fine. We don't need you telling us how to run our neighborhood. Nobody elected you. You're not even from here."

"Oh, I see. Is that what your letter to the Cardinal was about?"

"As a matter of fact, it is." The councilman smiled again. "Now, back to Garden Towers." He turned from the priest "I'm asking for your support of this project. It's an important step in the upgrading of the neighborhood. We'll take a vacant lot that's become a menace to the community and put it to good use. What could be better? I'm always out there working for you, looking out for your interests. It's the community first for me. Everybody knows that."

Chico groaned, and Rolón turned toward him. "Have you got a problem with that, brother?"

Chico stepped toward Rolón. "Actually, I do have a couple of questions for you, Councilman. Like, what are rents going to be? Who's going to live there? And how much money is Action for Housing making? And don't you think you've got a little conflict of interest on this deal? I'd really like to know. We're not stupid. Give us the figures, José."

Rolón glared at him.

"This ain't about helping the community. It's about real estate. Come on, Councilman, I'm waiting for your answers. We're all waiting for your answers".

"Chico, since when are you against low-income housing? Oh, that's right! You're with the anarchists now, aren't you?"

"Come on, Councilman, that's not the issue; we're not talking about me. Answer the question. Tell us, what's in it for you?"

"The issue is, do you support low-income housing, pure and simple. Either you do or you don't. These are homes for poor and working people we're talking about. Yes, the builder will have an opportunity to make a profit. That's the American way. Do you have a problem with that? Action for Housing is a private corporation and it doesn't have to reveal anything about its finances. But that's not the point. There's a big risk involved here, investing in this neighborhood. There's got to be rewards for the risk takers. But I'm sure the brothers and sisters don't want to hear a lecture about economics. They just want to know what the plans are. Take a look at these pictures I brought. Garden Towers will be a first-rate, modern facility." Rolón pointed to the drawings that his aide held aloft.

"No, I want to know what the numbers are and how much goes into your pocket," Chico's eyes burned into him.

Rolón turned and sputtered. "You suggesting I'm doing something illegal? 'Cause if you are, I'll sue your ass so fast your head'll spin. That's libel, my man. Everything I do, everything, is perfectly legal. I got a lawyer on my staff, Chico. You understand? Don't accuse me of anything unless you can prove it or I'll haul your ass to court. Now, do you support low-income housing or not? That's the point. Do you know how long it took to put this package together? Look, if H.U.D. thinks the community isn't behind this, they'll pull out the money and do it somewhere else. Believe me, there's a dozen neighborhoods in the city that would kill for a project like this. If we pass it up, who knows how long we'll have to wait?

"And let's face it, if you want to make an omelet, you've got to break a few eggs. You lose *El Jardin*, which has been taken over by scum anyway, but you gain the housing. It's a simple cost versus benefit situation. Check it out."

Someone shouted, "We want both," and Angie cried "Bread and roses," but it sounded unconvincing in the general silence that greeted Rolón. The crowd that had seemed so full of spirit and ready to fight before Rolón's entry was subdued now; demoralized and cowed.

"Anything else?" His aide was rolling up the drawings. Rolón ignored a smattering of catcalls. They left the podium and walked to the exit, along with others, a steady stream heading out of the auditorium. Some stayed behind, mostly the core of grassroots activists who Chico knew he could depend on, as well as a few squatters and punks, including Catherine.

"Hold on! We've still got lots to talk about. What now, folks?" Chico practically pleaded from the podium. "*Qué Pasa?* Where do we go from here?"

Angie Lopez spoke up. "We can't let him get away with it. People got to know that the man's making out like a bandit. We've got to get the facts out. He sidestepped all the real questions. He's a good actor; Rolón's slick. But he ain't gonna get over on us. We'll fight him at the Community Board."

"He controls the Community Board. We've got to protest." Catherine's voice rose.

"Sure, let's protest. Only a protest won't stop them, not even a riot. They'll come in with more cops than we have protesters." There had to be a way out, but Chico couldn't see it yet.

Chapter 5

The old woman sat on the nursing home bed, supporting herself upright with one arm, staring out her window at the river flowing north from the harbor, following an eastward bulge. The tide was coming in. She could see three bridges reaching toward the far shore, Brooklyn.

"Hi, Grandma," said Catherine as she walked into the tiny room. With some difficulty, the old woman turned to greet her, looking through clouded gray eyes deeply set in a wrinkled face.

"So you're here, darling," a smile illuminated the old woman. "Come, let me look on you." She had a trace of a Yiddish accent. "I have very few visitors these days. Your father, he comes once a month. But it's all right, I understand; he has his own life to lead. At my age you come to accept."

"Well, I'm just glad to see you Grandma. I live in the neighborhood now, so I'll try to visit more. We anarchists have to stick together."

Sonia adjusted the thick, white braid that hung down her back. "Anarchists?" she tilted her head and looked at Catherine. "Yes , I suppose we do." The old woman sighed again. "There's no one left but me. Ninety-three years. It was different when Sam was still around or before Abe died, but now … I outlived them all." She frowned and furrowed her brow.

Catherine, who was the old woman's great-granddaughter, settled into a worn armchair facing the bed. "Don't get upset, Grandma. Like, I wouldn't have come if I'd known it was going to upset you. I'm sorry I haven't been by sooner, but I've been busy. Anyway, it's great to see you. You look wonderful."

"I'm not upset. And if I was, it's all right. I'm a person who feels deeply; it's my nature. That's what they always said. 'Sonia, she's emotional. She wears her heart on her sleeve; she never holds back, speaks her mind.' And you want to know something, darling, I always did. I always spoke my mind. The bosses could never intimidate me. Oh, it cost me plenty jobs." A hint of a smile played across her face. "No one is left who even remembers what we stood for, how we had to fight in the beginning. Now there's nobody to carry it on."

"I'm here, grandma. I'm a fighter," offered Catherine. She rose from her armchair and embraced the frail figure on the bed. Sonia turned to look more closely at her great-granddaughter. Catherine's large, almond-shaped eyes made her seem vulnerable, and Sonia searched her face for some trace of the resolve one needs to be a fighter. There was something determined in the set of Catherine's jaw, and the old woman dropped her gaze, pleased with what she saw.

"Yes, darling, you're still here. I'm proud of you, darling. You're a good girl." She squeezed Catherine's hand. "Oh, yes -- we were always the most militant. The socialists and the liberals, they appreciated us for that. We were the ones there on the picket lines, the first to try and organize a new shop. And now I'm the only one left. The union?" she snorted, "the union is run by bureaucrats, all lawyers. No fighting spirit! And even the rank and file - all they care about now are wages and job security. No vision of a better world, no call for revolution. Nothing!"

"But Grandma, I'm still for all that. Like, revolution, a better world. that's what I'm all about."

"So your father tells me." The old woman smiled. "We have lots to talk about."

"I'd love that. Like, I mean, I knew you were in the union, but I guess I don't really know much else about your life at all. Nobody ever told me."

"So I'll tell. I want you should know. Have you seen my pictures? Open the drawer in the stand. Take them out, I'll show you."

Catherine opened the top drawer in the bedside end table and brought out a worn, black leatherette photo album with yellowed pages. "I think I might have seen it once when I was little, Grandma, back when you and Grandpa Sam lived at the Amalgamated."

"You were still a baby then. Here, let me see. There are so many things I want to show you, so many things you should know about." She took the album and placed it on her lap. Catherine sat on the bed next to the old woman to get a better look. Sonia turned the fragile pages and they stared down together at a sepia-toned photo of a large man with a huge mustache and full beard who was glaring out from beneath a fur hat.

"My father," said Sonia. "A nihilist, you know, a regular Narodnik,"

"What's Narodnik, Grandma?"

"A socialist, a populist, part of the Russian movement. We lived in a little shtetl named Proponie. Poppa came from a rabbinical family; his father was a rabbi. But he wanted none of that. He shunned religion and worked as a tailor. He was a rebel, and he was taken up with the ideas of the Jewish enlightenment, the Haskala, that came through the Pale like a whirlwind when he was a young man. He read Rousseau, not the Talmud; fell in love with the idea of freedom. Such a free thinker, my father was. The young people of the village flocked around him. People respected him, though maybe they didn't always agree. My momma, Esther, used to joke he had more influence than the rabbi. He was a brilliant man they always used to say. He tried to educate the people, to get them to forget the superstitious nonsense. Eventually, it got him in trouble. Momma worshiped him. She loved and served him, let him have his way with everything. I think she was a little in awe of him."

"He looks fierce. Cool hat." Catherine peered over Sonia's shoulder at the picture.

"He was an impressive man. Oh, darling, if you could have heard him speak. He was powerful, full of passion; a wonderful speaker. He held meetings, sponsored lectures, and distributed literature, pamphlets nechevand such, calling for an end to the czar, freedom for the serfs, rights for the Jews -- enough to send him to Siberia. Still, he spoke out.

"And you should have heard him sing. He had a beautiful baritone. He would sing peasant songs about Stenka Razen, Pugachev and Nechaev, heroes and martyrs of the people. These were the lullabies I heard from this man. Every night he would put me to bed and sing me a song. He looks very fierce in this picture, but he was gentle, a gentle man. A giant, six feet or more, and when I was little he seemed much larger. And always he wore the fur hat in winter, which made him look even taller. He was a like a great bear, covered in fur." Sonia sighed at the memory and stared past Catherine for a moment.

"What was his name, grandma?"

"My father? Solomon, but they called him Sol. When they tried to assassinate the Czar in Petrograd, the Okhrana, the secret police, came looking for him. He had nothing to do with it personally, but once he sponsored a lecture by somebody who did. There were informers everywhere, and he was a radical, a subversive, so we knew he would be arrested. We had to run away. I was so young I didn't really understand what was happening. And for my brother, Sasha, it was an adventure. But it was very hard on momma to go, to throw away everything. But she realized we had no choice."

"You ran away from the secret police? You're kidding!"

"Oh yes, darling. That night we slipped out of the village.

"Where is that town we came from, what's its name again?

"South of St. Petersburg, maybe 150 miles. And my shtetl, our town, was called Proponie. It wasn't much of a town, I don't know if it still exists."

"Like Fiddler on the Roof, or something, right?"

"Well, we were in the Pale, but nobody was dancing around on the roof, I'll tell you that." Sonia laughed.

"The Pail, Grandma?"

"The Pale of settlement, where the Jews were allowed to live."

"Grandma, this is awesome. Why didn't I know this?" Damn it. Why hadn't she been told before? "Nobody ever took me seriously back in Scarsdale."

Her parents treated her as if she was still a kid. She had dyed her hair orange, then green, and finally its current purple to prove she was grown up, that she wasn't sweet little Cathy who they remembered from grammar school, the little girl with dark curls surrounding an angelic face who stared down at her every day from a frame on the mantle in the living room. She hated that picture and, one day, smashed it against the fireplace.

Her mother was aghast, but it didn't take much to make her mother aghast. Orange hair; "Why, Cathy?" Body piercing; "A nose ring? Your eyebrow, Cathy? How could you mutilate yourself like that?" Her mother tried, but she could never really understand. Her parents were an embarrassment. Like in a certain way they were such fucking liberals. They listened to that stale old sixties music, and when Catherine was younger, her mom was always dragging her off to march for whales or whatever. They were always talking about the terrible things that the government was doing to those poor people in the ghetto. But her dad drove a Mercedes, and once, when she was about twelve years old, she had invited a man who she found sleeping behind a store at the mall to come home, and her mom had freaked on her. They were such hypocrites. Maybe she had been switched at birth, or adopted, or left on the doorstep by some stranger. She felt like an alien living in the big Tudor with the perfect lawn, and everything just so.

"Grandma, I really need to hear this, It's my history too, I mean, like, family stuff. Weren't you scared?"

"I was a very little girl, maybe not so scared. Poppa said it would be all right, I believed." The old woman shifted her position. "Darling, I've got to lie down, my back isn't so good. The doctor says I should sit up more, but it's hard." Catherine took the album from her and placed it on the end table. "You don't know,

57

but when you're my age everything hurts. It hurts to lie down, it hurts to sit up. But at least I have a window. Some look out at an air shaft. This place is hell, Cathy. To end up here, it's not right. I'm ready to go anytime. I've already lived my life. This isn't living." Sonia lay back and Catherine propped a pillow behind her head.

"I know, grandma, it's not fair. I wish I could take care of you."

"No, darling. You have your own life. I only wish I could take care of myself. I feel helpless, like a baby." The morning sun shone in her eyes and she shifted her position on the pillow.

"Well, you're old grandma, like, it's O.K. if you need a little help. What a life you had."

"Well I'm glad it interests you." Sonia took a sip of water from a glass on her bedside table.

Catherine twirled a strand of her hair and stared at Sonia. "I can't imagine. It's like, nothing I ever.. I don't know, Grandma! I feel cheated I never heard this before."

"So, I'm telling you now. It's just an old woman's story."

"But it's like this amazing adventure, grandma. It's incredible."

"Well, I'm glad you think it's interesting. Nobody at this place cares about my stories. They're just waiting for me to die so they can give somebody else my bed."

"Well I care grandma, I really care. I want to hear more."

"You, I'm happy to tell. You know I did a whole

oral history with your father when he was in college, with a tape recorder, for a course. I'm there somewhere at Columbia University. They made a transcript for me. If you really want to hear more."

"My Dad did that? Are you kidding? Like, I would love to see it."

"It's there, in the black binder in the drawer where you got the album. Take it, it's better you should read it then me try to remember and tell you. I was a younger women then."

Chapter 6

It was two A.M. and Catherine was walking home after work. The collar on her leather jacket was turned down. The cold snap had broken and for the first time in weeks she wasn't shivering. It had been slow at the restaurant, which was a drag because it meant not much from tips. She hated her job. The place was overpriced and pretentious, the manager was a pig and the customers, a bunch of yuppie scum, were lousy tippers. She felt like she was wasting her time there, and she was growing increasingly resentful. Of course she had to smile and act nice while she worked. "Don't want to scare the customers away," her boss said. The money was decent when they were busy, but those times were few and far between. She was starting to think that it wasn't worth the nightly humiliations she suffered.

Catherine walked up to the entry, dug the keys out of her bag, opened the door and went into the cluttered hallway. A stack of two by fours lined one wall. Boxes of nails were piled at the hallway's far end and a layer of thick plaster dust covered everything. She climbed the stairs carefully It was a long way down, she thought as she stepped across the chasm caused by a missing stair tread between the fourth and fifth floor. A bulb hanging from a droplight at each landing provided illumination. Catherine cast eerie shadows on the walls as she climbed the steps.

She was breathing hard by the time she reached the fifth floor, the top of the building. Walking down to the end of the hall and entering her apartment through an empty door frame, she cautiously skirted a hole in the floor that opened up into an equally devastated apartment beneath her. Catherine glanced quickly around the flat. The walls were down to bare brick. The floor had several gaping holes. The windows were wide open to the elements, lacking sashes and glass altogether. Home sweet home.

She walked to the rear of the apartment, opened a red door, and entered her sanctuary, the section of the apartment where she and Mike actually lived while they tried to rebuild the rest. It was a small room, 10x12, that held two metal folding chairs and a wooden desk, which they had salvaged from a burned out building. There was a single window that looked out over Avenue D. Against the wall, next to the window was a battered old 4 drawer metal filing cabinet they used as a dresser. A loft bed built from 2x4s took up most of the room. Under it they hung the clothes that wouldn't fit in the filing cabinet and stored several plastic milk crates full of their things and the covered bucket that, in an emergency, served as their toilet, though they avoided using it at all costs. An extension cord, their sole source of electricity, snaked through a thin opening at the bottom of the window caulked with foam rubber and ended in one of those jacks with six outlets that sat on the wooden desk. A radio, a hot plate, and a cord attached to the bare light bulb hanging from the ceiling were plugged into it, as well as an electric heater that glowed cherry red on the floor next to the desk.

Mike lay on a mattress atop the loft bed, reading by the light of the bare bulb. "Hi Cath. How'd it go tonight?" He asked as though he wasn't sure he wanted to hear the answer.

"It sucked!" Catherine sat down and took off her black combat boots. "Don't know how much longer I can last. Tonight a bunch of drunk yuppies started throwing pretzels at each other and I got caught in the crossfire. How was the meeting?"

"It was okay." He put down his book and sat up on the bed, almost hitting his head on the ceiling in the process. He was tall and thin, with greasy blond hair that hung past his shoulders, and an angular, unlined face with a boyish grin that made him look younger than his twenty-two years. "We decided Jesse has to go. Lisa saw him shooting up again. He was pretty pissed. What an asshole! I could never stand that guy. I'll be glad to see him out of here. He knew the rules, and besides, he never did any work. And it's not like he's got nowhere to go. He can move back to his folks on Long Island, or he can go crash at Raven's. Why should we take care of him? He's a fucking deadbeat."

"Yeah, all true. Is he gonna leave? He could be trouble."

"Well, he bitched a lot and said something about burning down the building."

The squat had almost no rules, but they had seen too many junkies and crack heads fuck things up, so they couldn't take the risk. Besides, she never liked Jesse anyway, and suspected that he had been dealing smack out of his apartment, based on the steady stream of strung-out looking visitors who passed through his door. She hoped he wouldn't cause trouble though. Their lives were shaky enough already.

She started squatting in the building almost a year ago, when she left Raven's. She and Mike had hung out together in the garden and at the ABC Club. She liked him right away, attracted by his lanky good looks and his languid, unflappable air. He had been living in the neighborhood forever, moving there from Queens when he was an art student at Cooper. He got an occasional job freelancing for an ad agency uptown where one of his buddies from school was assistant art director.

Catherine and Mike hit it off, and when he found out she was looking for a place to live he told her about the squat. She wanted to get out of Raven's as soon as possible so she moved in a few days later, after the group gave its ok. At first she had her own apartment, but it was in even worse shape than the one they shared now. When winter set in she became Mike's roommate, and his lover.

The squat was a loosely organized collective of eighteen people, there for lots of different reasons, and they had widely varying degrees of commitment. The basic idea was to fix up the building. Squatters had been living there for almost six years, but only one of them, Lisa, had been there for the duration. Not much visible progress was being made on repairing the building. The roof still leaked in spots. The stairs, halls and other common spaces were a mess, but people had managed to make some of their own apartments livable, as Mike had their back room. In fact some of the squatters had fixed up whole flats, and a few, like Lisa's, were really kind of nice.

"Who's gonna make him leave?" Catherine was dreading the answer.

"Well, we gave him a couple of days to move. And if he doesn't go, me and Bobby and Riff told him we'd come throw him out. We're gonna change the front door lock and put his shit out on the street!" Mike's jaw tightened as he spoke.

"Dude, why does it always have to be you? He's a junkie. He might get violent, have a gun."

Mike laughed and tossed his head to get his hair out of his eyes. "Don't worry. He's harmless. Besides, there are three of us; probably he'll go on his own. It's under control, really."

Despite his mellow demeanor, Mike had a macho side to him that Catherine hated. She suspected that he secretly wanted a confrontation with Jesse. Men were so stupid! Why were things always so unsettled here? Just when she was feeling like it was starting to calm down there was always a new crisis. Last week it was the electricity. Con Ed had discovered the line they had been tapping for power and, besides cutting them off, had sent them a bill for $6,000. Since then they had been running the whole squat off of extension cords that tapped into the bottom of a lamp post. Now, trouble with Jesse. What next? Oh well, at least she had a roof over her head, even if it leaked.

Things could be worse. They were worse in some of the other squats. Embryo Squat, which was what they called themselves, straddled the middle ground between the buildings that functioned almost like co-ops, with governing boards, long lists of rules and monthly "rent" payments, legal utilities, and all other kinds of formal structures and, at the other extreme, the abandoned buildings that served as temporary crash pads for anybody who claimed the space.

"What else did you do?"

"I went over to ABC's for a beer after the meeting."

While she worked her lousy job for an eight-hour shift, he went to a meeting and hung out at a club! It wasn't fair. But she stifled the impulse to start a fight.

It was late and she just wanted to go to sleep. She undressed, pulled on a flannel nightgown to help her stay warm, unplugged the light bulb, turned out the desk lamp and climbed into the loft bed. "Move over," she said, poking Mike in the ribs.

He slid over to make room for her and then rolled over back on top of her.

"Not tonight Mike, I'm not in the mood." He rolled off of her.

"Jeez, you're never in the mood these days."

"I'm tired, Mike, that's all. Like, I had a long night. Let's go to sleep. Don't make a big deal out of it, okay?"

He pulled away and turned his back to her.

While it was true that Catherine was tired, sleep did not come easily. She worried about the garden, and most of all, the paper. *The Avalanche* was the most important thing in her life, and Raven's threats chilled her. "Get the fuck off my paper!" She tossed and turned until her weariness overcame her anxiety and she slept.

She woke a little after ten. She could see blue sky out her window and Mike was stirring beside her. She glanced over at him and elbowed him in the ribs. "Get up sleepy head!" Mike groaned and turned away from her. "Dude, come on, it's work day!" She shook him. Mike stretched his arms over his head, yawning mightily.

"Slave driver."

"You bet. Somebody's got to get you lazy boys working or nothing will ever get done." She said it like she was joking, but she meant it.

"Hey, I'm living in a squat so I don't have to spend my whole life working, so why should I spend my whole life working on the squat?"

"The problem is instead of getting better, the building's worse. It seems like every time we make a little progress a new problem crops up." It was like they were slowly losing ground, being eaten at by the entropy that was gradually consuming the whole neighborhood.

Catherine got down from the bed and dressed quickly in jeans, one of Mike's old chamois shirts and her black boots. She pulled out a plastic milk crate from under the loft and dug out a battered old tea-kettle.

Sometimes she despaired. She loved the old tenement, and wanted to save it. She shouldn't be so pessimistic. They had accomplished a few things. They painted a great mural on the side of the building last summer, and planted a garden in the vacant lot next door. It was just that they were missing basic stuff, like running water. She tipped a five-gallon jerry can to fill the teakettle. And real electricity. She plugged the hot plate into the extension cord that ran through her window and put the tea kettle on the hot plate. Catherine rummaged through the milk crate and came out with a bag of coffee beans, a small electric grinder and two chipped cups. She ground the coffee while the water boiled and when the kettle whistled she poured the water over a filter that rested on top of one of the cups and then repeated the operation. "Breakfast is ready, honey!" she cried out cheerfully. Mike poked his head over the edge of the loft.

"Great!" He swung himself down to the floor. He was wearing his thermal underwear. He pulled on a pair of torn jeans and a red buffalo plaid shirt with a quilted lining. He laced his black boots and slurped down his cup of coffee. "Delicious, I'm ready to go."

Catherine took another few moments to finish her coffee and then pulled a wooden box full of tools from under the loft. Since working on the squat she had amassed a decent collection of hand tools, an old skill saw and an electric drill. Still learning carpentry, she was proud of the fact that Mike and some of the others in the building came to her with their questions. She hoisted the toolbox and she and Mike headed out into the hallway.

There was a crew working down on the ground floor. She could hear them clearly from the stairs. The group had decided to fix up the two storefronts that flanked the building's main entrance. Charlie the Rag Picker was snapping a line for a sill so they could start framing one of the walls. Charlie was in his late forties and had lived on the Lower East Side since the 60's. In many ways the building's patriarch, he got his name because he earned money by picking through bales of discarded clothing at a warehouse on Clinton Street and re-selling the stuff on the sidewalk up near Cooper Square. He had also once worked as a carpenter, and Catherine was relieved to see him there.

"Hey, Charlie, how's it going?"

"Ok, Cathy, but we could use somebody who knows what they're doin' cuttin' some studs. I don't want to see nobody lose no fingers here. Can you handle it?"

"Sure." Catherine thought that the project was dumb, that they should prioritize the work that needed doing. And the storefronts would be near the bottom of her list. But someone decided that if they fixed up the storefronts they could rent them out and make some money. The group's enthusiasm for any project had a short life span, so she went where the general energy was. People were hot to refurbish the storefronts.

Lisa, a young black woman, with her seven-year-old son by her side, was at a pile counting out two by fours. Catherine walked over to her. "Hey Lisa. Hi Jamaal. What's up? You helping out Momma? Working hard, Jamaal?"

The little boy ran to her, jumped up and embraced her. "Me and Mommy went to McDonalds today and I got a toy with my muffin!"

"That's great," Catherine laughed as she hugged him. "You helping Mom, huh?"

"Of course," He was looking self-important with a tape measure dangling from his belt. "I always help Mommy."

Of all the people who lived there, Catherine liked Lisa and Jamaal best. Lisa was one of the original group who had started the squat almost six years before. She was made homeless by a suspicious fire in a neighboring building. Social services sent her to a shelter for temporary housing and it terrified her. The single room occupancy hotel she tried next was no better, so she joined the squatters intending to stay only until she found another apartment she could afford to rent. Unfortunately with gentrification sweeping through the neighborhood the affordable place she was looking for never materialized. But she came to like the squatter life style. Even though there were hardships, she had been there long enough to fix up her apartment with some nice things she had found on the street.. And she loved the freedom and the sense of self-reliance living in the squat gave her. The City housing bureaucracy was the worst and at least she was out of their clutches now. She got food stamps and aid for dependent children so she was doing all right.

More than anyone else, Lisa was committed to the building and making it work. The others had options, but this was the end of the line for her and Jamaal. It was Lisa who insisted on the rule against hard drugs. She had seen the destruction wrought by the addicts in the S.R.Os, and even though she felt sorry for them on a certain level, she wouldn't ever live with junkies again if she could help it. Catherine looked up to her.

Most of the others working that day were, like Catherine and Mike, young people who had moved to the squat by choice, not out of necessity, though there were lots of different reasons why people made that choice.

Bobby and Riff, who shared a flat on the third floor and were currently busy tearing up rotted floorboards in the storefront, were both from Babylon, out on the Island. They had a band, and the Lower East Side was the heart of the music scene. If they rented an apartment though, they would have needed full time jobs to pay the rent, and then they couldn't have afforded a rehearsal studio either, let alone found the time to rehearse. They were Mike's best friends, so Catherine never told them how bad she thought their music was.

Catherine put down Jamaal and began to pull two by fours from the pile. She looked for ones that weren't too warped. "Want some help?" Mike was tagging along behind her hoping to make himself useful.

Mike was all right. He did his share. It was Mike who designed and organized the painting of the mural on the side of the building. She felt bad about their fight last night, so, even though she knew that he would slow her down, she put him to work measuring and marking the studs. He flashed her a hopeful smile that reminded her of a puppy she had when she was a kid, eager to please, as he borrowed her tape and found a broad carpenters pencil in the bottom of her toolbox.

"Dude, you know Raven went psycho on me the other day." They worked side by side. "He started yelling and threatened to throw me off his paper if I write my story about the garden. What a fucking maniac that guy is! It was scary. He really is sick!"

"Yeah, tell me about it! What got him so worked up?"

"Nothing really, just some history from my article. He's all uptight about those *La Cabaña* guys getting credit for starting the garden. It was weird. He flipped. He went off on a whole power trip. Like, he was the publisher and what he says goes, 'if you don't like it, get the fuck off my paper!' His paper, can you believe it? He's in a dream world. Publisher my ass! There wouldn't be any paper without us. I should've told him off, but he was scary. You know how he gets. Just before, I almost started feeling sorry for him too. But this is it! What a shit head! I think we ought to pull the whole thing right out from under him. He's a pig!"

"Yea, Cath, he's a pig, but he's our pig!" Catherine scowled at him. "What are you thinkin?"

"I don't know, Dude. Maybe we need to get together with Paula and Josh, talk about it. I think we've got a real problem. Like, I couldn't sleep thinking about it. I realized how much we do depend on him, or at least on his money, and how much power that gives him. There's got to be another way." She picked up the skill saw.

"Sure, an office, a phone, Xerox machine, computer, laser printer, press; we'll just pull it all out of a dumpster."

"I said I *started* thinking about it. I don't have any answers yet! Let's get together and see what we can figure out. I know Paula has her doubts about Raven too. I mean his latest 'Shining Path' shit! Come on, Dude! We can't let him intimidate us anymore!" She attacked a two-by-four; the skill saw whirring.

"Hey, take it easy Tiger!" Mike grinned.

"Mike, don't you care about this? It's your paper too! Think of all of the work we put into it! You willing to let Raven fuck it all up? I'm not! Come on!" She put the saw down and faced him.

He couldn't argue with her. It was important. But it also seemed like another one of Catherine's lost causes. "Uh-huh."

But she wasn't going to let it go that easily. "Like, are you with me on this, Michael?"

"Sure, let's get together and talk about it."

"This is important Mike! Like, it could be a really good thing to get out from under him. I mean I see your point but we can figure out a way to make it work. Back me up on this. The others respect you; they'll listen. I'm telling you, I saw a side of Raven you've never seen, and it was scary."

"I know the guy's an asshole, but he bankrolls the whole operation."

"It's not just his usual asshole behavior, this was something else. Like he flipped; it was like Dr. Jekyll and Mr. Hyde. He was acting like he was the boss, whatever he says goes, he told me. You know that's not the way we operate. Is that what you want? Raven for your boss? I don't. The paper is too important to be held captive to his ego. We've got to set him straight. Dude, we all agreed that editorial decisions would be made collectively. If he can convince you all that I should change my story I will. Otherwise... Oh, forget it!"

"Look, don't worry about it. We'll see what happens. It'll be cool."

They worked side by side in silence until they pulled, measured, marked and cut the rest of the studs. Catherine was still brooding about their conversation while she put away her skill saw and she and Mike carried the lumber over to Charlie.

They spent the rest of the afternoon framing and sheet rocking. People drifted in and out of the crew, but she, Mike, Charlie, and Lisa stuck with it and finally the walls were completed. At the end of the day's work Catherine and Mike trudged back up the stairs with their tools. They were covered with sawdust and plaster dust.

"Let's go over to ABC's and get a burger." Mike shook sawdust out of his hair.

"Sounds good, Dude, but I want to stop by Paula's first and take a shower, I'm itching all over."

"Cool, good idea. I could use one too." They threw some clean clothes into a daypack and walked the three blocks to Paula's apartment.

On the way there they passed *El Árbol que Habla*, who stepped out in front of them on the sidewalk and began to recite a poem. He had hundreds of poems, maybe thousands of them, memorized, all in Spanish, all his own work. And the poems ranged from very good to miraculous. For twenty five years he had wandered the streets of Loisaida, declaiming on street corners and in doorways, through rain and night, summer and winter, calling out visions of palm trees and sandy beaches; mountains covered with mist and bananas.

Mike dug into his pocket and handed the old man a quarter. Then he and Catherine walked past, while Langdon shouted his closing stanzas after them. "I wonder what he wants?" said Catherine.

Paula, a recent Sarah Lawrence graduate, made decent money as a copy editor and rented a flat on Seventh, between B and C. They rang her bell and when she buzzed them in they entered her recently renovated building. Catherine noted, with some envy, how clean everything was. No plaster dust, no missing stair treads, real lights in the hallway; but the full impact of Paula's affluence always struck her when she entered the apartment; white walls, no holes in the floor, heat, and best of all, hot running water.

"We figured you wouldn't mind if we came over and took a shower. Then we're going to A.B.C.'s. You want to come?"

"Yea, sure, Cathy. Be my guests." Paula was average height with close cropped dark hair, dark eyes and an air of quiet intensity about her; not brooding, but thoughtful. She wore a variant on the punk uniform;

black jeans and a black turtleneck. Her apartment was lined with books, and a cluttered desk almost filled the small studio. There was a futon on a frame that pulled open serving as both couch and bed.

Mike and Catherine headed immediately for the bathroom. "Back in a minute." Catherine shut the door. They undressed in the cramped quarters and then turned on the shower, stepped into the tub together, and pulled the curtain closed behind them. The hot water felt wonderful as she and Mike scrubbed each other's back. She felt herself getting turned on when Mike washed her bottom, but she slapped his hand away.

"Dude, not now! Come on, I'm hungry. I promise we can make love at home tonight." Mike stopped and reached around and began to soap her breasts and then moved down to her belly and her vulva. She couldn't help it. She gave in and turned to face him under the stream of hot water.

They kissed and embraced. She took the soap and began to rub it on him. She soaped his erect penis, and, lifting one leg to the side of the tub, she put him inside her. He gasped with pleasure.

"Be quiet," she whispered in his ear. "Paula's in the next room." They giggled and kissed and then moved together slowly, lost in the water and steam and feelings that engulfed them until they both climaxed. They held each other tight and continued to kiss until he slipped out of her.

"That was nice."

"Yeah, we should do it more often. I'm still gonna hold you to your promise about tonight." She slapped him with a wet washcloth and they both laughed. They rinsed the soap off and then washed each other's hair. She luxuriated under the stream of hot water for a few extra minutes while he dried off and got dressed.

When Catherine came out of the bathroom she found Mike and Paula sitting on the futon, where Mike was rolling a joint. "A little appetizer before dinner?"

"Why not?" He fired it up and passed it to Paula, who inhaled deeply. Catherine took a toke and passed it back to Mike. By the time the joint was done she was stoned. It was in that state that they walked to the corner of Seventh Street and Avenue A.

They stepped down into the dark interior of the club like divers descending into a shipwreck. It was a former Polish social hall that was crusty with age. The bar dominated the room. The counter was dark wood, burnished over time by the forearms of honest working-men. The wall was lined with booths and there was a small stage at the rear. Light came from several bright neon beer signs hanging over the bar and reflected in its mirrored back. The bar was full. So were most of the booths. It was early, about seven o'clock. Most of the crowd at the bar was drinking beer and a haze of cigarette smoke filled the room.

The clientele was young and clad almost entirely in shades of black. They found an empty booth and squeezed in, but not before saying hello to half a dozen people. A song by the Fine Young Cannibals was blasting on a jukebox to their right, but it barely cut through the din from the bar. Catherine spotted Josh, the other member of the Avalanche collective. She waved, and he walked over to the booth. "Hey, Dude, what's up?" She had to shout to be heard.

"Not much. What's shakin'? You see the new issue? Looks pretty good."

"Not bad. But we need to talk. Just us, without Raven. You free Saturday night?"

Josh, who was short with curly red hair, raised his eyebrows and shouted back "Yea, I guess so. Why?"

"Come by the squat," Catherine yelled. "I'll make coffee and we'll talk about it. It's important."

The Dead Kennedys replaced The Cannibals as Catherine sunk back into the booth and hugged Mike's arm. "Let's order. I'm starved."

Chapter 7

We left behind everything we couldn't fit into one suitcase and rode in a neighbor's cart. The four of us, me, Momma, Poppa, and Sascha lay together under a load of straw, we didn't dare to move. We could hear our neighbor clucking to his horse while we went slowly down the road. But what ruts! We bounced around like crazy back there. It was fall and the night got very cold, but the heat from our bodies all huddled under the straw kept us warm. The cart jounced along, and all around were sounds of the night: dogs barked when we approached farmhouses; faint music drifted to us when we passed an inn; the horse whinnied, and I peeked out and saw a troika rush past, carrying one of the gentry on to his dacha.

We rode there a long time, and I got hungry and nibbled at the loaf of challah that Momma had grabbed before she closed the door of our house for the last time. What with the rocking of the cart and the warmth of Poppa's arm around my shoulder, it was almost cozy. Under the straw, I fell asleep.

The next day we got to Volochek, where Poppa had a comrade, a baker, who agreed to hide us and help us arrange to leave Russia. Our neighbor dropped us at the baker's. "Hurry out now!" he said. He took a big risk you know. We crawled out from the wagon into the bright afternoon. We brushed the hay from our clothing, then followed a skinny man with a beard up a flight of stairs. We walked into a small kitchen with a cast iron cook stove. The baker's wife, very plump with cheeks like small red apples, she smiled, and said to sit.

"Eat, Eat." She told us. Cabbage borscht, steaming hot, a platter of fresh bread, with a bowl full of schmaltz next to it. "Poor children, you must be starved," she fussed over us. She plucked pieces of straw from my hair while I devoured the soup. I'm telling you, I never tasted anything so delicious since that meal she gave to us.

Then we rested but not for long. After we were done eating, Momma and the baker's wife picked up the dishes and carried them to a basin. Then the grownups gathered around the table talking in low voices. It got dark and the baker lit a kerosene lamp that hung from a beam in the ceiling.

I sat on a featherbed in the couple's bedroom with my brother, Sasha. He read to me, a book of fairy tales. I dug through the carpetbag until I found my wooden doll that came apart with another doll inside it, and then another and another. Suddenly, the door to the tiny kitchen burst open. A boy, I remember corduroy knickers, ran in. "The secret police are looking for you. My Poppa overheard at the magistrate's." He was panting.

"Quickly, downstairs to the bakery!" the baker's wife yelled, and we ran down the steep stairway, me and Sasha first, urged on by Momma and Poppa with the baker and his wife behind.

The lower room was open, with a long wooden table and a huge domed oven built of stone. The baker opened the oven door. "Get in," he told us. Inside we climbed, followed by Momma and the baker's wife. Poppa barely fit through the opening and then finally the baker followed him, pulling the door closed. I began to cry. "Quiet!" the baker told me. We squeezed together, there in the dark, listening.

To this day, I remember. We huddled very tightly, silent for what felt like hours but was really probably only a few minutes. We heard the door to the bakery crash open and the sound of boots on the stairway above, and the shouting, oh such shouts, such voices, bloodcurdling! Then the sounds of furniture crashing, and breaking pottery, oh, I trembled! We heard boot steps rushing down the stairs and orders being shouted, then the crack of the baker's table being splintered and ripping sounds as bags of flour were slashed open. At last the door slammed and it was quiet.

We waited in the dark for an hour, in case the police had left a guard. But there were no further noises so the baker opened the oven door a crack and peeked out. Slowly, he made it wider. Then he worked his way out. We followed him. "We hid there once before," he told us, "during a pogrom."

Once we were out, I could see that the whole place was destroyed, a wreck. And now the baker and his wife were in the same boat we were. I remember my mama started to cry and Poppa tried to comfort her.

We left the bakery that night, out the door and down an alley, to the outskirts of town. This part I don't remember, but Momma told me we slept in the woods at night and, in the day, walked the roads like any other peasant family, except Sasha was with the baker and his wife walking a little ahead of mama, Poppa, and me, so the police wouldn't suspect -- they were looking for a childless couple and a family with two children. We walked this way for days, buying food with money that mama and the baker's wife had hidden in their bosoms.

The road was very dusty, with steady traffic. We mingled with others on foot or riding in carts pulled by horses or oxen. When we got close to Petrograd, the road grew wider and was joined by other roads until the dirt and gravel changed to cobblestone. Here, we split off from the baker and his wife.

Poppa had a name and address for some comrades. He just hoped they hadn't been arrested. That evening Momma, Sasha, and I, all very scared, sat drinking tea at a table in front of a fireplace at an inn. We looked up every time the door opened, hoping to see Poppa return.

It was dark, and I was tired. Momma held me close and whispered an old folktale into my ear, the one about the wolf and the samovar. Finally, the door opened and there, we could see by a lantern hanging in the courtyard, thank goodness, stood Poppa in his long coat and fur hat. What a relief. He came to the table smiling, followed by a young man.

"Come on, it's time to go. This is Mischa. We'll stay with him tonight." Poppa told us. He picked up our carpetbag, and we followed Mischa through the winding streets. Those streets and alleys of the workers' quarter still confused me even after we spent almost a month there, moving to a different flat every few days, until Poppa announced over a meal of cabbage and bread that we were leaving. "The plans have been made; it's time to go.

The secret police, they have informers, they use unspeakable tortures. Nowhere in Russia are we safe."

At the station we waited on the platform, Poppa pacing back and forth, while the first-class passengers and their baggage were loaded on the train. Momma hugged me in her arms, singing softly. Once we were on board we took our seats on a wooden bench that ran the length of the coach. I was so scared when the whistle sounded and the steam locomotive began to chug away from the station. It was my first train ride. Poppa squeezed my hand and smiled at me.

From Petrograd we went to Orenumbaum and from there, over the ice to Katlin Island and Kronstadt. We went on a sleigh, drawn by horses hauling supplies, for about five miles. It was a sunny day, but cold. There was a garrison there, full of soldiers and sailors, many of them very radical. It was homeport for the battleship Potemkin, you know, and later they revolted there against the Bolsheviks.

The sailors. They were very kind, the sailors. I remember that they played with me and Sasha in Anchor Square. They were practically children themselves, peasant boys. We felt safer there, for a few days. Then, one night, a young sailor came to lead us away, to Finland. It was early in the winter, December I think, so the ice wasn't so thick. There were cracks we had to walk around.

The night was clear and very cold. Sasha and I rode under a pile of blankets heaped on a small sled that Poppa pulled. The moon was coming up, huge and orange, hanging just over the horizon when we headed out onto the gulf; a full moon, it cast shadows on the snow covered ice. The moonlight was soft, bright enough to see clearly, but different from daylight. I'll never forget that moonlight, there was something magical about that night. I felt so small on the sled, huddled under the blankets with the whole of the Gulf of Finland stretched before us, under a sky full of stars. It was so cold, and in that moonlight our breath left a trail of vapor. We passed right under the guns of the garrison, which were manned by sympathetic comrades that night, with no sound but the sled's runners scraping on the ice. We saw no one else and walked well west of the outlying islands, out onto the empty gulf, guided by the young sailor, Alexei, I think he was called.

Anyway, after a few hours we lost sight of Katlin Island and could see nothing but ice, surrounded by silence and moonlight. The sailor pulled his compass from the pocket of his greatcoat to make sure that we were walking in the right direction. The night grew colder, so cold, and when the wind picked up further out on the Gulf, it cut through the blankets covering me and Sasha. Momma, Poppa and the young sailor turned up their collars and gritted their teeth against the wind. We walked all that night, not daring to stop. When the sun came up, we could see a distant coast, a thin line on the horizon. And that was where we headed, after we took a rest. The sailor lit a kerosene lamp that he pulled from a bundle on the sled, boiled water, and made tea. Oh, how I savored it.

We walked most of the rest of the day. The crust of snow over the ice was not too deep, and the day warmed up as the sun rose higher. We were all thankful for the warming, but no one more than me. The night's cold had chilled me to the core and my toes felt numb. Twelve, fifteen miles we walked until we ar-

rived at Terijoki, in Finland. Oh, were they surprised to see us, amazed. They had seen plenty refugees from Russia before, but they arrived on the train. They had never seen a family come across the ice; smugglers, yes, but a family, never.

I remember the warmth of the fire and a hot bowl of soup; the feeling of relief. Poppa cried when he looked out across the gulf, back to Russia. Home, everything we knew was back there, and now it was as though none of it had ever existed. We knew we could never go back. And ahead, who knew what waited ahead?

Recorded: March 5, 1967, transcribed: March 23, 1967, For: Columbia Oral History Project, Immigrant Voices.

Chapter 8

Chico's forehead was creased and his eyes were brooding as he opened up *La Cabaña* and entered the lobby. The meeting Friday night had been a disaster and to top it off, he had just seen the latest issue of *The Avalanche*. He held a folded copy of the paper under his arm. "Shining Path Declares Class War on the Lower East Side". Those punk kids were right, there was a class war being fought on the Lower East Side, but it couldn't be won with violence. He thought about the girl with purple hair who called Rolón a poverty pimp.

Chico knew all about poverty pimps. He had watched the government pump millions into the neighborhood; the New Frontier, the War on Poverty, the Great Society, the New Federalism, millions and millions; money for education, job training, housing. And things just kept getting worse, like the money disappeared into a black hole. He couldn't help but be cynical when he heard yet another new program announced. Now he had faith only in the grassroots.

A few weeks after he got out of Attica, Chico joined the Young Lords Party and began to patrol the neighborhood in a brown beret. They started a summer free-lunch program for the neighborhood kids. Chico ran it out of a vacant lot.

When he began working with his own group it was loose; a bunch of friends who got together to talk about the neighborhood and its problems; some old buddies from the gang, a few comrades from the Lords, and a couple of neighborhood kids who went to City College.

They started putting some things together. They organized a rent strike on 11th St., where most of them grew up, and started a protest against police brutality after the shooting of a homeless woman. Then they had run out some smack dealers who had a shooting gallery in an abandoned building on their block. Chico and the others handed out leaflets to support the farm workers grape boycott. And they organized a march on City Hall to demand low-income housing for the neighborhood.

But Chico had seen early on that protest wasn't enough, and if they waited for the City to move, they'd wait forever. Sure, they had to keep protesting, keep the pressure on. But they had to build something of their own at the same time, like *El Jardin*. Their neighborhood was dying. They had to create a counter force -- life to oppose the death all around them.

Meanwhile he had watched some of the guys he knew from the gangs, like Rolón, go into the poverty business and they usually brought the same rules with them that they learned in the street: look out for number one, watch your back, take care of your boys, and get over on everybody else. Things had gone from bad to worse, and the poverty programs hadn't helped. Back in those days Chico knew lots of people who enlisted in the war on poverty and wound up as casualties.

"Hey, Chico, 'sup man? What you doin' hangin' around? *Coño*, it's cold out here! Let's go in and turn on some heat." Angela Lopez entered the lobby and grabbed his arm. "It was pretty bad the other night, huh? I guess Rolón got over on us. Damn bro, that's not right!" Angie was New York born, like many of the young Puerto Ricans in the neighborhood. In contrast to Chico, her voice only hinted at an accent.

"Tell me about it. We been fighting twenty years for decent housing in the neighborhood and now they say they're going to build it in *El Jardín*?" He grimaced. "I wonder how much he's going to make on the deal. Councilman Rolón!," Chico shook his head. "He's the same *pendejo* he was when we ran together in the gangs. But he's going to make us look bad; any way we go on this we're going to get hurt. He is one slick bastard, I'll tell you that."

"Yeah, it's a tough one. What can we do?"

"We've got to get the people in the neighborhood

to speak out, then we go to the Community Board, maybe march downtown to H.P.D., put some pressure on. Rolón's not the only one who can make things happen."

Chico opened the office door and headed for his desk. Angie had already turned on the donated computer and was checking the answering machine for messages. Chico lowered himself into his chair. "We got to set a date for another meeting and get some flyers out. Then start some petitions. Can you handle it? I'm going to call around and see if I can find out what's in it for Rolón. I smell a fat rat."

"Sure, I'll take care of it. I'll see if some of the youngbloods in the after-school program can get the posters up today. *No Hay Problema.*"

Chico sat at his desk, depressed. He had been in Leshko's that morning eating eggs when a guy he knew from the block asked him why he was against low-income housing. Chico drummed a pencil on his desk blotter.

"Chico, man, you won't believe what's been going on down here while you were away upstate." Chico was just a week out of Attica when Jorge, a comrade from the Lords, had clapped him on the back. "Motherfucker landlords been jacking up the rents. I mean milking people."

"Jorge, that's not legal. We got rent control down here."

"I know that, man, but most of the tenants don't - half of them right off the plane from the island anyway. Motherfuckers getting away with murder. Tenants don't know their rights, landlords stop repairing the buildings. When a boiler breaks, it stays broke, and people try to heat their houses with their kitchen stoves. Motherfucker landlords don't pay their taxes to the city, and keep on milking rents. That goes on for a couple years 'til the city gives a final warning that they gonna take the building. Then the motherfucker landlords send in somebody to torch it so they can collect fire insurance. Finally, they strip it clean; plumbing, copper pipes, wire, anything else worth anything, leave a burned-out shell. It's like a regular routine. Been goin' on all over the neighborhood. Some blocks look like they been bombed."

Chico's part of the Lower East Side, the blocks east of Avenue A from 14th Street south to Houston, had been hit the hardest. By the early seventies almost half of the buildings had been burned out and abandoned.

Years later Pedro was hanging out with Chico in the park over by the band shell one afternoon. "Man, things are tough; no work, and I been livin' on canned beans for weeks. I mean ham and eggs for me would be like a lobster dinner or something. My rents due tomorrow, and I'm broke."

"Why pay rent?" Chico jumped up, excited. "I know this sounds crazy, Pedro but there's apartments all around us for free. We'll go into the burned-out buildings and fix them up."

"But we don't have any money, Bro, you need equity,

you know, cash, to do something like that."

"We got our sweat; our labor, our own work."

He began to scout the neighborhood for a likely building. He talked to Hoffman about it. "What about conservation and solar energy, Chico? You could be the first." It was 1974, the "energy crisis" was in full swing, with cars lined up two blocks down Houston Street waiting to buy gas.

Chico liked the idea. "We'll be on the frontier, the new pioneers in Loisaida, urban homesteaders!"

They went back to 11th St., a building where he lived when he was a kid, before the landlord torched it, and went to work. The first job was just to clean out the building. The city started to hassle them right away, sending the cops to kick them out and seal it up. But Chico and the others always came back. It took six months of steady work, and fighting with the cops and the housing department, but they finally got the building gutted.

Then the real work began; the rebuilding. Chico convinced some of the union guys in the neighborhood to train them. He went back to Jack Hoffman, who helped them design the energy systems. The pieces were starting to fall into place for Chico's greatest success, Sweat Equity Urban Homesteading; housing by the people and for the people; a way to create life out of death.

Chico used his press contacts to get some media coverage of the project, the City got interested. In fact

H.P.D. started falling all over itself to co-operate. Things were moving, but Chico had to line up some money for materials. He finally found a small dairy co-op upstate, run by an old socialist, that promised him a no-interest loan to set up a low-income housing co-op. The day Chico got word of the loan he offered to purchase the building from the city for one hundred dollars. They had no choice but to accept, given the publicity surrounding the project.

They rebuilt the whole house, from top to bottom; new roof, new floors, plumbing and wiring. People left the group for different reasons, and new people joined. Everybody wanted a decent place to live, but it was hard work. There were all kinds of hassles; decisions that had to be made, a budget to manage, city inspectors to deal with. Folks argued and marriages broke up. Three and a half years later, when they finally finished, only six of the original crew were left.

But, those who stayed learned how to work together, how to make decisions and help each other. When they put the solar collectors on the roof they threw a party for the whole neighborhood.

They managed the building collectively, and everybody had to put in one afternoon a week of sweat equity for maintenance. There were still problems, but for the most part, things worked. The building attracted a lot more attention, stories on T.V. and in the papers. *Newsweek* called them a new model for urban renewal. Then everybody in the neighborhood wanted buildings. Chico set up technical assistance projects and a construction co-op to share tools. People took over forty other buildings.

The City was overwhelmed. They had to respond when the press covered a series of sit-ins and protests organized by Chico and the other groups. Besides, it was clearly to H.P.D.'s advantage to fund the projects. They were creating low-income housing at one quarter the cost of what the government spent. H.P.D. set up an "experimental program" where the squatters got legal title to the buildings they seized and a fund of low interest loan money to finance renovations. The Sweat Equity Urban Homesteading movement had become a force in Loisaida.

Angie interrupted his reverie. "Earth to Chico! Where you at, man? You all right? Your brow is all creased, brother. 'Sup?"

He stared out the window at a flock of pigeons descending to the roof of the building across the street. "That bastard Rolón!"

It had been an exciting time; people beginning to feel like they could control their own lives, instead of being helpless victims. They had started holding "town meetings" every few months, to bring together the homesteaders and the gardeners with neighborhood artists and health care activists, people trying to a start a neighborhood credit union and others. Out of these meetings grew new projects; a food co-op, a fuel oil co-operative, a neighborhood recycling center, a youth center. It was a way for people to learn democracy, make it work every day of their lives.

Neighborhood artists understood. Poets and playwrights wrote about their lives on the Lower East Side. They performed everywhere; in vacant lots, in the parks, in storefronts and on street corners. They talked about gangs and drugs and winos and rent strikes. The murals that surrounded *El Jardin* were only a few of the dozens painted around the neighborhood, showing famous moments in local history or familiar themes of neighborhood life. Local graffiti artists painted some of them. Chico had begun to feel like they were making real progress.

They created cafes and performance spaces where folks could discuss and argue, where news and gossip were exchanged. People discovered who their neighbors were and saw what they could do working together. They created a sense of community. Chico knew that was the start for any movement about real change.

Gardens blossomed in vacant lots all over the neighborhood. At first he worried that the gardens would be vandalized. But any hint of mischief brought an instant response from the grandmothers on the front stoop or the kids playing under the open hydrant down the block. Each garden was more elaborate than the next; one with brick paths, another with a shrine to the virgin, another with a rustic garden shed, or a series of trellises. Some simply provided a green space to sit and relax, offering refuge from the unrelenting concrete; others grew food, organic vegetables. The transformation of the environment, the kind of thing he and Jack Hoffman had spent long nights discussing, was beginning to happen.

The successes of the movement; the gardens, the murals, the shift from death to life, was part of what made the neighborhood so attractive to the gentrifiers. The Lower East Side was happening, lots of exciting things were going on.

Then it started to slip away. Chico watched the movement lose the initiative, their energy turned against them by the jiu jitsu of the real estate market. The neighborhood started changing, fast.

At first it was artists and students looking for low rents. They created little enclaves and were soon followed by the bars, restaurants and clubs. The sixties had left a hip residue on Lower East Side that the newcomers grafted onto and transformed. By the early eighties a counter-culture of punk rockers and anarchists flourished east of Avenue A. When the landlords saw what was happening, rents began to go up and buildings that had been on the market for years began to sell.

The clubs along Avenue A and the galleries that sprung up on the side streets began to attract the limo set, down slumming. The ads for apartments in the *Voice* started to call the neighborhood "Alphabet City", and suddenly it was a cool place to live. Big developers got interested. Chico remembered a building on Avenue B that sold for $12,000, then $60,000 and finally, without being fixed up at all, $300,000 over a period of fourteen months. Landlords forced out poor tenants to make way for the gentry.

Chico and others in the movement fought back. They protested and tried to pressure the Community Board and the City. But it was a losing battle. Chico realized that their first move in the early days should have been to secure community ownership of all of the abandoned properties. Suddenly they were a hot commodity and the City wanted to sell them to the highest bidder.

By then the neighborhood had been hit by what Chico thought of as the four plagues; gentrification, homelessness, crack, and AIDS.

Chico looked out his office window as a woman walked by, pushing a shopping cart full of her belongings, screaming obscenities to nobody in particular. He knew that by mid-morning a line of people would form, waiting for the church soup kitchen to start serving. They dressed in layers of rags and huddled together on the street corner to stay warm. Always a presence on the Bowery, now they sat on the sidewalk and in doorways all over the neighborhood. Their jaundiced eyes pleaded with passersby who stepped over them without a word.

Nor was the third plague without precedence. Drugs had always been part of life on the Lower East Side. But the crack epidemic was something else again.

Local kids were sucked up into the trade. The choice was obvious when you could flip burgers at Mickey D's for $4.50 an hour or earn a thousand dollars a week as a runner or a lookout for the local crew.

The drug's power was incredible. Chico remembered Jorge, one of his oldest comrades. He'd always had a little drinking problem, but he kept it together, until he was seduced by crack. They had been forced to kick him out of *La Cabaña*. It had nearly killed Chico to watch helplessly as Jorge's personality disintegrated, and he began to cannibalize the group. The last straw had come when they caught him trying to steal their computer.

Cars from New Jersey and Connecticut cruised the neighborhood, and held up traffic while the runners filled their orders. Chico remembered Willy, killed just a few weeks ago right down the block. Chico had known him his whole life. He wasn't a bad kid, only fifteen. Eleven and twelve years olds were packing Uzis and Tech Nines, child soldiers in the drug war. Crack was bleeding the neighborhood dry, and there was no end in sight.

Totally unprecedented, though, was the spread of the AIDS epidemic. Chico had buried three friends in the past year. The H.I.V. virus was spreading faster in the Lower East Side than in any other neighborhood in the city, and there seemed no way to stem the tide. They tried education. They set up a needle exchange. Chico and a few of the fellows handed out condoms outside the high school every week. The word in the neighborhood was that the AIDS epidemic was a C.I.A. plot. Chico wasn't sure, but people just kept on dying. The System was winning.

Folks fell away, got lost, and slipped through the cracks. Brothers and sisters got drawn back into the mire of the streets. Sometimes he felt like it was hopeless. Chico worried about them all. He took everything personally and often his broad shoulders sagged under the weight of his concern. There were times when he felt it was all he could do to save one person; to help a burned out family find an apartment, get a job for a brother, help somebody kick a heroin habit or stop drinking themselves to death. He was an organizer, a psychotherapist, sometimes a baby sitter, helping with child care so that a sixteen-year-old could visit her daughter's father in prison. People came to see him with their problems and he did what he could to help. All this in addition to earning his living on a late night shift driving a gypsy cab. His work in the community consumed him, but somehow he never felt that he was doing enough.

Chico flipped through his Rolodex, crammed full of contacts that he had made over the years, and then picked up the phone. He dialed the number of a sympathetic staffer at the office of H.P.D. "Hey, Rod, it's Chico Santiago," he said into the phone. "What's the deal? How you been man?...Yeah, that's good...Me? I'm fine... Listen, Rod, I need some information... *El Jardin*, the housing for there... What took me so long? You were expecting this call?... Yeah, uh-huh...I figured as much...Like a pig rolling in shit...Do tell...You bet, all the gory details." Chico sat drumming a pencil on his desk, listening for several minutes. "That bad, huh? Well, I figured something had to be up. Okay, thanks Rod. I owe you a beer sometime...Sure, give me a call. See you." Chico hung up the phone. He did not look happy.

"Well? What's goin' on?" Angie leaned over his desk.

"It's Rolón, and it's bad." Chico shredded a piece of paper. "Just like I thought. His outfit, Action for Housing, gets the contract. They build it under a J-21, they get the land free and HUD loans them all the money for construction at 1%. They don't pay taxes for twenty years. Half of the apartments have to rent to low and middle income for eight years, and he's guaranteed a fat management contract. The other half- whatever the market will bear. Then, after the eight years are up, he can go market rate with all the units.

"It's a total fucking scam, and a gold mine for Rolón. And, according to my buddy Rod, there's nothin' we can do about it. It's perfectly legal. Plus, he wins big time politically. Anybody who comes out against it he can claim is against low-income housing and with the punk rockers and the anarchists, who he's been trying to get rid of anyway. And we lose *El Jardín* for good. Next he'll come for *La Cabaña*, he's had his eye on this building for years. Meanwhile he scores points with his real estate buddies uptown, and they crank things up another notch. Beautiful! We're gettin' squeezed from all sides, and I don't like it!"

Chapter 9

Sonia coughed. "Cathy, darling, can you get me a glass of water, please? My throat gets so dry when I talk. Probably because I don't talk so much here. I have no one to talk to. Most of them here are a little, you know... not all there. Oh, the staff are nice enough, they treat me well, really. But they don't want to hear me talk. They don't want to listen to my stories. They don't indulge me like you do. No one else wants to know. But your being here is wonderful. I wouldn't be so happy if someone gave me a million dollars."

"It's easy for me to get here Grandma. I can't stand the thought of you all alone. I love you." She leaned over and hugged the old woman.

"I know, Cathy, I know you do. But do you really have the time? I don't want to keep you from important things. You're not working today? You've got nothing better to do than to sit all day with an old lady?"

"No, Grandma. I can stay for a while. They put me on a dinner shift so I've got plenty of time. Can I get you anything else?"

"No darling, I'm fine. Not the least tired. Just the water, and maybe you could put up the back of the bed for me? So I can see you better." Catherine cranked the back of Sonia's bed to a more vertical position and then poured a glass of water from the pitcher on the end table.

"Thank you, darling, thank you", Sonia took a sip, her wrinkled hand trembling. "Tell me what's with you? Your life must be very busy. I remember what it was like, seventeen years old."

"My life? I guess I am kind of busy, like with the squat, where I live. We're trying to fix up the building, and I work on *The Avalanche*,"

"What's a squat, Cathy?"

"You know, like, we're squatting in an abandoned building."

"You live in an abandoned building?"

"Yeah, but, were like, fixing it up. It's a great place to live."

"I hope it's safe, darling."

"Don't worry, Grandma, it's safe."

"OK, Cathy, if you say so. And what is *The Avalanche*?"

"It's a paper."

"Really darling, a newspaper?"

"Yeah, like an anarchist paper, you know. I love it, I mean, like, I write articles, and I'm on the editorial collective."

"A collective? How wonderful."

"Except for this one guy, he tries to boss everybody around."

"Oh yes, I know darling, there are always some difficult personalities..."

"This guy's beyond difficult Grandma, like, he's a real asshole. He threatened to kick me off the paper."

"But you said it was a collective!"

"I told my boyfriend Mike that we should, like, get rid of this guy."

"Oh, sounds to me you should have a meeting to work this out."

"You know how sometimes you can't, like, get somebody to hear you? To listen to you? This guy doesn't listen...ever. It's hard to even talk around him, he takes up a lot of space . He sort of dominates the meetings, always gets his way."

"This person is an anarchist?"

"I guess; he says he is."

"But this is no way for an anarchist to behave."

"Yeah, like, I know. He thinks he's a leader or something. I'm so sick of him bossing me around. Seems like I'm always getting bossed around; when I was in school; at work; back in Scarsdale..."

"The world is full of people who want to be boss. But this is not a leader. You need to speak out, darling. It's a matter of principle!"

"Last time I tried to talk to him he started screaming at me, and threatened to fire me."

"Then let the collective make a statement to him"

"Good idea, grandma." Catherine smiled and took Sonia's hand. "But grandma, I want you to tell me what happened after you escaped to Finland. I brought a map, I looked." Catherine pulled a page with a map of Scandinavia on it from her Mexican bag.

"Oh yes, but you know I need a magnifier, and even then, the writing is so small.."

"I'll show you" Catherine leaned over with the map and traced a line with her finger from St. Petersburg across the Gulf to the Finnish shoreline. "See, Grandma, it, like, made your story come alive for me. It helped me visualize it."

"Darling, it's just an old lady's story. I don't want to bore you."

"Bore me?" Catherine was astounded. "Grandma, I want to hear more. I want to hear it all."

"O.K., darling, I'm so glad you're interested. I want you should hear, so you can remember. Memory and imagination, they hold the key to everything. Nothing is impossible, but somebody has to remember, to learn from the memories, a whole lifetime full. But really, you should read the oral history. I try, but the details..." Sonia paused for a moment, to stare out the window.

"I've been reading it, Grandma. It's great. I'm so glad my father did that."

"Yes, darling, it was a wonderful project."

"But I still want to hear from you, Grandma"

"Ok, so I'll tell, what little I can remember. From

Terijoki we went to England."

"You lived in England? Like Karl Marx, huh? I haven't got to that part yet."

"Just like Karl Marx," Sonia gave a little laugh. "Noise everywhere, down the narrow streets and alleys between the buildings. It was always loud there, overwhelming. We had lived in a shtetl, a tiny village, and then we were in London. Only, despite all the hustle and bustle in many ways it was still like a shtetl."

"What do you mean, Grandma? I went to London with Mom and Dad when I was in the sixth grade, it's huge, as big as New York."

"We lived there in our own little world, all the people were Jewish. If it weren't for Poppa we would never have seen the rest of London, but he insisted. Whenever he had a day off he would take us out; museums, Piccadilly, Covent Garden. Every Saturday, we went somewhere, and a bigger world started to open up for Sasha and me."

"How old were you?"

"At this time, I must have been six or seven. Listen, darling, could you please pour me another glass of water? My throat is so dry. But it's good to talk, to remember all of this. Some days I try, but I can't remember the details. But today, with you, it's like I'm there again." The old woman's voice was cracking.

Catherine poured more water from the pitcher on the bedside stand and handed it to Sonia. "Are you O.K., Grandma?"

"Yes, darling, please. Just let me have a drink." She swallowed a few sips. "After a few years in London, Poppa left us to go to America, earn money and then bring us over. It was very stressful, the whole time we were separated. Finally he saved enough money to send for us to join him."

"You know, it, like, helps me put things in perspective ...reading your story, and talking to you."

"What do you mean, darling?"

"Oh, like, when I start feeling sorry for myself about the paper and stuff, and then I think about all the things you went through in your life."

"You know, it's true, I've been through plenty in my life, but also many wonderful times. We had our parties and fundraisers; dances with different themes; Peasant Balls where we would dress like they used to in Russia and dance late into the night. And the Yom Kippur Balls, every year on the highest holy day of the Jewish calendar. We rejected religion, of course. 'Neither man nor God above us,' They would say.

"I never felt that comfortable with the Yom Kippur Balls, but they would all laugh at me. It wasn't that I believed in God, but the religious, and even the not so religious -- the ones who went to shul only on the high holy days- they were offended. We mocked them, it was very disrespectful I thought. We drove away people who might have listened to us otherwise. I didn't see the point of it. It seemed, well.., unnecessary. We had enough enemies; the press, the politicians, by this time even some of the other socialists, the Marxists especially. After some years we stopped having the Balls. Oh, I'm not saying I convinced anybody, but the movement came to realize that maybe it wasn't such a good idea."

Catherine shifted in her seat, thinking about the meeting at the old school she had attended, and the way the Puerto Ricans had reacted to her and her friends. What were they doing that drove them away?

Sonia coughed. "I must be boring you, darling."

"No Grandma! I was just thinking about something. I want to hear more, if you're OK."

"Yes, darling, I'm fine. " Sonia coughed again. "We were very experimental. The arts too, the artists were extremely attracted to us. Freedom, they understood it. Writers, poets. painters, sculptors, playwrights, musicians, all free spirits. We supported them; we published them; we encouraged the avant-garde. It was only natural that they were drawn to us. What a time it was! We were at the heart of the movement, on the cutting edge of change. I often spoke about this. I felt so lucky to be there, to be involved with the movement. I was alive, really alive; part of something bigger than myself."

"I know that feeling," Catherine smiled, thinking about the paper.

"Do you darling? Then you are very lucky, because most people never do. I've been lucky too. I've felt that way my whole life. I know we didn't make the revolution yet. But we made many things change; working conditions, hours, wages, civil rights, women's rights, sexual freedom. None of it would have changed without us. And most important, we've kept the dream alive. Without the dream people would have nothing. Through all history people have had a vision of a better world; freedom, peace, enough for everyone. These are the things we fought for against the State, the capitalists, the bosses and the owners."

Sonia sighed. "We had our influence. Just reforms, you might say. But I don't feel that I wasted a minute, not even a minute. There would have been no change without us fighting, pushing, demanding. Yes, it's true, some things discourage me. But as long as there are still people who dream, who believe in the principle of hope, who feel like you do darling, than I can die a happy woman. Because I helped to keep the dream alive."

"Yes, you did Grandma." Catherine, gazed into Sonia's clouded eyes and squeezed her hand.

Sonia turned her head and stared out the window at the river; rolling green, brown and blue, reflecting clouds and sky, shadows and light. Catherine sat there for a long time. Finally Sonia spoke. "I do need to rest now, darling. You should go, you've spent your whole morning with me. Come back soon Cathy, don't forget me."

Catherine kissed her cheek. "Goodbye, Grandma, I love you." She left the room, closing the door gently behind her and walked down the steps of the nursing home onto the windy street. She was lost in thought and her steps carried her, without conscious direction on her part, toward the basement office of *The Avalanche*.

Chapter 10

They worked in the office until almost 9 o'clock. "What are we going to do, Angie? It don't look good. I'm not even sure the other community groups will back us up on this one. I guess it's just us and the punk rockers, huh?" They both laughed.

"Let's go somewhere," Angie got up from the desk. "I could use a beer."

"Yeah, good idea."

"Let's check out the Café."

"Bet, I could use a cold one too right about now."

They walked over to Third Street and Avenue C, where they entered a storefront painted by a neighborhood graffiti artist. Huge letters above the door spelled out "Poets Cafe."

The club was jumping and Chico started to feel better as soon as he walked in. There was a bar along one side and the rest of the room held round tables packed close together. The room was full of noise; music, laughter, and clanging beer bottles. At one end was a small stage and a dance floor that was crowded with couples moving to the salsa that echoed through the room. The lights were low, but Chico could make out that the crowd was mostly Puerto Rican, though there were whites and blacks there too.

Chico and Angie were met by shouted greetings when they walked in. Chico squeezed his way through the crowd to the bar and got them each a Bud. He joined Angie and the poet, Pedro, who were sitting at a small table at the edge of the dance floor.

A Ruben Blades song came on and Angie grabbed Chico's hand, pulling him to his feet. He placed his hands gently on her hips and they began to dance. He took her hand and as they moved to the clave he began to twirl her through an intricate series of turns and dips. She was a fluid dancer who made it look easy. Through all of the twists and turns she never missed a beat. Chico liked the effortless way she anticipated his next move. When the dance was over they applauded themselves wildly and the crowd shouted "*Vaya!*" Chico was breathing hard when he sat down, but Angie laughed and pulled Pedro up onto the dance floor when the next tune began. "I'll wear you both out before the night's over!"

True to her word, she danced with one or the other of them until the music ended and the stage lights came on. A man wearing a white shirt, a red tie, and a porkpie hat walked to the microphone on the stage and started to address the crowd, but his words were lost in a screech of feedback. He jumped and waved to the soundman seated in the D.J. booth. "Testing," he said, and his voice reverberated through the room.

"All right! I know you've been having a great time tonight, but it's about to get better. We're going to start the poetry now. We've got a lot of wonderful poets here tonight; ready to read. But if you're not on my list and you want to recite something too, that's cool! Just come see me to sign up. It's an open mike and you're all in for something special. So, let's get started, here's our first poet for tonight," he glanced at his list, "Jorge Caballero."

There was a smattering of applause from the audience as a skinny young man nervously approached the mike. "Go for it, brother!" someone shouted in encouragement. The young man adjusted the height of the microphone and then began to declaim. His poem was in rhyming couplets. It was a declaration of love for a woman named Maria and it was a terrible poem. Maria was present at a table not far from Chico's, hiding her face in her hands and trying to sink beneath her table while Jorge read. The audience laughed, cat-called and booed.

Next up was a middle-aged white woman, heavy set with straight black hair, worn long. She read a poem about walking in SoHo. It was an angry poem and she touched something in the audience because the room became suddenly quiet and the people attentive, hanging on every word. When she finished, there was a moment of silence and then applause and cries for more. So she read another, this one about a woman and her cat. It was a sensual poem, full of sexual imagery, but perhaps less accessible than the first. People listened respectfully, but the response was polite rather than enthusiastic, so she sat down.

Next Pedro was called to the mike. He and Chico had first coined the name Loisaida years earlier, in a moment of linguistic genius which had simultaneously Hispanized the name Lower East Side and made reference to the town of Losada, a place outside of San Juan from which some of Loisaida's residents hailed. The name was important, a commitment to the place; a statement of identification for the people who lived there; a way of saying "This is our town."

Pedro greeted the crowd like they were old friends. He made a joke about Maria and the painful love poem her boyfriend had read. The crowd laughed and Maria blushed crimson at this renewed attention. But it was all in good humor and Pedro set her at ease before he drew a deep breath, waited a moment, and began to recite.

> *"Loisaida, what next?*
> *I walk your streets day after day*
> *and I wonder what will you bring?*
> *Will it be life or will it be death?*

So many brothers and sisters gone now
victims of your cruelty
ground down by the weight of your mean streets
buried in the rubble of your tenement buildings
left to die like rats by an uncaring world."

"Loisaida, what will it be for me today?
Life or death, love or hate?
You hold it all and who can say?
You have no reason
only the cold logic of your streets
the brutal calculus of a time
that never should have been
Loisaida, what's next?"

The room went wild. Chico clapped him on the back when he sat down. "Well said, Brother Pedro, well said." They ordered another round of beers and waited for the next poet.

Chapter 11

From Terijoki we took another train, this one to Helsinki. We stayed a few days, at a hotel, near the train station, while Poppa booked us passage on a steamer to England, London. The next day we bundled up and headed for the docks. Now we had a trunk with some things from the refugee aid society in Terijoki. I remember looking up at the huge boat that was to take us. It seemed enormous to me, but it was just a tramp steamer, not the ocean liner I thought. The ship's name was written on the bow. I couldn't read it, but when we walked on board Momma told me it was the **Finnish Star**. They showed us to a stairway that led down to the depths of the hull. Dark, damp and cold, those are my strongest memories.

We sailed around for over two weeks, stopping in Oslo and other, smaller ports too, loading and unloading cargo. When we stopped we would go out into the town to buy food, but for the most part we stayed down in the hold and tried to stay warm. When we reached Copenhagen, we knew the trip was nearly over. Three more days, across the North Sea and down the coast to London. We docked at Gravesend, we cleared immigration and customs and we took a trolley to the East End.

Whitechapel Road. We stayed there almost five years. Poppa and Momma both found work in the garment industry. The streets were narrow, cobbled, they all twisted and turned. No logic, it was a medieval section of the city. The stone houses were ancient, three and four stories, cold, damp, with the first story, like a basement, sunk below street level. We played in the roadway, there were no sidewalks, dodging horse drawn wagons and pushcarts, piles of dung and garbage. The neighborhood was full of Yiddish voices, so noisy, always with the haggling and arguing. The shops hung signs in Hebrew for dry goods, tobacco, religious items, provisions, bakeries, kosher butchers, and tea shops.

We lived in one of the basement flats, dark, cold. And always damp, so damp. My brother Sasha and I would lay under a quilt filled with goose down. In the kitchen a group of Poppa's friends would argue around the table. I remember the voices. "Sol, you're crazy! They'll never kill the Czar, he's too closely guarded. And if they do, what then? I tell you education is the key, the peasants must be educated!"

Poppa would answer "Oh, is that so Mr. Know-It-All? Change in Russia needs action, not just talk. Believe me, just a year ago I was there. From London what can you know? Tell me, I'm listening!" I must have heard the same argument a dozen times before, but I still found it fascinating. It had been the same in the shtetl, only I was too young to understand then.

I would pretend to be asleep with my eyes closed under the covers, but I listened to their discussions. I remember the smell of their pipes and cigars, and the sound of the spoons tinkling against their glasses when they stirred their tea.

Poppa was very active in the radical community. What a collection of people it was; Nihilists; socialists of all stripes; Chartists, Marxists, Anarchists; reformists and revolutionaries. I was dragged to all the meetings and then Poppa and his friends would come back to our kitchen table and argue through the night about this point or that speaker. All of the problems of the world they solved around our kitchen table. Not just the problems of Russia, or the workers. Art, literature, religion -- Poppa was very scornful of religion -- science, evolution, politics, philosophy. These were not educated people, but they certainly weren't ignorant. They were self-taught, interested in everything. All the new developments they wanted to know. So we went to all the lectures, all the speakers, almost every night a meeting.

One in particular I remember, What an impression this man made. Momma, Poppa, and all the others had come directly from the factories where they just spent twelve hours cutting coats or piecing together dresses. They were exhausted, but Poppa lifted me to his lap so that I could get a better look at the speaker, Rudolf Rocker, skinny, balding, dressed in a suit and tie, really not much to look at, kind of a nebbish.

But then he began to speak, "Comrades, fellow workers!" even though he wasn't Jewish he spoke perfect Yiddish. "I have come to talk to you about the promised land," he told us. Not the heaven of the bible, but the heaven on earth that we, the exploited working men and women of the world could create for ourselves. He told us to seize the means of production; fight the capitalists and the bosses; take what is rightfully ours; reclaim our humanity, our birthright! And to do that we needed a weapon, the most powerful weapon we had at our disposal -- the general strike!

I was entranced. I had been to lectures with Poppa before, but never had I heard anyone like this. This speaker seemed to get bigger as he continued, until he looked to me like he was ten-feet tall. His voice filled the hall, and with every word the crowd became more alive.

"Anarcho-Syndicalism will be the vehicle through which we will gain our freedom!" he told us. The crowd was silent and then applause and shouts rang out through the auditorium. It was that evening I decided I was an anarchist.

His words stayed with me for days afterward. I lay awake at night thinking about the workers' paradise Rocker had described. After hearing his call for revolution all of the others, the socialists and Marxists seemed bland and uninteresting.

Rudolf Rocker, he was the one. We had to organize the workers into syndicates, unions, and back up our demands with action. Oh, he was really something.

It was hard being there. As long as we stayed in the East End it was fine, everybody spoke Yiddish and we could get along with no problem. But when we went out, English made no sense. It was just sounds; noises. Oh, we knew a few words, but not enough to really talk, and we couldn't read the language, not at all. So, soon Sasha started to learn English, and to teach me too.

He took me to the library. The building was like a castle, or a temple. Carved stone, with massive oak doors. Oh, I felt over-whelmed, the main reading room was huge, a cavern. A woman with dark hair in a tight bun, and glasses perched on the bridge *of her nose glared at us from behind the circulation desk. Sasha took my hand and asked her for newspapers. She was not unfriendly; she pointed us toward a rack of papers. Sasha chose* **The Daily Mail,** *and then we sat at one of the tables that filled the reading room. The woman with the glasses watched us from behind her desk while he read to me, very softly.*

Every day we returned. Oh, how I looked forward to our visits! It was quiet there with the tables and all the books; my sanctuary, a place to escape from the noise that filled the neighborhood, the streets, even our flat. We became regulars and the librarian who had greeted us that first day learned to expect us every afternoon. She began to help us, suggesting books. My favorite was Dickens; **Great Expectations, A Tale of Two Cities,** *a*nd **Oliver Twist.**

This was the most wonderful gift that anyone ever gave to me. Sasha was very able. We attended classes at the Jewish settlement in the morning, and then we would go to the library and he would help me. We were very lucky, most of the other children had to go to the factories or do piece work at home. But Poppa insisted. He valued learning. He came from a rabbinical family, you know. My English came along, slowly at first. But soon I was able to translate for Momma and Poppa when we went out of the neighborhood.

When we lived in London, life went along okay. But then there were hard times, economically, you understand, a recession, and Poppa lost his job. Also, I think he was restless, and a little disillusioned maybe. He thought life outside Russia, in the West, would be a wonderland. He thought it would be an enlightened place, where workers would be treated with respect and there would be real democracy. Well, we were better off in London, at least we didn't have to worry about the police -- but freedom and democracy? No, that we didn't find. We were still exploited and oppressed, and Poppa, always the dreamer, was still looking for utopia.

So one night over dinner he announces, "We're going to America". Just like that! I suppose he talked it over with Momma, but this was the first Sasha and I heard of it. America! The golden land! It sounded very exciting. But then he explained to us that he would go over first, find a job, and then send for us. I was so upset; the thought of life without Poppa, even for a little while, and to break up the family, after all we had been through together! I couldn't stand it. I cried and begged, but in the end I had no choice. I had to accept it.

It was common then, the husband would go, find a job, save money and then send for the rest of the family. Only sometimes they wouldn't send, they would just disappear into that strange land called America. We had all heard stories. Not that Poppa would ever desert us, though maybe that fear was part of what upset me so much.

But it was decided, Poppa would go first, to New York, then we would follow. In six months they said, though it turned out to be almost two years We put him on a train to Liverpool one warm night in July. I cried the whole way home from the station. He had a ticket for a boat that sailed the next day. It was two months before we got his letter saying he had arrived safely. A week later we got another saying he had found work, and he was living with a cousin and some other comrades in a place called the Lower East Side in New York, twelve of them sharing a flat to save money. He was working in a coat factory. Until that first letter arrived, every night I lay awake worrying, convinced I would never see Poppa again.

I remember how excited I was, and a little scared too, when Momma told Sasha and me that we would be leaving for America soon. This time we sailed on a real ocean liner, **The Brussels**. But if anything, conditions were worse. We came over steerage, of course.

Oh, it was a horror, an absolute horror! To begin we had to go down the narrow stairway into the hold and when we went the passageway door slammed shut behind and the last ray of sunlight vanished. I held onto the hem of momma's skirt, and when my eyes adjusted to the darkness I couldn't believe the scene. The hold was full of people, frightened families like us, clutching suitcases and holding tight to crying children. A few kerosene lanterns provided the only light. It looked to me like a Bosch painting of hell that I had seen when Poppa took us to the National Gallery.

Momma had to elbow her way through the crowd with me and Sasha, until she found our beds. Three hard slats, with mattresses thin as cardboard, stacked one on top of another, and barely room to stow our suitcases underneath. Then we collapsed, exhausted from moving and saying goodbye.

When the ship left the dock everybody down in the hold burst into applause. Voices called out. "We're on our way!" "Off to America!" "The promised land at last!" "Next stop, New York!" But they changed their tune once the ship was at sea. Our hold sat atop the stirring screws, and the screeching of steel railings and hawsers was so loud you couldn't even think. And within an hour Momma called for a bucket. She gagged and vomited into a pail the whole trip. And she was not alone. All around us, people green with sea sickness. The sounds of retching became a regular part of the voyage, and the smell was constant. The scene was like a Roman vomitorium after an orgy.

I was one of the lucky ones, with me the sickness came and went. I could keep down a little kasha. For many others it was constant. Two people died on the voyage, and one night we all lay awake to the moans and screams of a woman giving birth. They had to pry the stillborn baby from her arms and sent it up to be disposed of overboard like the buckets of vomit. Can you imagine? They wouldn't let us up on deck with the fancy passengers. I think most of them didn't even know we were on board. Like cattle they treated us

It was a nightmare. We spent twenty seven days in that hellhole, twenty seven days of torment. Momma, Sasha and I tried to keep our spirits up by talking about Poppa and our new home in America, the Lower East Side. I knew it would be better than London. America, after all was the land of freedom, the land of opportunity. We had come so far, traveled so long already, been through such hardship. Surely we would find our true home and happiness in New York. Rocker's workers' paradise danced in my head and that hope was the only thing that made our passage bearable. That, and the fact that we would be reunited with Poppa.

Finally we arrived in New York. When we left the hold and walked on deck we got our first glimpse of the city, the buildings shining in the sunlight. We trudged down the gang-

122

plank with our suitcases in hand. Sick, exhausted, filthy, but still excited; they herded us into a big room at Ellis Island. And then suddenly it seemed a hoax, a big joke. The immigration people were no better than Cossacks. They treated us like we were animals. They hosed us down and inspected us, poked at us, even our private parts. Sasha and I spoke English, so it wasn't as bad for us as for most of the others, who couldn't communicate with them at all. But in the end it didn't matter. We were in America! And soon we would be with Poppa. America, the streets paved with gold and freedom and opportunity for all!

Recorded: March 6, 1967, transcribed: March 23, 1967, For: Columbia Oral History Project, Immigrant Voices.

Chapter 12

It was two A.M., and Catherine was glad to be heading home. It had been a long week. Things were getting more unbearable at work. The weather had been bitterly cold, and she had been fighting with Mike. Then there was the situation at *The Avalanche*, and to top it all off, the garden!

She was pissed off at Mike because they hadn't been spending enough time together; that and the fact that he was a macho asshole. He and his buddies, Bobby and Riff, had evicted Jesse earlier in the day. It was nasty. Jesse pulled out a baseball bat in the end, not a gun, thankfully. But Mike took a direct hit in the side and Catherine was sure that he cracked a rib. He refused to go to the emergency room for an x-ray. Catherine could see him wince with every step he took, but he insisted that he wasn't hurt. Men were such jerks.

Catherine passed Enrique Langdon, who had a hood pulled up over his sky blue helmet. He swept his arm with a flourish to allow Catherine to pass. He spoke to her in Spanish. It almost sounded like a poem, or something. But she couldn't be sure.

All the Puerto Ricans knew Langdon. Kids followed him up and down the block, mocking him. Grandmothers loved him and brought him rice and beans and cafe con leche, Buscuello, dark and rich, smelling of the Island. His poems reminded them that they were still *Jivaros*, tied to that lush and cruel land to the last. And they made their children listen, so that they would not forget that, even though they were born in New York, they too were still Puerto Ricans. And the poets of the neighborhood whispered that he was the best; their Whitman, their Neruda, their god.

He cast his gifts every day before the deaf and blind like Catherine, who never stopped or listened, or even really looked at him. He never published a poem. He recited and wrote, wherever; street corner, park bench, front stoop, whenever the spirit moved him. *El Árbol que Habla*, The Talking Tree, chronicling the lives of his brothers and sisters, his sons and daughters. Everyone in the neighborhood knew him, grew up hearing his chants and incantations holding back the evil, keeping the neighborhood safe; he lived in a sacred space inhabited by madmen, beggars, and poets.

Catherine walked by him, and was so deep in thought that she was almost home before she realized that a fire truck and two police cars were parked in front of the squat. She ran up to a young cop who was standing by the front door. "What happened? Is anybody hurt?"

"Yeah, sure. Everybody's okay. Don't worry. You live here?"

"Yeah, I do. What's going on?"

"It was a fire." The cop stated the obvious, Catherine could smell the smoke and see the splintered door. "Somebody saw a guy wing a molotov into that empty storefront. He was wearing a leather jacket, they didn't get a real good look at him. The front door was locked, fire department had to bust it in, but they got the fire out. Nobody hurt. You know anybody who'd do that? Anybody got a thing goin' with you people? Problems with the neighbors? Any dealers in there? None of your pals there would tell us nothin'. Damn lucky somebody phoned it in right away. Old building like that'll burn fast. You know anything about this you better tell me. "

Was Mike okay? How about Lisa and little Jamaal? Her mind began racing. Somebody set the fire. Who? Some psycho, somebody mad at them, really mad. Jesse? He swore he would burn the building down if they evicted him. But she would never give any names to the cops regardless. The State had no place in the squat. If there was a problem they would solve it themselves.

She was frantic to get in and see how everyone was. She tried to walk past the cop, but he blocked her way. "You think of anything, you give me a call, Okay?" He handed her a card.

"Uh huh." She stepped around him and entered the hallway. Mike was talking with Charlie and Riff at the far end of the hall. She ran toward him through puddles of water.

"Mike! You all right?" She hugged him hard.

He let out a scream. "Shit, my ribs!"

She let him go. "Sorry, I forgot." Then, for the first time she really looked at the damage. The hall smelled of smoke and gasoline, and there was the water on the floor. She saw dark smudges on the new sheetrock wall they had put up over the weekend. The whole area was marked off with crime scene tape.

"That psycho, that fuckin' junkie son-of-a-bitch!" Mike was red in the face. "He could have killed us all! I'll kick his fuckin' ass up and down the block when I catch up with him!"

"Uh huh," said Catherine, hesitantly. She wasn't sure. Jesse proved that he was violent, but he was impulsive, somebody had planned this. Then she heard Charlie, the voice of experience, speak up.

"This sucks, It's gonna bring heat down on the building. The cops are already here. The fire Marshal too. They'll use this as an excuse to boot us. You better get ready people. I'm tellin' you. Wait and see. I know what I'm talkin' about. I've seen it before."

Great, just what she needed. Things were going from bad to worse.

Mike sensed her mood. "Don't worry, There's no

real damage, and Charlie's just going off. The City doesn't give a shit. They won't try to throw us out, you'll see."

Catherine remained unconvinced, and she brooded as they climbed the stairs to their apartment.

They slept late the next morning and when they woke up at around noon, decided to walk over to Leshko's on the Park and treat themselves to a real breakfast. Catherine did all right with tips the night before and she was hungry. Mike was always hungry.

They both ordered kielbasa with scrambled eggs and pirogis. Mike read the *Times* while Catherine stared out the window at the passing street scene. She noticed Chico Santiago coming toward them, tapped on the window and waved hello as he walked by. Chico barely nodded his head in response and kept on walking. He had been planning to go into Leshko's for lunch, but the last thing he wanted to do was chat with the young anarchists.

Catherine wondered about Chico. He stood up to Rolón at the meeting, one of the few who had, and it confirmed her opinion that Raven was wrong about him, as he was wrong about most things, she thought. Their plates arrived and Mike dropped his paper and started wolfing down his food. Catherine began to eat as well; with better table manners but no less relish. She was starving and the sausage and eggs tasted great. They emptied their plates.

Catherine sipped a second cup of coffee. "How do

your ribs feel today?"

"Okay," Mike picked up his *Times* and started reading again, shutting off all communication before it began.

"Michael! Don't read the paper now. I want to talk with you. Like, we haven't had a conversation all week." He looked at her over the paper. "You really don't think they'll kick us out of the building?"

He lowered the Weekend section and glared at her. "No, I don't think so. Look," he grimaced, "just let me finish this article, O.K.? It's about Madonna."

"Madonna! Who gives a shit about that bimbo?"

"I think she's sexy."

"Really? After all these months I discover that you're a Madonna fan."

"I'm not a fan, I just think she's sexy. Didn't you see her book?"

"Reading about Madonna is more important than talking to me, huh? That tells me a lot about our relationship!"

"You want to talk about our relationship?" He folded the paper and put it down.

"No, not really, I just want to talk. I'm worried. Like, what'll we do if they throw us out?"

"There's nothing to worry about. They're not gonna throw us out. Nobody's gonna throw us out, and if they do we'll find another building to squat."

"Don't you ever wish we had a real apartment? Like Paula's; some place with a shower and a toilet and a phone?" She brushed a strand of purple hair out of her eyes.

"What a lot of bourgeois crap. Are you going soft on me, you little bourg-monster?"

They both laughed and Mike winced. "Your ribs still hurt, huh Mike? Why don't you go up to Bellevue?"

"They're just bruised or something. They'll be better in a day or two. Besides, I don't have any insurance and it would mean about twelve hours hanging around the emergency room, and I hate hospitals. Stop bugging me will you."

"Okay. I won't say another word. But, Dude, you know it's going to hurt if we have sex. Like, I don't wanna be responsible for your pain."

"All right, all right. I'll go up there tomorrow or something."

They laughed again, and Catherine started to feel better.

"What do you think the collective's going to decide about my story and the paper?"

"I don't have a clue. It's a shitty situation, but what are the alternatives? If he won't agree do we just walk away and turn the whole thing over to Raven? That sucks. I don't know, Cath."

"But we're supposed to be a collective, like, that means we make decisions together."

"I know, but what if he won't go along? You come up with any ideas?"

"Yes, one or two. But it really depends on where

people are at."

"What are you thinking?"

"You'll find out tonight. Like, I don't want to talk about it till then. What do you want to do this afternoon?"

"Let's go up to the Met. It's a free day and there's an exhibit I want to check out."

She agreed. They finished their coffee, left a tip, paid the bill and walked out into a gray afternoon.

Chapter 13

Sonia awoke suddenly with the sun shining through her window. She was too old to be bedeviled with dreams. She rubbed her eyes, recalling the details before they faded. She had been walking through the streets of her youth; pushcarts and horse drawn wagons crowded the avenue, and peddlers called out to the people jostling for a better view of the merchandise on display. But she was not interested in the buying and selling that was a constant feature of the neighborhood. Her step was quick. She was searching for someone; she wasn't quite sure who. Yiddish voices called to her from all sides, "Come back! Be careful! You've gone too far!" But she ignored them and kept walking, almost running now, with a feeling of desperation growing in her chest.

And then she knew that she would never find who she was looking for. Emptiness overwhelmed her, she felt hollow, and it was at this point that the morning sun woke her.

It had been years since she had the dream. She couldn't remember how long, but she was certain it was a long, long time. It was a dream she could never forget, one that had haunted her on and off for most of her life. She sat up, propping her head with a pillow.

Suddenly, the door opened. "Hi, Grandma, how are you today?" Catherine was cheerful. "You OK?" Her voice lowered when Sonia turned and she saw her face. "You look upset."

"No darling. I'm fine, I'm fine. I just woke up from a little nap, that's all. I was dreaming. You know I don't dream much these days. I'm an old lady now, and I sleep all the time. But a dream, that's unusual for me."

"Really? What were you dreaming about?" Catherine, removed her beret and leather jacket, throwing them on an empty chair.

"Ah, an old woman's dream. Nothing important. But how are you, darling? Everything all right?" Sonia brightened, throwing off the shadow of the dream. "How is work? Your boyfriend, how is he? Do I get to meet him? What have you been doing? Tell me darling. I sit here all day, and I sleep, but that's all. Bring me news. What's the world like these days?"

"I'm fine Grandma, nothing much happening. Mike's good. I'm working on a story about a new housing project they want to build. I've been a little upset though. There was a fire in our building. We don't know if the city's gonna try to kick us out or not" She sat down in the chair next to the bed.

"A fire? Darling, are you all right? Are you safe there? Maybe it's better if you find a new place."

"I'm fine Grandma, everybody's all right. No one was hurt and there was no real damage, just some scorched sheetrock. Please don't worry about it, I'll be O.K. I had to come see you though. I've been reading the binder you gave me. It's awesome! What a story. It really was another world."

"Yes it was, darling, we created alternatives. We built our own world on the Lower East Side. We had co-operatives, for food, anarchist black cross, prisoners aid, lots of projects and like I told, our own school. We organized the unions. We had our paper, the *Fraye Arbayter Shtime*, published for seventy years. Did you bring me a copy of your paper darling?"

"I'm sorry, Grandma, I forgot." Catherine looked at the floor. "I'll bring one next time I come, like, I promise. But I want to know about your dream. What was it?"

"It's OK, Cathy, don't worry. The dream? It's nothing darling, nothing. About Emanuel, your great grandfather, that's all. You shouldn't concern yourself. It was so long ago, ancient history." Sonia sighed.

"Emanuel? You mean Sam, don't you?"

"Oh, no darling. Didn't I tell you? You didn't get to that yet in my story? Sam raised Abe, and we were together for many years. But Abe's real father was Mannie. They never knew each other. Mannie was gone by the time Abe was born."

"You're kidding Grandma! Nobody ever told me this. What's the deal? Who was this guy? Like, what happened to him?"

"Darling, it's many years ago I saw him last. A lifetime ago. It was another world... Still, it pains me when I think about him. A wonderful man. He's dead a long time now. But he was very precious to me." Sonia smiled faintly at the memory.

"He died? He left you, or what? Come on Grandma!"

"All right, darling, if you insist. I'll tell. Get the album. I have pictures of him."

Catherine took the photo album from the drawer, sat on the bed and placed it between them. Sonia turned the brittle pages until she came to a photo of a laughing teenager with lustrous dark curls. The girl was embraced from behind by a smiling young man looking over her shoulder.

"That's Mannie. We were so young. Not even your age."

"And that's you Grandma. You were beautiful." Sonia's face in the photo was radiant. Her eyes sparkled and her smile was playful, slightly erotic, hinting at joy and pleasure. Dark hair framed the young face with ringlets. "You were really hot, Grandma."

Sonia laughed. "Hot, you think I was? But so innocent, Cathy, I was maybe sixteen when we took that photo. We were going to a picnic sponsored by the Workmen's Circle. I remember like it was yesterday.

135

Mannie was a wonderful man. He was very intelligent, a wonderful writer and speaker. He was very well thought of. And handsome! He was so handsome, you can see in the picture."

Catherine looked again at the yellowed page. "He was handsome grandma, kind of a hunk. I mean with those big arm muscles".

"Oh darling, he was very strong. Lots of other girls would have liked to be with him, but he only wanted me. In the movement then we talked a lot about free love. We sponsored Margaret Sanger at the Great Hall at Cooper Union, and we packed the place. She, Emma Goldman and others were arrested for teaching about birth control.

"We were very big on freedom to love who you wanted. Marriage, that was for the bourgeoisie and the religious. We scoffed at that. But for all our talk, our love of freedom, our radicalism, Mannie was always true to me." She glanced down at the picture again.

"Me, I have to admit that once I made a mistake; a comrade from Philadelphia, older, famous in the movement. I wouldn't say he took advantage, but I was very young. We drank some wine. Mannie was out in Stelton visiting his parents. I told him when he came back home. He never said a word. He didn't reproach me. After all I was a free woman. But I could see in his eyes that he was very hurt. I felt terrible; never again! I couldn't stand to hurt Mannie, I loved him so." Sonia shook her head slowly.

"Don't feel bad Grandma, I'm sure he forgave you. It wasn't your fault. Guys are all dogs when it comes to sex. Mike is obsessed."

"Yes , darling I'm sure you're right, he forgave me, but I still felt bad. I still do, to this day. Will I ever get to meet this Mike?"

"I don't know grandma, I guess. I mean why not? I would love for him to meet you. You're definitely the cool one in the family. I, like, told him all about you. I think you'd really like him; he's an artist, and he works on the paper, too. I mean, like , he can be a jerk sometimes, but...he's all right."

"That would be marvelous, Cathy, to meet him. A loving relationship is a wonderful thing, that's what Mannie and I had, it helped us in the movement. We thought we would be together forever." Sonia stretched her neck and sighed. "I get so stiff sitting here."

"Do you want to go up to the lounge, Grandma? I could like, take you up there in a wheelchair or something."

"What a lovely idea, Cathy. You wouldn't mind?"

"Of course not."

Sonia pressed a call button and an orderly entered the room, a large, black woman, who helped her into a wheelchair. Catherine pushed her to the elevator and they rode to the nursing home's top floor and a pleasant sun-filled room that looked out over the river, the co-ops to the South and the tenement rooftops, gleaming with ice to the North.

Catherine settled into a vinyl covered chair opposite Sonia. "So, like, what happened with this guy Mannie, Grandma?"

"I'll tell, I'll tell. Don't be so impatient. It takes me time to gather my thoughts," Sonia laughed. "We had only been on the Lower East Side a year or two. I was still a little girl when I first met Mannie. We lived on Eldridge Street when we first came over. It was always crowded, worse even than the black hole of Calcutta, and loud there. And smelly, it smelled always of horse manure. Poppa was working as a cutter in a coat factory, a sweatshop. This was before the union. A terrible place; dark and full of dust, worse than in the East End, worse than Russia even, in a way. Momma also had a job there, sewing buttonholes. Can you imagine, sewing buttonholes twelve, sometimes fourteen hours a day? They worked so hard! I don't know how Poppa managed but he still found time for his comrades from the old country.

"There was a whole group of them living on the Lower East Side then; even real old timers. Some had been quite famous in Russia. I can't remember them all, but there was Lvoff Hoffman, he tried to kill the Czar on the Moscow Railroad, smoked very smelly cigars, and Degaieff, who lived on Eldridge Street also.

"This is all in the papers, you should read it there."

"I want to hear it from you, Grandma. If you want to tell.

"Well, They had a special club where they all met to

138

talk politics, an old storefront over on Center Street. I remember when the newspapers found out they called it a bomb club. They always make everything sensational. Really, Poppa and his friends talked, and they sponsored lectures, raised funds for political prisoners, tried to educate. Some got very active in the early days of union organizing. It was through the club that I met Mannie for the first time. At a dance, a fund raiser.

"I was very proud, wearing my finest clothes, a gray shirtwaist with a white collar, that Momma made for me. They had rented a hall on Rivington St. It was dark and narrow, but they hung blue and white crepe paper, and to me, I was only ten years old, it seemed like a grand ballroom. A boy with curly red hair, he was very cute, I had noticed him earlier in the evening at the punch bowl, came up to me. He asked if maybe I wanted to dance.

"He took my hand and led me out onto the floor. It was a Klezmer band. The adults all gathered around us, clapping. When the song ended they all laughed and applauded. I was so embarrassed darling! I turned bright red and ran back to my seat. Mannie followed me.

"I saw him a lot after that, when we went on outings with the club, or when I went with Poppa to a lecture. Mannie would tease me. Sometimes, if a lecture was boring we would go together to the store for a little treat; a cream soda or a pretzel, or some penny candy." Sonia remembered the salty pleasure of the big, soft pretzels they sold.

"Poppa and his friends always had a project. They were involved in everything. Not just politics, but where ever there was a progressive idea. Later, we helped to sponsor a school, an anarchist school, based in the ideas of Francisco Ferrer. I attended lectures and meetings there, Mannie too. The school started out on St. Marks Place, right next to the offices of *Mother Earth*. We used to go visit Alexander Berkman, who was great fun. He would always stop what ever he was doing to come and talk with us. He would join in a circle with the children and sing. But Emma Goldman!" she rolled her eyes. "Oh, if she was there everyone would walk very quietly."

"You're kidding! You knew Emma Goldman?" Catherine's eyes were wide. "Like, she's famous. You really lived history, Grandma!"

"I don't know about that darling. The school was wonderful though, artists and writers, radicals of all stripes. Will Durant was school director for a little while, very skinny, from Yale. And Man Ray went to art class, only then he was Mannie Radnitsky, from Brooklyn. Big Bill Haywood, Elizabeth Gurley Flynn, Eugene O'Neill, they all came to the center."

"Man Ray! How cool! Mike has a book of his photos." Sonia looked puzzled. "You know, my boyfriend."

"The children really ran the school. The whole city was their classroom. They went to all of the museums and the libraries. Visited factories and talked with workers. It was wonderful. We wanted them to experiment."

"You mean it was like a free school?"

"Yes, darling. That's just what it was. Oh, the children learned English, Math, and Science too, but when they wanted to, in ways that were fun. We moved the school around, uptown to Harlem, and then out to Jersey, the Stelton Colony. Mannie's family moved out there. Every Summer we would go and visit, once I stayed there for a month. It was all farmland then, gardens and chickens. The houses weren't much. Cottages really, but the comrades supported each other.

"We had our own bookstores, cafes, magazines, co-operative farms. We had our poets and writers," she took a sip of water. "There wasn't a night of the week that we didn't attend a meeting, a lecture or fundraiser, some kind of event. And it wasn't just the Jewish anarchists. Then there were the other groups; the Italians, the Germans, the Russians. In the ghetto there were socialist and Marxists too, but we were the most popular. This is before the Bolsheviks took over in Russia, of course. That changed everything."

"What about Mannie, Grandma?"

Sonia stared at the wrinkles on the back of her hands for a moment. "You see. I can't even remember from minute to minute. She shielded her eyes from the glare off of the roofs.

"Grandma, do you want me to move you out of the sun?"

"Maybe just turn me a little so it's not in my face."

141

Catherine rose and shifted the wheelchair.

"Build the new society in the shell of the old,' this was an I.W.W. slogan; free, without bosses, or money. We tried, we really tried. That was what Mannie and I lived our lives for. That and for each other." She paused for a moment, staring out at the river.

"Of course there were others who saw things differently in the movement. Some of them preached violence. It was mostly rhetoric, but a few took it seriously, like poor Alexander Berkman. Such a devoted man, but he spent fourteen years in jail. He tried to shoot Frick, Carnagie's lieutenant at Homestead, the one who called in the Pinkertons that killed all those steelworkers. But his gun misfired.

"Oh, we were no angels, don't get me wrong. We would wreck a piece of machinery, we would fight back when the police attacked a picket line. But to take a human life, this is not right. We valued life more than anything, certainly more than the capitalists did. Of course the papers made us all out to be bomb throwers. Mannie was opposed to that, so was I. In fact, I have to tell you, darling, in all the years I've been alive, in the movement I saw the kindest, gentlest people, people with great love in their hearts. They really were. Oh, we worked and sacrificed for the revolution. We thought it would come when the workers rose up in a general strike, and the police and the soldiers, even if they wouldn't join us, at least they would step aside. You can't force revolution on people. You can't hold a gun to their heads. Reason would convince them."

"Do you really believe that, Grandma? I'm not sure I do. I mean like, look around, people are so screwed up. It's all such a mess."

"Of course I believe it, Darling! People can be good, it's society and the state that make them behave badly -- that's what Mannie always argued. Even though we supported Berkman, we knew that violence was not the way. The movement knew. But we were anarchists so we couldn't tell others what to do. And anyone who called themselves anarchist, well, we had no rules or official members, we weren't a party so what could we do?

"That boy who assassinated McKinley, he called himself an anarchist -- nobody knew him. What, he went to one of Emma's lectures? Oh, what a mess that caused. They wanted to lynch all the anarchists. We had no control over him. We were peace-loving people. Lots of them were pacifists, Tolstoyans. Even vegetarians because they didn't want to kill animals. You think all of that is new? It's not new. For the most part anarchists were gentle people, peaceful people, idealists."

"But Grandma, isn't revolution violent? Like, how else can we get things to change?" She thought about Raven, how uncomfortable he made her feel, and how she always thought that was her problem; a weakness in her.

"Oh, no, Darling. Martin Buber said it very well,

'How can you take an apple tree, cut it down, turn it into a war club, and still expect it to bear fruit?' You can't kill people to end killing. Ends and means, you know?" Sonia stifled a yawn.

"You look tired, Grandma. Do you want to go back to your room?"

"Tired?, a little, Cathy. Back to the room might be best. I shouldn't exert myself, you know, I live such a busy life." Sonia laughed.

Catherine pushed the wheel chair back to the elevator, wheeled Sonia to her room, and, with the help of the orderly, got her back into her bed.

She looked down at Sonia. "I should let you get some rest."

"You know, I am tired, and the doctor is coming to check on me. I could use a little nap first. I'm sorry, darling; you don't have so much energy when you get to be my age. But thank you, Cathy, thank you so much for coming. You do me a world of good, you're my best medicine. Next time bring me a copy of your paper. I love you."

"I love you too, Grandma. Rest. I'll come back soon. I want to hear more. You take care of yourself." She leaned over and kissed Sonia on her cheek. As she left the room she looked back to see her great-grandmother staring out the window at the East River.

Chapter 14

When Catherine walked into the squat later in the day she saw Lisa on the stairs. "Fire Marshal came again. Looked over the rest of the building, wrote a bunch of things down in a notebook and left. I asked him what the deal was but he wouldn't say nothin'."

That evening the four core members of *The Avalanche* collective squeezed together in Catherine and Mike's room. Josh arrived first with a box of cannolis from Veniero's. Catherine filled the kettle with water and plugged in the hot plate. Paula straggled in shortly after Josh. Catherine brewed fresh coffee for them. By seven thirty they had finished their pastries and started to talk. Mike was in the desk chair and Catherine had pulled out plastic milk cartons for the rest of them to sit on.

"Like, it's not just that Raven's a bastard. I've known that pretty much since I first met the guy." Paula was nodding her head in agreement. "He's really gone off the deep end. He freaked out on me last week, like he thought he was my boss or something. He actually told me to change my story or leave the paper! Can you believe it? The guy is in la la land. Like, he really thinks he's the publisher! We're supposed to be a collective, decide things democratically."

"Well, he does own all the equipment and he pays for everything." Josh looked sheepish.

"Bullshit!" Catherine shook her head. "He paid for the computers and the press, but the collective owns them. He doesn't even know how to use 'em! Property is theft!"

"Yeah, yeah." Josh had heard it before. "But the fact is he bankrolls the whole operation."

"Not really. This last issue more than paid for itself. Every time we come out we sell a few more papers. There's enough cash in the account to put out another issue." Paula kept the books.

"No shit? Really?" Mike almost dropped his coffee cup.

"Oh, definitely, over $500."

Catherine sensed an opening. "That's not all, I mean the Shining Path? Class war? Do you really believe that?"

"Raven's line. We let him get his way, as usual." Paula shook her head.

"Yeah, Maoist terrorists who kill more Indians than they do ruling class," Mike snorted. "What does that have to do with anarchism?"

"You can't be such a purist," countered Josh. "We've got to support other revolutionaries. It wouldn't hurt to shoot a few landlords down here."

"You're insane!" Catherine glared at Josh. "You sound like Raven! It's that macho little boy shit! Cowboys and Indians. Do you honestly think that would help us?"

"We gotta do something to wake people up. The Yuppies are taking over the neighborhood. They're pushing us out. We gotta fight back!"

"Of course we do. But this Shining Path crap will just backfire on us. Believe me. Now they'll call us terrorists." Mike stood up.

"They're the terrorists!"

"I know!" Mike was annoyed. "But the point is that anything we do that even sounds violent they'll use against us. We've got to find a way to talk to people in the neighborhood, not scare them."

"The people voted for Rolón," Josh was insistent. "We need a revolutionary vanguard to lead the way."

"A vanguard?" Paula rolled her eyes.

"I'm for what works, for what get results, and I don't care what you call it! I don't agree with Raven about everything, and yeah, the guy can be an asshole. But he might be right about this. Make 'em think twice before they come down here."

"Yeah, let's just kneecap some Yuppies.. Come on, get serious!" Catherine shook her head. "We've got a paper. That's an incredibly powerful thing."

"What? You want to be some kind of theoretical journal or something?"

147

"No! I'm for action, you know that, but we've got to think things through more. Where do the actions go? What are we trying to do? What's our strategy?"

"Spontaneity!" Josh exclaimed. "That's our strategy. We just keep things stirred up and eventually people will get the message. We gotta tear down the old shit before anything new will happen. Keep the pressure on the cops, the Yuppies, the developers. Raven's right about that."

"Yeah, we do have to keep the pressure on, but not how Raven says," countered Catherine. "We've got to find some way to connect with the people who live here. The Puerto Ricans, the community groups."

"They're a bunch of poverty pimps." Josh was derisive.

"Not all of them. I went to a meeting at the old school on Ninth Street the other night. Rolón showed up. Some of those people stood up to him. We've got to find out how to talk to them. They seemed really cool. We're just gettin' more and more isolated the way things are going."

"Bullshit!" Josh was on the edge of shouting. "We gotta fight back. Take it to the streets! You're beginning to sound like a bunch of liberals. You're just gonna get swallowed up by the system."

"No, Dude," said Catherine. "That's not it! Like, I just don't think we're gonna get anywhere by scaring off people who are our natural allies. It won't bear fruit."

"What are you talking about?"

"Oh, never mind. Just something my Grandma

148

said. The point is Raven is an asshole and a loser and he's totally out of touch. Like, He thinks it's still the sixties or something." They fell silent for a moment, thinking about what Catherine said.

Finally Josh spoke, "I can't say I agree with everything. But, maybe you're right about Raven. We all agreed we're a collective. The only problem is I don't see any alternative. Without Raven there is no *Avalanche*. It's a bitch, but that's the way it is. We're stuck with him."

"But he needs us!" said Paula. "Who's he going to find to do the work, his dime bag dealers? The paper will fall apart without us. We've got some leverage, let's use it, remind him about our agreement, draw up a list of demands. If he doesn't go along we'll quit!"

"And just turn the paper over to him? No way!" Mike was irate. "It's ours! There are four of us and one of him. All he did was bankroll us. Does that make it his?"

"It's worth giving him a chance to come around," Catherine considered. "But I'm with Mike. If he doesn't respond I'm definitely not for just turning it all over to him. Like, we worked too hard and put too much into it. If he won't go along with us, I say we kick him out. He goes, not us. That's democracy! Sound fair?"

"Oh, sure! The office is in his house. He owns the computers, the laser printer and the press, but we'll kick him out. Then what are we left with?" Josh

149

paused for a second. "Nothing! And you can't put out a paper with nothing."

"That's true. You can't put out a paper with nothing." Mike looked at Catherine and shrugged his shoulders.

"Like, who says we've got nothing?" Catherine wagged a finger in Josh's face. "We're the people who do all the work aren't we? Like, we've got the bank account. Paula's an official signature, same as Raven, and she says there's enough in there to bring out another issue. The computers and press? They belong to the community. Like the money to buy the stuff came out of the pockets of the people in the neighborhood. He doesn't own anything, except the office, and we can find another one. We could move everything out in a couple of hours."

"Raven would never let us take the computer equipment".

"Josh, I'd like to see him try and stop us." Mike relished the idea.

"I bet you would. Maybe this time you'll get hit in the head with a baseball bat!" Catherine glared at him.

"Very funny!"

Catherine smiled. "We'll outsmart him. Like, if it comes down to it we'll get him out of the house and take the equipment when he's gone."

"Well, hopefully he'll listen to reason; see things our way and play by the rules," offered Paula.

"Yeah, hopefully." Catherine sounded unconvinced.

"Now all we need is someplace to move the office."

"How about the storefront downstairs?" offered Mike.

"Not if people are going to keep tossing in Molotov cocktails,"

"You got a better idea?"

"Not yet, Mike. But we'll come up with something. There's got to be some space somewhere."

"Yeah, some place he can't come get it back," cautioned Josh. "Raven will blow his top, and you know how he gets when that happens."

"He'll probably listen," offered Paula "We're not asking for anything outrageous, just a little respect for collective process, and some democracy. He's supposed to be an anarchist. It'll look really bad for him if he won't go along with us."

"Then we agree," said Catherine. "First we try to be reasonable, and if that doesn't work, we take direct action. We'll liberate *The Avalanche*."

"Yeah!" said Mike.

"Okay." Paula was with her.

"I guess," answered Josh.

Chapter 15

Mannie went to work in the garment trades to organize for the union. He was I.W.W., a Wobbly, most of us were back then; "One big union".

That's when we really started to see each other. I was sixteen. I was working in a millinery factory and we were organizing too. I lost so many jobs because of the union it's hard to keep track. They tried to blackball me, but there were hundreds of sweatshops in the neighborhood, I could always find a place where they didn't know who I was. We went to a picnic sponsored by the Workmen's Circle, they were mostly socialists, but we cooperated, and there was a group of anarchists that published **Fraye Arbayter Shtime**, *the Free Voice of Labor, a paper which Yarnofski was editing. He was very talented. That was our paper. We started our own group, the Fraye Arbayter group. We published some pamphlets. Whenever there was a strike, we were there. They depended on the anarchists like nobody else because they knew that we would lead a strike, walk a picket line, even fight with the Cossacks, the mounted police, when they came to break up a strike. I myself, I used to carry a* bag of marbles. The horses would slip on them. I always felt sorry for the horses, but their masters showed us no mercy.

I remember a strike on Broome St. from those days. I was sixteen years old, barely five feet tall, but I was full of fire. It was a very cold day, blustery. I had to turn up the collar on my coat against the wind. Mannie and I were picketing with workers marching outside of a shirtwaist factory. We had signs in Yiddish and English: "Unfair to Garment Workers"; "One Big Union". I was arguing with the owner, very fat, wearing an overcoat with a velvet collar and a homburg hat, when I heard the sound of horses' hoofs. I looked up in time to see a troop of Cossacks come around the corner and up onto the sidewalk. The fat man ran toward the doorway of the sweatshop, and everybody else scattered. They began to swing their billy clubs. I tried to use my picket sign to fend them off, but a cop on a big brown horse knocked it away. Everyone dropped their signs and ran for cover. I looked for Mannie and saw him kneeling on the sidewalk beside a fallen comrade. It was Max Birnbaum. Dead! The goniffs killed him!

I ran towards him, but was knocked off of my feet by one of the mounted cops and dragged to a paddy wagon. They took me to jail. In court it was a joke, a big joke. They charged me with disorderly conduct, and assaulting an officer. At first the judge couldn't believe it. "This little thing?" he said. "She can't weigh more than ninety pounds." But when the cop told I was over on Broome Street he changed his tune. "Oh, one of the reds! Maybe thirty days in jail will teach the little Yid bitch a lesson."

"But your honor," I said, "they attacked us. They killed

Max Birnbaum! I saw it! An unprovoked attack on honest working people, your honor. I was there! He was just marching for a fair shake! We did nothing wrong, our cause is just..." But he cut me off, banged his gavel. "Make that sixty days. Next case!" I tried to protest, but they put on handcuffs and dragged me off.

It's just the way it was in those times. We believed that the workers would rise and make a revolution, but we were wrong. They never did. They were mostly interested in higher wages and a shorter work day, even then. We thought the union would be the way to build the movement, but from the start the reformists tried to use us. Mannie was one of the first to see it.

Mannie and I got a room on 5th Street. Not so different from what's there now, except we went in through an alley and used an outhouse in the backyard. We loved each other so much, but we didn't marry. This was very unusual in those days, but we were very principled. Who needed the State? We knew who we were and why we were together; two free people, together by choice. Those were good days. We had some victories; we organized some shops. The union started to grow. Mannie and me were by then with the Amalgamated Clothing Workers.

We were the most popular of all the groups among the Jews. I think maybe what anarchism stood for was a little bit more exciting. Mannie used to say that the Jews were a messianic people, waiting for the messiah, looking always for salvation; Utopia, the kingdom of heaven here on earth. That's why they left Russia to come to New York. And when they lived on the Lower East Side what they found was, you'll pardon my language, shit. They got tired of waiting. We lived in America, but

154

we really didn't fit. What we offered most of all was hope. The idea that a better world was within our grasp if we would just reach out and take it."

Recorded: March 12, 1967, Transcribed: April 3, 1967, For: Columbia Oral History Project, Immigrant Voices

Chapter 16

Catherine was walking west, toward the *Avalanche* office. The wind was always strong near the River and she shoved her gloveless hands deep into the pockets of her leather jacket. The squat was cold. She needed to go someplace warm. As she walked she found it hard to believe these were the same blocks she had wandered in a heat-induced trance last summer.

It had been mid August, the hottest weekend in an unusually hot summer. The traffic was heavy; a festival down at the South Street Seaport was attracting huge crowds, with a million people expected for the fireworks display that night. Two days before she had seen a digital thermometer at a bank over on Second Avenue that read one hundred and three degrees, and there had been little relief since then, not even at night. Sleep for her and, judging by the crowds that spent their nights in the park or down on the block, most everyone else, was impossible. The demand for air conditioning had Con Ed working overtime, leading to brownouts, and even worse pollution.

Catherine walked down toward the river hoping to find a breeze, but had no success. Given the heat, the exhaust fumes, and the stink of rotting garbage Catherine felt like she could hardly breathe. She had allergies ever since she was a little girl, and now her chest hurt whenever she took a breath, while her eyes burned constantly. Sweat poured off of her, making her wish that she could jump in the stream of one of the fire hydrants local kids had opened, but she didn't dare.

As she turned on Tenth Street, walking back to the Squat, a new smell came to her, something she couldn't identify. She passed a social club that had put its tables out on the sidewalk and heard a radio. "Well, New York," the voice of an announcer enthused, "if things aren't bad enough for you we've just received word that there's a fire raging out of control at a tire dump in Staten Island. Fumes and particulate matter are drifting towards Manhattan. City air quality monitors are concerned about the effect of this added pollution on our already unacceptable air quality index. They are advising that anyone with respiratory problems stay inside with their windows shut. Stay tuned for further details." A tire dump on fire! That was the acrid smell she had noticed, burning rubber!

She suffered through the sweltering night, inside with the windows shut. The forecast called for the heat to break and a westerly to clear the air. But the next day was even hotter than the two before. A hot air inversion, that's what the paper called it. What the hell do you do when the air quality is unacceptable, stop breathing? There was a little girl who lived in the building next to the squat who had a bad case of asthma. She died that night. By noon the next day the emergency room at Bellevue was filled with people gasping for breath.

Catherine was out on Avenue A with the sun beating down through the haze. She had almost hacked off her hair the night before in the vain hope of relieving her discomfort. Every step took a conscious effort. She felt like she was sleepwalking, or slogging through quicksand that kept trying to suck her in. Her chest burned with every breath and the haze that engulfed her was a sick shade of grayish green and so thick that she could barely see to the end of the block. Tiny flecks of black rubber covered everything, and they were still falling from the sky like a light rain, particulates from the burning tire dump. People were staggering down the street, looking for relief that was impossible to find. There had been a blackout that morning when the demand for air conditioning had finally caused a short somewhere in Con Ed's vast system of relays and transformers.

Catherine walked over to Houston Street and the entry ramp to the F.D.R. Drive, she looked down on the traffic motionless on the highway below her, spewing more poison into the already toxic air. The front page of the *New York Times* she had picked out of a trash can that morning read "Hot Air Inversion Continues-Public Health Emergency Declared". The article said that only cars with two or more passengers on essential business should be on the road, but she saw at a glance that the order was being ignored. She wiped the sweat from her eyes and looked up at the sun, visible only as a hazy disc in the sky, but beating down unrelentingly on the city, soaking the concrete with heat that radiated back all night long.

Walking home, Catherine saw an old lady carrying a bag of groceries collapse on her front stoop. A neighbor bent to help her, and Catherine joined the crowd that gathered around them. An egg carton fell out of the grocery bag on to the sidewalk and the broken eggs started frying. Word on the street was that ten more people died in the neighborhood that day.

The next morning, after a restless night, she awoke on the roof of the squat, where she and Lisa and Jamaal had gone to escape their stifling rooms. Over Brooklyn the sun rose, an iridescent orange smear through the morning haze, promising more of the same unbearable weather.

She bought an iced coffee at a local *bodega*. Farther down, on Avenue C, people milled around a storefront Pentecostal church where the preacher, standing on a folding chair, was shouting out a sermon about the end of the world, and that Jesus offered the only route to salvation. Ordinarily Catherine would have laughed and walked on, but today she stopped and listened for a moment.

That evening the streets were packed with people forced out of their apartments by the heat, wandering listlessly with nowhere to go. Catherine was hanging out in the garden with Mike, Raven, and some others. They heard a scream.

"Folks are freaking out," said Lisa, "and I can't say that I blame them. This shit is too weird." The setting sun radiated an otherworldly glow that had turned the sky orange, red, pink and purple. It looked like what Catherine imagined the aftermath of a nuclear explosion would be.

The next day Catherine was on the corner of 10th St. and Avenue B when it started to rain; warm wind came first, blowing in from the river, rattling the garbage cans on the street and blowing old newspapers up from the gutter. Then the smell of the rain; like dark earth, moist and sweet, mixing with the smells of the street; garbage, dog shit, exhaust, grease. Then came the rain, falling lightly at first, then driven by the wind, rustling the leaves on the locust trees in Tompkins Square, pursuing the chess players who fled their game to seek shelter from the huge drops that plopped on the puddle forming in a corner of the basketball court. Pouring down suddenly with a burst of lightning high over the Christadora, sky darkening and water coming down in buckets, in bathtubs, in volumes far beyond a normal storm, and still that hint of warmth, even in the rain, and the smell of soaked sidewalks wafting into the lobby of the tenement where Catherine had sought refuge, mixing with smells of mildew and plaster. The rain beating against the glass of the door was deafening, a stream formed in the gutter carrying the water to the storm drain on the corner, soon clogged with debris. The water creeped up the curb, and threatened to overflow the street onto the sidewalk. And then, more suddenly than it began, the rain ended, the sky cleared, the flood receded, and the sun shone brightly, enticing Catherine out of her sanctuary. Steam rose from the sidewalk and in the sky above, arcing from the East River to somewhere uptown, hung a rainbow, huge and bright above the city. She took a deep breath; the air, clear and sweet, filled her lungs. She ran down the block towards home with her hair flying in the wind that still blew from the river and sent puffy white clouds sailing through the blue sky high above her.

The memory faded as Catherine turned the corner and shivered when the wind caught her full on. She could see the entrance to Leshkos, and decided on a hot cup of coffee before she submerged herself in the office.

Chapter 17

Once Mannie made a speech at a May Day rally. I will never forget, I was so proud. Union Square was packed. Red and black flags flying in the breeze. It was very warm for May. There were signs and banners everywhere, written in Yiddish, Italian, German, English, Russian, even Chinese. Mannie walked to the podium, he wore his curls greased flat. Very distinguished. He was representing the Amalgamated Clothing Workers. I had managed to work my way to the front of the crowd and stared up at him on the stage. So proud I was of him! Love and pride rose inside me to the point I felt light-headed. I barely heard the words of his speech, but I hugged him so when he joined me in the crowd. He was just a young man, but he had a very fine reputation in the movement.

Our lives were not all strikes and meetings though. Second Avenue had six theaters. Yiddish Broadway they called it. My father sang in a men's chorus at the Workmen's Circle, Yiddish songs, and they traveled all over, Philadelphia, Paterson. We would always go hear him. Of course there were picnics and outings in the summer. We would take the ferry and then a train to Stelton to see Mannie's family and the comrades there. Or we would swim in the East River. In the winter they would flood Tompkins Square and make a skating rink. Mannie was a wonderful skater, people would stop to watch him.

Our big lectures we had at Cooper Union. I already told you Margaret Sanger, but we sponsored lots of others; Kropotkin when he came to America, Rocker, Malatesta. We would pack the Great Hall, thousands of people.

And we had our special cafés. The one Mannie and I liked was on St. Marks Place, not too far from our apartment. We had a regular table in the back corner. Mannie would go there often to read or to write. And always with a pot of tea. . Saul, the owner, was a comrade and he let us sit in the café for hours over a five-cent pot of tea, he filled it with hot water whenever it was empty. He provided a big service to the movement, I'm telling you. We would meet there almost every night and then go to a lecture, or a meeting, or the theater. Ibsen, O'Neil, whatever was experimental. Mannie would joke with me, "Every night Sonia, it's one thing or another! Just once I'd like to spend a night at home!" It was true. We led very busy lives, not a moment to waste.

We were real internationalists you know. We were for the workers everywhere. The State was an abomination that pitted the workers against each other. Mannie even learned Esperanto, the international language. We wanted to break down the borders, create solidarity world-wide. What a beautiful vision we had!

A world of plenty; peace, no wars or violence; no bosses or police. We would do away with money! The unions would provide for all and organize production. *Decentralization, true democracy and complete respect for the individual. Freedom! It was intoxicating, and it seemed so close at hand. Not without a struggle of course, nothing without a struggle. All over the world people shared our ideas, and especially on the Lower East Side.*

We had an impact, we had a major impact. We were the conscience of society. That's what Mannie used to say. Whatever the issue, we always had the radical position. It forced the others, the social democrats, the Marxists, even the liberals, it forced them all to the left. They had to look at things a little more radically to compete with us. And not just political issues or labor. On all of the social issues of the day, the anarchists were for freedom!

Mannie and I were very happy, but then came World War One. We were anti-militarists. We protested the draft, we protested the arms buildup, and when America entered the war we organized a huge demonstration at Union Square. All of those boys on both sides dying for the profits of the capitalists. The workers of the world had to stand in solidarity. But some in the movement couldn't make up their minds; Kropotkin, first he was against it, then he was for it. Mannie and I knew where we stood. We gave speeches on street corners. We handed out leaflets, we wrote articles. We opposed it strongly. All the time we made propaganda against the war. And this was not an easy period to be a radical. There was war fever.

One night we were out putting up posters in the neighborhood. I stood on the corner mixing the wheat paste while Mannie brushed it on the posters. He stuck one to the side of a building and three thugs started shouting. "Hey, Jew-boy, what you doing? What you got there?" I will never forget,. When Mannie faced them, they surrounded him. "Look at this!" The tallest one said, and he tore down the poster. "You red Kike bastard! What do you mean `War is a Crime'?" he was shouting in Mannie's face. "My brother's over there in France!" I smelled the liquor on his breath from ten feet away.

The tall man took a wild swing, which Mannie ducked, but then the other two grabbed him, and the tall one began to punch him in the face. Blood spurted out of Mannie's nose. I rushed toward the man punching, but he threw me off and I landed on the sidewalk and hit my head on a lamppost. They kept beating Mannie. I tried to sit up. I saw Mannie fall to the ground and the three of them kicking him there. When he lay still they finally left, slapping each other on the back and laughing. I managed to get up and I knelt beside him. Poor Mannie! He groaned and raised his head. His nose! His beautiful nose! I wiped away the blood with a handkerchief.

Everybody was flying flags. All over town, even in the ghetto they hung them out. It's a very powerful thing, war. It infects people. It makes them act crazy, like a sickness that affects their minds. The newspapers attacked us and the politicians screamed. They stirred up bad feelings against us. The offices of our paper had a brick thrown through the window and someone burned down the Anarchist Library. The government was putting lots of people who spoke up, mostly immigrants, in jail under the Alien Sedition Act. We were afraid that they might come for Mannie, he had been very public and very vocal. But at that time they were just going after the leaders."

We worried, but we kept on working against the war. We

165

had no choice. It was madness, the greatest slaughter ever on earth. They used poison gas on the battlefield and dropped bombs on civilians. It was barbarism.

And then we got word of the Revolution in Russia. We had expected that the German workers would rise, but Russia, the home of the revolution! We couldn't believe it. We were delirious. We danced in the streets all night. I can't begin to tell you what it meant to us! It was like a dream come true! Mannie wanted to leave immediately, right away, to help defend the revolution.

But there was work to be done here, and my Poppa had died just the year before. It was a blow to us all, but Momma really suffered. She had a stroke and we took her in with us. Right away Mannie was concerned, not just about the Whites, but about the authoritarians as well. He had great faith in the Soviets, the collectives, but he had seen the socialist bureaucrats operate in the Unions and he didn't trust them. We stood with the radicals; the left Social Revolutionaries, the Bolsheviks, and most of all the anarchists. We were so full of hope!

Then in October, when we heard that the Bolsheviks had seized power, some of our friends rejoiced. But Mannie was very skeptical. He had a bad feeling from the first. It was confirmed by reports from comrades who went back. They were throwing anarchists in jail, dismantling the Soviets. There was no democracy, it was a disaster. But for most people on the left the Bolsheviks were heroes. They were making a real revolution. Everyone admired them for that. Lenin was a god to these people. And they were willing to overlook the authoritarianism. They turned away, or made excuses for it. Lots of people became communists, lots of anarchists even. Many of the best people in the movement went over to them. It was hard to resist, but Mannie and I remained true to our principles. I might have considered going over, I must admit, but Mannie was certain. He was very smart about these things, very instinctual.

Well, we heard about Mahkno and his anarchist militia being crushed in the Ukraine by Trotsky, and War Communism. Mannie's worst fears came true. They were betraying the revolution. And before you knew it we were fighting against them in the union. They tried to take over. So we made a coalition with the social democrats and we kept them out. Mannie was not happy with that either. He felt we were being co-opted. Maybe he was right. From that time on the Fraye never published another article criticizing the union bureaucracy, never again talked about democratizing the union. Rose Pisota even became a Vice President of the I.L.G.W.U!

Then came a horrible year, 1921. The repression of the movement grew even more terrible. The war was over but the Bolsheviks threatened the bourgeoisie. The government was terrified that revolution would break out all around the world. It was a regular red scare. And we were all reds to them, communists, and anarchists alike. They used the Alien and Sedition Act to come after us. The Attorney General, a real son-of-a-bitch named Palmer, wanted to become President. So he started to arrest radicals.

One night that spring, it was very warm, Mannie and I were walking down Avenue A, late to a meeting of the Fraye Arbayter group. When we turned the corner onto Seventh Street we knew that something was wrong. The street was barricaded and there were police cars in front of our office. They were dragging people out and carrying away boxes full of files. I had to hold Mannie back to keep him from joining the comrades. I told him we've got to get home, get rid of names at our apartment, so nobody else would get in trouble. We walked by, like we didn't belong.

We had both been arrested before, plenty times, and we weren't so worried. The only thing, I was pregnant at the time. We talked about trying to run away, go underground. A lot of people did. But Mannie thought maybe my condition was too delicate.

We walked back to our room and began gathering papers in a box. Without even a knock, police, led by a big blond man in a bowler hat, broke in the door with an axe. "Get that," the big man told them, pointing at our hutch full of dishes. They smashed it with the axe. Oh, what a mess! Broken pieces of china all over!

Mannie stopped me from charging at them, I was so angry. Funny, more angry than scared. He held me back, and we just stood there, watching the destruction. They toppled our bookcase and overturned the desk, covered the floor with books and papers. The big man in the bowler hat knelt down and pawed through the mess. He saw the carton we had begun to fill with our papers, and leafed through the stack. "This is it!" he ordered the others. "Take this downstairs, and bring him down too." At first he barely looked at me, or poor Momma lying on a bed in the corner, behind a hanging sheet. Two cops handcuffed Mannie, and when I called out, another one held me. The big man told them to hurry, they had more visits to make that night. They led Mannie out of the apartment with his hands chained behind his back. He looked over his shoulder. I tried to break free from the one holding me, but he was too strong.

They took Mannie to prison. The comrades all chipped in and we had a big defense fund, for all of the anarchist prisoners. We got a lawyer, a good one who had helped out the movement in the past. But it was hopeless, there was such hysteria. There were newspapers saying they should be executed.

The trial was in the court house downtown. I went every day. Mannie told me not to come, because of my condition. But of course I went. I would visit him in prison too. To nobody's surprise they were found guilty. The punishment was deportation. They were sending them back to Russia! I wanted to go with him, but he argued. I was seven months pregnant at the time, and my Momma needed me too, he said. We talked that I could join him after the baby was born. I didn't care, I wanted to be with him. I should have gone, but I suppose in the end I lacked the courage to insist.

I'll never forget the day they sent them; a misty morning in June. The boat was a rusty hulk, the **Atlantic**, over on the dock at South Street. The wind was gusting and the river was choppy. I stood behind a wooden barricade and a line of police. They wouldn't let us get any closer. I tried to see over them and have one last look at Mannie. All I could see was the back of his head and the cardboard suitcase he carried when he walked up the gangplank. The sun was trying to burn through the fog. The boat's whistle wailed, like a sound a ghost would make, a sound that would haunt me for years; still haunts me. I tried not to cry,

169

*in case Mannie was watching, but I couldn't hold off when the ship pulled away from the dock and headed out into the harbor. The Brooklyn ferry crossed in front, and the **Atlantic** tossed in the wake. I watched, sobbing, until the ship sailed through the Narrows and out of sight.*

They sent 450 of them. Men and women, mostly anarchists, but some Bolsheviks also. I thought my tears would never stop coming. My Mannie was gone! I had lost him! They had taken him away from me.

I heard just after New Years. He had been killed in November, at Krondstadt, defending the revolution against the Bolsheviks. Where my exile began his had ended. Trotsky came with a force across the ice. My Mannie was no more; my dear, dear Mannie.

Recorded: March 15,1967, Transcribed: April 3, 1967, For: Columbia Oral History Project, Immigrant Voices

Chapter 18

Late at night Councilman José Rolón sat in the leather driver's seat of his Mercedes, talking on his car phone. He hung up when he saw a young man walking toward him across Avenue D. The boy was about 16 years old, medium height and solidly built. He wore a leather bomber jacket with an elaborate appliqué of the New York Yankees logo, baggy blue jeans and a pair of black Air Jordans. There was a thick gold chain around his neck and a Yankees baseball cap was turned backwards on his head. He opened the door on the passenger's side of Rolón's car and got in the front seat, placing a brown paper shopping bag between them.

"'Sup, José?"

"What the hell do you mean 'sup?' You supposed to do a job for me and you blew it. So don't 'sup me, all innocent-like. I don't play that shit and you know it! When I say do a job I want it done right; you fucked it up! A simple little job too, something any twelve year old could have handled. I picked up the paper, I didn't see no story. That building's still there and those punks are still in it. What happened, bitch? Can't I count on you to do anything right? Do I have to find somebody else?"

"No, José! It's not my fault man! I did just like you said!" There was an edge of fear in the young man's voice. "Somebody called it in. They must've seen me or somethin', 'cause the fire department got there right away, before the place could really start to burn. Man, I'm telling you I didn't do nothing wrong. Don't be trippin' on me, I held up my end!"

"Bullshit! If you held up your end those freaks wouldn't still be in that building. Stop cryin' like a little girl. Excuses don't cut it! I need people who can get the job done, period. No excuses, no shuckin', no jivin'!"

"Give me another chance, José! I swear I won't fuck up!"

"It don't much matter now. The Fire Marshal's probably gonna get them out of there soon enough. But I want to make sure. That loudmouth girl with the purple hair, I want her gone. You hurt her, scare her bad, get her out of that building, send her screaming right back to New Jersey, or where ever. You know what I mean?" Rolón stared hard at the youngblood.

"Sure José, bet. What ever you say man."

"Take care you don't fuck it up this time! You hear me?"

"Yeah, no problem. It's cool!"

"All right then, Roberto" His tone softened a bit.

"Everything Okay?" he asked, nodding to the shopping bag between the seats.

"Bet!"

"It's all here?"

"Yeah, bro. Nobody short you, you know that!" Roberto sounded hurt at the thought.

"Good, the new shit is on the back seat."

Roberto turned around and picked up an attaché case.

"Get your people to move it faster this time. I'm gonna drive by that corner and I don't want to see nobody sitting around, or trying to fuck with me. You remind them about Willy on Ninth Street if they get any ideas, all right? Any problems?"

"No, I keep it all under control. It's a little slow, that's all. Cold weather and all, you know. We doin' all right though, don't worry."

"Okay then, get out of here," Rolón dismissed him, and he left with the attaché case, heading straight for the corner bodega.

Roberto was a smart kid. He reminded Rolón of himself at that age. Smart, tough and streetwise. The worst the kid could pull would be two years at Spofford. They had to let him out when he turned 18. Gang kids weren't scared of prison, certainly not reform school. In fact it was a badge of honor, and, if necessary, Rolón could make it worth the kid's while to keep his mouth shut.

Even though he was making big money in real estate Rolón couldn't give up the trade. He had to maintain his ties to the street. It was like an addiction. Now that he was a councilman he thought about getting out. But it wasn't about money. The action gave him an adrenalin rush he loved. It was like listening to winning returns coming in on election night.

Of course he was into making money. Between the real estate and crack, his Councilman's salary was icing on the cake. And now he was in a position to do favors for people who, in turn, could help him. He was living the American dream. He looked into the grocery bag beside him. The rows of bills were neatly stacked and bound with rubber bands. He would count it when he got home, but he was sure that Roberto wouldn't try to short him.

He knew that a seat on the City Council would have its rewards. Real estate developers were by far the most appreciative constituency he helped, and, of course, by helping them he was also helping himself.

For years they had worked to gentrify the Lower East Side. And the old City Councilwoman fought them every step of the way. With Rolón in office they finally had somebody who was ready to play ball, and they were extremely generous in their support of his efforts on their behalf. He suddenly had access to a whole new level of money, influence and power. He loved it. But he had to deliver, he knew that from the streets, where, after all, the rules weren't all that different. If you couldn't deliver, you didn't last long. That was the lesson he was trying to teach Roberto a few minutes before. It was a lesson that Rolón learned early, and it had served him well.

Cleaning up Tompkins Square, grabbing *El Jardin*, getting the squatters and the homeless out of the neighborhood; they were all part of delivering what his new friends needed. Gentrification was de-railed by the depressed real estate market a few years earlier, but now things were back on track. Rolón was impressed. His new friends planned, and he too was starting to think long-term. Garden Towers would put him over the top. He was learning to play it smart, to go for the big payday.

He based his election campaign on a "family values" theme. And it worked for him. He painted his opponent, a twenty-year incumbent, as an "ultra-radical", who was out of touch with the decent people. When the boundaries of the council district were re-drawn to include Gramercy Park, his election was assured.

He had first connected to the political establishment through Action for Housing, his development company. He built his power base there from a tiny Church sponsored not-for-profit to a major player in the Lower East Side real estate market. He did it through partnerships with big developers looking for a toehold in the neighborhood, the artful use of public funds, and, of course, with bribes and kickbacks to politicians, H.U.D. officials, and Mob-owned construction firms. He was living proof that in America anyone who was ambitious and worked hard could make it; that the system works.

And he saw his crack business as another proof of that same entrepreneurial spirit. Capitalism was his ethical touchstone, and he always made sure that he followed its first commandment; buy low and sell high.

The neighborhood had been at the center of the city's drug trade for twenty-five years and by the mid-eighties crack was king. Rolón always watched the trends and early on he took over a lucrative block, 9th St. The corner bodega was the distribution point. He had lookouts stationed on all the corners, young kids acted as runners for the street level dealers; salesman really, to an eager clientele drawn from the neighborhood and out of town. A steady stream of cars with plates from Jersey and Connecticut cruised the neighborhood, and shoppers didn't even have to leave their cars. For less mobile consumers, his crew had an abandoned building on the block they could use to smoke their purchases. And Rolón covered all of his bases by making payments to a contact on the police department's Lower East Side Drug Task Force, as insurance.

Rolón thought of himself as contributing to the community's development through his efforts. He was hiring a good number of young people, connecting them with a growing market, and paying them top dollar. Yes, he was making money, but he was really providing a public service. He knew a great opportunity

when he saw one. Crack was seducing a whole generation; perhaps twenty five percent of the neighborhood
was either buying, selling or using it. He knew how to
put together an organization, and how to keep the
players in line.

He paid his people well; a runner, usually a twelve
or thirteen year old, could make $100 a day. Rolón
used only proven gang members, like Roberto to head
up the crew. Things went smoothly for him. The occasional problems were handled with outlays of cash and
a slick lawyer. Rolón stayed way back, usually not as
close as he came tonight, but he needed to talk directly
with Roberto, and straighten him out about the squatters. Only rarely did he have to take extreme measures,
like with Willy, who had run the crew for him until he
was disciplined, permanently, on 9th Street a few
weeks earlier. An unfortunate incident, but Willy had
been stealing from him.

He had to make sure discipline was enforced, or it
could all unravel very quickly. He had seen it happen
to others. That was why he kept a Glock Nine Milli-
meter under the front seat of his car. Roberto had to
be slapped down, but not too hard, he was a useful
member of the organization. He would do his job,
Rolón felt confident.

He found that the winning-through-intimidation
style that served him so well in the gang and on the
street was ideally suited to his management of Action
for Housing. The church that sponsored the group

wanted an authentic grass-roots leader to run the organization. He renounced gang life and declared himself rehabilitated in order to land the position of Director. He moved quickly to consolidate his power over the agency by staging a coup on the board, replacing the Board Chair, the pastor of the sponsoring church, with one of his own cronies.

He loved the role. He had a good rap and he scored grant money and church dollars right and left. He was small time at first, hustling funding to organize tenants associations that never quite materialized and offering "leadership training programs" for local youth who then spent the summer painting his office. He was investigated during the Carter Years for misappropriation of funds, but never indicted. He got fat off of dollars from the public trough, but all of that changed when Ronald Reagan took office. Suddenly the Federal pipeline dried up.

Rolón was resilient though, and lucky. One afternoon he received a visit that changed his life. A well-known developer from uptown stopped by his office with a proposition. H.U.D. was going to start pumping housing money into the neighborhood again, but through locally based housing development corporations, and minority contractors, not the commercial developers. He proposed that Rolón form a for-profit-development wing at Action, and that they work together as partners. The man guaranteed that Rolón's proposals for projects would be accepted. Rolón jumped at the chance and almost immediately lucrative contracts were coming at him from all directions.

His new status helped him make more contacts and soon he was serving as a "consultant" to a half-dozen other firms scrambling to get into the suddenly hot Lower East Side real estate market. Before too long his contacts went all the way to the United States Senate, where New York State was blessed with a Senator who had strong connections to H.U.D. The cycle of corruption extended from the burned out tenements of the Lower East Side to the town houses of Georgetown and even into the White House. Rolón discovered that he could relate to politics. He was in his element, and it was then that the idea of running for office himself first crossed his mind.

However, in politics, as on the street, you have to always remember to watch your back, and to take care of business. He had obligations to his partners and his new friends. He had to deliver. And he wasn't going to let anyone get in the way. The punks alone posed no real threat. They were hated in the community, he had seen to that. What he didn't want though, was an alliance between the community groups and the squatters. That could make for some problems, at the very least it would slow things down at a time when he had to keep them moving. It was true that if he didn't get the project approved soon H.U.D. would take the money it had committed and spend it elsewhere. With the H.U.D. scandals he and his partners no longer had the clout with the agency that they once had. So it was crucial that the project get final approval, and begin soon. He was prepared to do what ever he had to do to insure it.

Ordinarily he would have never gone to a meeting like the one at *La Cabaña*. But Rolón felt that things went pretty well there. No major organization had come out against Garden Towers. The "low income housing" smoke screen kept potential opponents confused and divided. He wanted to make sure that it stayed that way. His assignment to Roberto was a part of his strategy.

The girl had a smart mouth, she had dissed him, called him a poverty pimp, and it seemed like she was speaking for the squatters at the meeting. If he could get rid of her, the bottle throwers would take over again, and play right into his hands. And an added benefit of getting rid of the girl and the others squatting in her building would be the addition of one more vacant property that he could grab through Action for Housing.

Chico Santiago was another matter. Rolón knew he couldn't scare him off. He was able to tar him with the anarchist brush at the meeting, but Rolón knew it wouldn't stick. He was sure that Chico was planning his next move right now. He needed to neutralize Chico. He had a grudge against Santiago that went back to their gang days together.

And, if he could get rid of Chico he could grab *La*

Cabaña, the old school, prime real estate. They wanted to develop it as a centerpiece for the neighborhood. It was right next door to the Christadora House. It would make a great health and racket club. There were millions to be made on the school, and Santiago was the only obstacle.

Things were really going his way these days. He just had to stay on top of them and follow through. He started his car and pulled the big Mercedes out onto Avenue D. He dialed his car phone. "Hola, Mommi, you need anything from the *bodega*? Okay, I'll be home soon. See you then. Love you moms."

Chapter 19

Catherine walked East on Houston St. until she saw the river beyond the sunken highway, shimmering in the morning sun, whitecaps tossed by the freshening breeze blowing in from the ocean. She remembered Sonia's old apartment on Grand Street; the Amalgamated they called it. When she was a kid her family went there every month or so. Catherine always knew that they were there by the smells wafting down the hall; cabbage borscht, pot roast, sometimes roasting chicken. The grownups sat around the small table in the kitchen, talking about relatives who Catherine barely knew.

When Sonia went into the nursing home located on the river, just North of the Amalgamated, their visits became less frequent, much less frequent. It was as though Sonia had disappeared. Catherine could only remember visiting her there once or twice with her parents.

And now she found herself thinking about Sonia and her stories all the time. When she walked through

Tompkins Square she swore that sometimes she could hear Yiddish voices calling out to her, though she didn't know what they said. She passed by the same buildings Sonia told her about. Maybe she knew people living in the apartment that Sonia had shared with Mannie. She was drawn into Sonia's world; She felt like Sonia's past and her future intertwined.

She reached the nursing home, took the elevator to the fourth floor, and opened the door without knocking.

"Hello darling, you're here again so soon. I wouldn't be so happy if someone gave me a million dollars! Look at you!" Sonia sat with her bed cranked up to support her back. "Tell me about your week now. Bring me news of the world. You wouldn't believe what's been going on around here all morning. The man across the hall, Mr. Goldfarb, had a heart attack. They just took him out a minute ago. The nurse told me. I heard the noise and I knew something was going on. He's a nice man, not all there anymore, but nice enough. I hope he's all right. But you get used to people dying around here. That's really what the place is about. They all die." Sonia shook her head slowly.

"But enough about me, darling. What's new? You never brought me your newspaper like you promised. I have a magnifier, I could read it. Or I could have an orderly read me your story. Don't tell me you forgot again?"

"No Grandma, I brought it." She pulled a copy out of her Mexican bag. "I did all the data entry, and I have a story on page 6, about gentrification." Catherine handed Sonia the *Avalanche*. "I'm sorry it took me so long, Grandma. You're amazing! You reminding me about things; it's supposed to be the other way around!"

Sonia looked carefully at the front page, and then turned to page 6, "I'm just glad to have it. It looks beautiful. I'm going to read the whole thing and then we'll have a talk about it." She placed it on an end table. "But darling, gentrification?"

"Rich people taking over the neighborhood, Grandma."

"What, they don't have enough? They can live anywhere, why here?"

"It's close to Wall Street, like, it's very convenient for them. They buy places cheap and fix them up, force all the poor people out. Yuppie Scum!" Catherine snorted.

"Ah, Wall Street, the biggest crooks on the planet!"

Catherine laughed. "How are you, Grandma?"

Sonia sighed. "When you're ninety-three everything hurts. But otherwise, I'm wonderful. What could be wrong? My Cathy is here for a visit today." Sonia's eyes sparkled with excitement.

Catherine took off her beret and shook her head to get her purple hair out of her eyes. Sonia's album was open on an end table and Catherine saw Sam, her great grandfather, staring back at her. She remembered his trick of making a rabbit out of his handkerchief and using it as a puppet to play with her. In the picture his dark hair was slicked back and he had a thick mustache. The face was much younger than the Sam she remembered, but easily recognizable.

"He was a fine man" Sonia spoke softly. "He took good care of me and he was a wonderful father to Abe." She shifted her position on the bed.

"Can I get you a pillow, Grandma?"

"No darling, I'm fine, just fine. He was always there, for me, the baby, even for Momma. So, one thing led to another. He kept telling me that Abe needed a father. I was already living in the man's house and most people assumed we were man and wife anyway. We had many wonderful years together. We finally got married in the sixties, for the Social Security. Your father was at the wedding. I'm surprised he never told you about it. It made a big impression on him."

"How cool, Grandma! He never told me about any of this. He never told me anything about when he was younger, or really about the family at all. Like, he hardly ever talks to me, too busy with his law firm." She chipped away at her black nail polish.

"I can't believe it!" Sonia's nostrils flared. "He was such a good boy, a principled young man. He spoke out against the war. He organized protests at his college."

"You're kidding! My father? Like, I knew he was against the war, but an organizer? That is awesome! I don't believe it!"

"Oh yes, I remember we had long talks about him not burning his draft card. I was a little disappointed, but it was his decision to make, and he didn't think he could get into law school if he did. And then of course you were born. You were so adorable, darling. You used to come visit me and Sam at the Amalgamated."

"Uh huh, I remember. I used to go under the piano, and you guys would play Scrabble after dinner." Catherine remembered the shadows embracing her, as she rested in the semi-darkness, staring at the legs of the grownups around the table in the kitchen. Catherine thought about the pot roast they used to have.

"I read your history, Grandma, like, about Mannie being deported. I couldn't believe it. You must have been devastated."

Sonia shifted on her bed again, trying to find a comfortable position. "That I was darling, truly, the worst time of my life. Losing Mannie, and me with an infant at the time, after a very difficult carriage. A real low point, and if it hadn't been for Sam…"

"I can't imagine, Grandma. What a strong person you are."

"I tried, darling, after all, what can you do? Life must go on, I had a little baby to care for. And after the deportations and the red scare, if all of that wasn't bad enough, there were the Communists." Sonia's eyes narrowed. "They had a lot of appeal. They made a successful revolution, nobody else could say that. Of course we knew from early on that they were authoritarians. We heard news from Russia, and we saw how they acted here."

"What do you mean, grandma? Like, how did they act?"

"Before, the different tendencies on the left, we argued, but we got along. We co-operated. But this was warfare. The CP wanted no rivals, no critics or skeptics. They were impossible to work with. Sometimes I thought they fought us more than they did the bourgeoisie.

"Everything was the Bolsheviks. Lots of people stopped taking us seriously, but we never lost faith. We knew what to expect because it was the same over there, in Russia, as it was over here. They betrayed the revolution. And this was all under Lenin and Trotsky, forget about Stalin! They cared nothing for freedom!

"At first they used our slogans. In *What is to be Done?* Lenin sounded like an anarchist. But once they seized state power, all of that ended. Really, for them, the concern all along was for power and control. That isn't our way; we want power with, for everybody to have and share power, not power over. Here, they took their orders direct from Moscow, the party line all the way."

"Power with, Grandma? I just want to get *rid* of power." Catherine sat on the edge of the chair.

"Darling, I'm afraid this you will never do. There will always be power. We need it to make decisions. The question is who has the power? A boss or Commissar, or people acting collectively? An individual, or all the people together? That's why I say power with.

But the communists...I personally had bitter fights."
She coughed and sipped from a glass of water on her
bedside stand.

"My brother Alex -- Sasha -- joined them right
away, right after the revolution. We argued terribly. I
felt betrayed. And after Mannie was killed, well... He
said that the revolt at Krondstadt was counter-
revolutionary and the Bolsheviks had no choice. I
never forgave him for that. We didn't speak for many
years, until right before his death. It was wrong. Their
whole approach was wrong. And look what happened.
But at that time on the Left it was very hard to speak
out against them. You were called a reactionary if you
criticized."

"You are, like, so right on, Grandma!"

"Well, I don't know about that, but I always stood
up for my principles. Yes, the Communists were a big
problem. When Abe was accepted at Bronx Science
for high school we were proud of him, but it put him
back in touch with the Marxists. He was a good boy
though. We had been very close, but now, well, he was
growing up and he had to go his own way." Sonia
shifted her position on the bed."

"So, things went along for a couple years. Times
were hard, but we survived. Then, in 1936, in Spain, at
last, an anarchist revolution. The comrades in Spain
were rising! Three million workers in the C.N.T., the
biggest workers syndicate, with the real militants also
active in the F.I.A., the anarchist federation. They took

over whole provinces, ran factories. While they fought a civil war against the Fascists they set up collectives, and abolished money. It was an incredible moment for us. In the countryside whole villages collectivized. They would burn all the records in the town hall, drive out the priest, and declare libertarian communism!"

"Libertarian communism? I thought you were against the communists, Grandma."

"Libertarian communism, or libertarian socialism, free communism, that's another term for anarchism. What they called it in Spain. We were for communism, true communism, from each according to their ability, to each according to their need; but not for the party, or the state. Sam wanted to go fight. But I begged him not to. I had already lost one husband and I didn't want to lose another. The comrades in Spain were crushed and the Civil War dragged on. Then came Hitler.

"Abe went away to the war in Europe even though I told him he should refuse the draft. He left City College, where he was an excellent student, and enlisted in the infantry. It must have been terrible for him, he was a different person when he came back. Sad, always with an underlying sadness. Then he married Ruth, they had your father and moved to Westwood.

"He was always a good boy, Abe. He would help me with anything I would ask. But his heart wasn't in the movement. Maybe it was the war, it took something out of him. I don't know. I always thought that was why he got the cancer.

"The war did something to all of us. The world changed. Suddenly the hope for revolution died. When we first found out about the camps, I remember, I wondered, I doubted for a moment whether the social revolution was really possible. That such evil, such brutality could exist in the world! That a whole nation could stand by and allow it to happen; it made me wonder."

"I wonder too, Grandma."

"Do you, Darling? Wondering is OK, but never give up hope. Like Sam reminded me, there has always been evil in the world, and the job of the movement is to confront it, to not allow it to go unchallenged. It helped me to remember that. Of course by then it seemed like there wasn't much of a movement left. We still had our newspapers and magazines, but not much else. They said anarchism was a thing of the past, that it died in Spain, that it was a nineteenth century philosophy, and the future belonged to government and the State." She poured more water from the pitcher on the end table. Her hand shook and it splashed on the floor. Catherine got a paper towel from the bathroom and cleaned it up.

"We had very few young people joining us. Just a bunch of old timers. We were very close, even some of the old arguments were forgotten. There were so few of us left. Comrades moved away, out of the neighborhood. And they started dying. When you live to be as old as I am you've seen a lot of friends die, believe me."

Sonia stared out of her window, sighed and turned

back to Catherine. "Will you braid my hair for me, Cathy? The nurse's aide here tries. But she doesn't know the way I like it, a French braid. Can you do it darling?"

"Of course, Grandma," Catherine brushed the shiny white hair and marveled at its thickness. She plaited it into a substantial braid. "Are you tired, Grandma? Would you like to rest?"

"No, no, I'm expecting another visitor soon. In fact I'm glad you're here. I want you should meet him."

"Who's coming, Grandma, somebody else from the family?"

"An old friend. Somebody I know from the period I was just telling about, Jack Hoffman. Maybe you heard of him? He's famous. A writer."

"I've heard the name, but I never read any of his books."

"He's a wonderful man. Brilliant. He's in his late sixties now, but still very active. Jack's a wonderful teacher. I can't wait to introduce you!"

Chapter 20

The door opened and a man peered in; a tall, thin old man, bald except for a fringe of long gray hair. He entered Sonia's room, said "Hello", walked to the bed, bent, embraced her, and kissed both her cheeks. He had full lips, a prominent nose, and the bushiest eyebrows that Catherine had ever seen.

"Sonia, you're as gorgeous as ever!" he roared in a gravel voice.

"Jack, you always were a flatterer and a big exaggerator. But it's good to see you anyway. It's been a long time."

"I'm so busy these days. I'm working on a new book and responding to my critics, who are legion as usual; a bunch of ignoramuses. Nobody understands what I'm saying. I'm sorry it's taken so long between visits. But I brought you some of the Nova you like from Russ and Daughters, on a bialy with a schmeer. I thought it would be easier for you to chew than a bagel. It's a peace offering." He extended a sandwich wrapped in wax paper.

They laughed and then Sonia grasped Catherine's hand. "This is my great-granddaughter, Cathy. She lives in the neighborhood now. She's an anarchist." Catherine stared down at the floor, embarrassed.

"Really?" Hoffman tilted his head and cast an appraising eye on her.

"Oh yes, she writes for a paper!"

"Fascinating, what paper?"

"*The Avalanche*." Catherine looked up.

"Oh! You're one of those! A spray can anarchist! You think you can make a revolution by spray painting on the walls. One of the ones who wears the leather jacket with a circle A but doesn't know what it means!"

"I know what it means!" Why was this man attacking her?

"Sure you do!" He snorted. "You probably think that setting fire to a trash can is an act of revolution. What have you read? Who's philosophy do you draw on, Groucho Marx? That creature Raven puts out your paper, doesn't he?"

"We're a collective! And, like, anarchy is in the streets, not in a library!" She didn't like this man.

"Spoken like a true moron! You children should grow up. You give anarchism a bad name. You think it's a style or a look. You'll be married and home in the suburbs in a few years. If you last that long. Or you'll land a job working for a publisher, a career move. I've seen it before, lots of times."

193

Sonia was shaking. "Calm down, calm down, both of you! Jack, Cathy is a good girl. Very committed. We need more like her in the movement."

Hoffman removed a pair of glasses from a case in his top pocket, put them on and took a closer look at Catherine. He noted her long black fingernails, and snorted. Catherine looked Hoffman over as well. What makes him such a big deal? She knew he had written some books, and she knew Sonia thought he was special. But as far as she could tell he was just some skinny old fart who looked angry, in a tired sort of way. Like he would be angry if he had the energy for it. Another old guy who thought he had all the answers and wanted to tell people what to do. He kept staring at her. Fuck you, she felt like yelling. Who gives a shit what you think? But he was Sonia's friend, and she was beaming at them while they glared at each other from across the small room.

"I'm so glad you two had a chance to meet. I wouldn't be so happy if someone gave me a million dollars!" Sonia took Catherine's hand and squeezed it. Her old gray eyes glistened. "Jack is a true revolutionist darling, a man of principles. You've never met anyone like him before, this I guarantee. We've been friends for almost forty years now, I think. Right Jack?"

"Over 40 years, the Libertarian League, remember? I'll never forget it. I was just coming out of my Trotskyite phase. You took me under your wing."

"Oh, nonsense, Jack. Nobody ever took you under their wing."

Catherine was growing weary of their reminiscing. Did Sonia really think she had something in common with this nasty old fart? He'd called her a moron! She looked at his sagging face. Jeez, when he talked his eyebrows looked like they were alive; wooly caterpillars perched above his eyes. What a creep!

He had to hold back a sneer. It made him angry to even look at her.

"So," Sonia lifted a cup, "would anybody like some tea?"

"It's okay, Grandma. I have to be going now anyway," Catherine grabbed her jacket. "I'll see you again soon." She backed toward the door, and glared at Jack Hoffman. "Nice meeting you." Her voice dripped with sarcasm. Then she wheeled and walked out of the room.

Hoffman watched her go. "Sweet kid! I hope she grows up." He began to lower himself into the armchair next to her bed.

"You were very nasty to her, Jack."

"Not really. Have you seen her paper? It's stupid! It confirms all of the worst stereotypes of anarchism. They're so thoroughly bourgeois, these kids, just posing as revolutionaries. I don't know, Sonia, I can't understand her generation. Oh, there are a few good individuals, I'm sure, but as a whole. They're anti-intellectual. They don't read. They're not only ignorant but they celebrate their ignorance. They reject reason.

195

They don't even know what socialism is!

"They present everything in the most simplistic way, with no sense of history; no understanding of how ideas connect to action. And this Raven who she's working with! I've known him for years. He tried to throw a pie at me once! He's mindless, manipulative, really a despicable person. Sick, full of hate and violence. He's done a lot of harm in the movement over the years. I know at least three promising organizations he's broken up. So if I was harsh with her, please forgive me. But I've seen their paper and it's unspeakably bad; a throwback to the worst of the sixties. They're calling themselves the Shining Path, after those Maoist gangsters.

"I don't even use the word anarchist anymore. I can't, the meaning has been so corrupted. I call myself a Libertarian Socialist. I'm sorry, but it is impossible for me to just sit back and watch fifty years of my life turned into a parody. I have to react. I'm sure that you, of all people, understand. It's a matter of principle." Hoffman's voice had risen and he was waving his arms to accentuate his point.

"You're from the old school, Jack, The young people today aren't like you. You frighten them. The theory doesn't matter to them. They don't believe in it. They've seen too many theories betray them. They just live day to day and respond situation to situation. I'm not saying it's right. That's just the way things are today. Your problem has always been that you expect too much from people. She's a good girl. She's smart. She needs encouragement from you, not venom. She's a product of her times, the same way you are of yours."

Hoffman snorted. "By the time I was her age I knew all of Marx, Trotsky, Gramsci, Lukach, and Hegel. I read them myself. I never studied them in school, but it was my responsibility to know. The movement was like a university; the finest minds, the highest level of discussion. And we weren't afraid to argue either!" He shook his head, took a deep breath, looked at Sonia and frowned. "Maybe you're right Sonia, these are terribly impoverished times. I'm glad I'm not her age." Hoffman was beginning to calm down.

Sonia looked at him for a long time. "You more than anybody know how important it is to educate people through the terrible times. She'll learn. She's a smart girl. You'll see, I'm sure."

"I hope you're right. I really do."

She looked pointedly at Hoffman. "Do you remember when you were young? When we first met? When you walked into the Libertarian League you caused quite a stir. We hadn't seen anybody new for a long time. Some of the others thought you were crazy. You told them the unions were washed up, and always talking about the ecology! But even then I knew you were somebody who could make a difference. So you see, I have an eye for these things." She smiled.

And she had been right about Hoffman. When they had met, after the war, he had been taking courses at night at Cooper Union, studying architecture. He had practiced for a few years, trying to introduce "new communities" planned in the utopian tradition of Kropotkin and Ebenezer Howard. But he watched suburbs spring up like mushrooms after the rain in Post-War America, and realized that design alone could never bring his vision into reality. He abandoned his architectural practice and turned to social theory.

He had written two dozen books over the years, grounded in the anarchist tradition, but also drawing on Marxism and Greek Philosophy. His work bridged the gap between the thirties, when anarchism had presumably died in Spain, and the sixties, when it was reborn with a vengeance in the counter-culture. His greatest contribution was a synthesis of anarchism and ecology that he had begun to develop in the 50s.

Scorned by the academy and the policy makers, he had predicted the health hazards of chemicals in food, the dangers of nuclear power, the likelihood of global warming and the impact of pollution on the planet. He published his warnings long before Rachel Carson's *Silent Spring* finally made environmental issues a legitimate concern.

But Hoffman was no mere environmentalist. His analysis rooted the cause of the environmental crisis not in flawed technical processes, but in the attitude and structures of social domination that they were built on. He understood that the logic of capitalism led ultimately to the destruction of the ecosystem.

And it was this radical insight that made his work so threatening to the powers that be.

Hoffman squirmed in the armchair. "So are they treating you well here?" he asked.

Sonia gave a little laugh. "Treating me well? Yes, I guess. Well enough considering that they're just watching for me to die. There's a waiting list for my bed. But you know what, Jack? I don't mind. I've lived long enough. It hurts to get up in the morning. Most of my comrades and friends are gone. There's not much left for me anymore. Can you imagine? A waiting list," She shook her head in disbelief.

"It's quite a world, Sonia. These are hard times, they wear people down."

"No, these times aren't good for much, are they Jack?"

They spent the next hour talking mostly about old friends and old times, better times, reveling in the memories. "It's good to remember, isn't it?"

"Yes, very good. It was wonderful to get your call. But you said over the phone that you had a special favor to ask me. What is it, Sonia? What can I do for you?"

"It's about Cathy." She hesitated for a moment. "I've been talking to her Jack, telling her things about my life and the movement. But, like you said, she's ignorant. She needs to know much more than I can teach her. I want you to help her Jack, educate her. She's full of potential, I can tell."

"Sonia," his voice was gentle. "I love you, but I'm

not a nursemaid. She's gone in a direction I don't approve of, and, to be honest with you, it's clear she doesn't like me. I don't know what I could do for her."

"You still have a group don't you?" She knew that over the years Hoffman had taught classes to small groups exploring politics, philosophy, anthropology, history, and ecology.

"Yes, a few of us meet every week, but I don't think your granddaughter..."

"Yes," Sonia cut him off. "That's exactly what she needs, something like that. She's a smart girl Jack. She's committed. A little ignorant, but committed. She just needs to be educated, and you're the one to do it."

"You can't educate someone who doesn't want to learn."

"She wants to learn. She told me. Promise me Jack, please. Promise me."

"I can't promise anything." Hoffman's tone admitted defeat. "But, for you Sonia, out of respect for you and our friendship, I'll try. I'll offer, but then it's up to her. Nobody can coerce someone to learn. You know that."

"Yes, I know. Thank you Jack, for indulging an old woman. It's important to me, very important."

Chapter 21

By three A.M. the rain had stopped, but a thick fog rolled in off of the river, a seamless mist swept along by the tide and leavened by the moon when it rose in the night sky. The neighborhood was enveloped in an otherworldly glow. Catherine's steps echoed down the empty streets as she walked home from work. She was weary; all she could think of was her bed. The squat was almost in sight when she heard footsteps behind her. Before she could turn around someone reached out and grabbed her.

A scream rose in her throat, but it was silenced by a forearm across her neck, then she was slammed up against a wall with a force that rattled her teeth.

"Make a sound and you're dead." He had a low, guttural voice that chilled her.

"There's money in my bag! Take it, what ever you want!"

"Shut up bitch!" Her limbs felt heavy, immobilized by fear, and her throat ached. She caught a glimpse of his profile. He slapped her across the face. She could taste the blood from her split lip. "You do what I say or I'll kill you."

Panic raced through her. She tried to run, but a fist to her midsection stopped her. Doubled over, fighting for breath, she cowered against the wall. Slowly a low moan built in the back of her throat. Her stomach radiated pain.

"Get the fuck out of our neighborhood, or next time you're dead!" He ripped the bag from her shoulder and she watched through her tears as he swaggered off and disappeared into the fog.

She raced to the squat, fumbling for the front door key in her pocket and looking back to see if he was following. Listening for his footfalls and hearing nothing, she stopped shaking just long enough to put the key into the lock. She reached the safety of the squat, sobbing uncontrollably as she staggered up the stairs to the apartment.

It was empty. Mike was out at a club with his buddies. She curled up on the loft bed under the green army blanket, shivering and crying. That was how he found her when he arrived home a little later.

"Mike!"

"What's wrong? What happened?" He was next to her on the loft.

She told her story and he gathered her into his arms, trying to calm her down. But it didn't work.

It was a fear that shook her to the core. Just the

thought of going out alone sent her into another round of sobbing.

"I'm gonna go out and find the motherfucker who did this!"

"No Mike! Please, just stay with me, I need you here now."

After an initial outburst of cursing he fell silent. They lay there, Catherine crying intermittently, enfolded in his arms until dawn, when exhaustion overcame her.

That morning Catherine and Mike lay in bed, finally asleep, when there was a sudden banging on their door. Mike called out groggily, "What do you want? Go away, were sleeping!"

A male voice on the other side of the door answered. "H.P.D., we want you out of here. You're occupying this building illegally. This building had been condemned by the Fire Marshal and slated for demolition. You have twenty-four hours to vacate the premises, by court order. I'll leave the papers on your door."

Catherine stiffened next to him. "Mike! What are we going to do?" tears were growing in her eyes again and her voice quivered.

"It's okay, Cath. They can't just kick us out like that. We'll organize. We've got plenty of support in the neighborhood. We'll resist! Charlie will know how to handle it. He's been through this before." But Mike's assertions sounded hollow. She looked around the room at their meager possessions.

"Where are we gonna go, Mike?" she asked through her tears.

"I don't know Cathy. We'll figure something out. Don't worry, it'll be OK."

"I'm poison Mike. What ever I touch turns to shit. Maybe I should just move back to Scarsdale, give everybody a break!"

"Don't talk like that! You're being ridiculous. You can't take this on yourself. It's the fucking City, and the cops. You didn't do anything. You're not thinking straight yet! You're still freaked out from last night. Don't say that shit Cath, I need you here with me. Don't even think about leaving!"

"I'm scared Mike." She huddled beneath the green army blanket. "I'm really scared. Like, yesterday I didn't think anything could hurt me; that anything bad could happen. But now, I don't know. I can't handle it Mike! It's too much; I need to feel safe! I can't live like this!"

"Come on Cathy! You're upset, it's only natural. You'll feel better later. We can't give up now, we put too much into this place! And what about the paper? All of our plans? How about us? We've got a great thing going, you and me. I love you!" He had never told her that before. "You can't leave me!"

"Oh, Mike! I don't know." She sobbed. "Like, I just feel so bad. I can't do this anymore. I need something solid in my life."

"We'll get an apartment. Telephone, running water, the works! If that's what you need we'll do it. I'll get a

204

straight job. I can make big bucks doing commercial art. Jimmy'll hire me at the ad agency."

"No Mike, that's not what I meant, and that's not what you want. I don't know..."

They lay together on the mattress. She stared at the cracked plaster on the wall of their tiny room. "I love you," he had said. But what did it mean, she wondered? That he couldn't wait for her to come home at night? No, that couldn't be it. Half the time she came home he was off with his buddies at ABC's or some after-hours club. That he would sacrifice for her, give up something he wanted so she could have something she wanted? Come on! He was the most selfish, stubborn person she had ever met. That he would protect her from danger? Well, he was protective, but she hated that. And it had more to do with his stupid macho than it had to do with her. Maybe he was talking about sex. He was obsessed with it. And it was pretty great when they made love, the best she had ever had. In fact he was the only man she had ever had an orgasm with. He excited her and he was responsive to what she wanted, at least most of the time. But was that really love? After all, he got as much pleasure out of it as she did.

When she was a little girl she used to think about growing up and falling in love all the time. Like the princess and prince in the stories her father used to tell her every night when he put her to bed. But it had never been like that for her. It was always her liking a guy and him being mean to her, or some guy screwing her and never calling again. Until Mike. Maybe he really did love her.

"Hey Mike, what did you mean when you said you loved me?"

He looked down at the mattress for a moment and she thought she saw him blush. "I don't know. I love you. You know what I mean."

"No, I don't Mike. Tell me."

Mike looked at her with his eyes wide. "You're awesome. I never met anybody like you. I mean, you don't fuck around; when you commit to something you follow through, you really do it; the paper, the squat, *El Jardin*. I really admire that in you. You're like a pit-bull, you don't let go. And you're really sexy, you turn me on, but I guess you know that. I never felt this way about anybody before."

"What does it feel like Mike? How does being in love make you feel?"

"I don't know. My hands get sweaty, my throat gets dry, my stomach gets queasy. Sort of like I'm coming down with the flu or something."

"Gee Mike, you really know how to sweet talk a girl, don't you?"

He looked hurt. "Come here Mike." She reached out, drew him to her and hugged him long and hard.

They lay together and she felt his warmth, but it could not stay the chill that made her shudder when she remembered her mugger, and when she started thinking about the building again. What could they do?

There was nothing much to say about it. The fact was, Catherine realized, they had little choice. As close to collapse as it was, it was all that they had. Cold in the winter, too hot in the summer, open to rain and wind, it was still home. Since she arrived in the neighborhood it was really the only home she had known. Well, there was Raven's, but that was just a place to crash when she was too tired to stay awake. That had been a place to try to leave, not to come home to. This was it. As unprepossessing as it might seem to her parents, or her old friends from Scarsdale, this was her home.

It wasn't fair. She knew she could find another place, and if there was ever a problem Scarsdale was still just a phone call away. She hated that; the fact that she was still connected to her parents, that she was certain they were just waiting for that phone call. She could practically hear her mother, "It's just a stage you're going through, Cathy. You'll grow out of it."

They were so fucking liberal! She knew they loved her, but why couldn't they understand, she wasn't like them. She wasn't going to give up; to get along and go along. She was going to fight the system, not buy into it. They didn't know what she had found on the Lower east Side, the people, the politics, the music, the life. She could never go back to Scarsdale. They just didn't get it, and she supposed that they never would. If only there was some way to make them understand.

She had invited them over to the squat once, a few

months ago, and they had come up for a minute before they took her and Mike out to dinner in Little
Italy. Catherine had seen the horror in her mother's
eyes when she walked in. She tried to hide it, "How
charming, Cathy. You know we have some of our old
furniture stored down in the basement, why don't you
and Mike come out and take whatever you can use. It's
just sitting there." Mike had been all for the idea, but
Catherine knew what she was really saying, "How can
you live like this, like an animal?" And she knew the
offer was really an attempt to draw her back into their
suburban orbit. Fuck that! She was here to stay.

Dinner that night had been torture. Her parents
tried to be nice, but they kept treating her like a child.
"Have some more pasta honey, it's good for you."
"Aren't you cold in that light jacket, don't you have a
sweater or something that you could wear?" And reminding her of the past she was trying to forget;
"Remember Harold Glickman, you went to school
with him? I saw him with his mother at Bloomie's the
other day. He just finished his first year at Yale. What a
handsome young man." They were so banal. She didn't
even know how to begin to connect. Could she tell
them about Raven, or the paper, or how great sex was
with Mike? She didn't think so. Next time she would
go visit them, it would be less painful that way. And
she was embarrassed, scared to death somebody would
see them getting out of her father's Mercedes. The
whole evening was a disaster.

And it wasn't made any better by Mike. "I think your parents are pretty cool. That was a great dinner too. Christ, we'd be lucky to get my old man to take us out for a big Mac and a beer. Why don't you want to go out there and get that furniture? We could use some decent stuff. You know, you were kind of rude to your mom."

"Michael! Spare me. You don't know them! He's a buffoon, and she's treacherous. Don't you see what they were trying to do?"

"Well...no. Like I said, they seemed pretty nice to me."

"Like, they're trying to control me, Michael. Get me dependent on them again, and then ship me off to college or something."

"Well what would be so bad about that? You could go to N.Y.U. or somewhere else in the city, still live here. That could work out really well..."

"Fuck you, Mike! I can't believe you're taking their side! You're just as fucking bourgeois as they are!"

"No, I'm working class, remember! My father drives a Chevy, not a Mercedes. What's your problem anyway? They just want to help you. Why don't you let them?"

"Pride, Michael! I have some pride. I don't need their help, or your help, or anybody's help!" She had slammed the door and stormed out of the apartment.

She and Mike had built a life here in the old tenement. There was a familiar look to the water stain on the outside wall and the crack in the ceiling that made her feel comfortable. They invested their sweat and their dreams. There was no way she could just walk away from it, though it was true that there wasn't much to pack. Her things would probably all fit in one suitcase. They could leave everything else, as far as she was concerned. The hot plate was worthless, the lamp a piece of junk that didn't work half the time anyway. They had found the chair and desk in a dumpster. And the mattress! She hated the mattress, the goddamn lumps kept her awake almost every night.

It was true; it would be simple to just move on. No great loss. She never believed in things, and these would certainly be easy enough to replace. And there was the mugging the other night, could she really stay somewhere she didn't feel safe? But there was something that held her back; that stopped her from just walking away. She thought about at the pile of two-by-fours outside the door. She and Mike had spent a whole day scrounging the lumber. They planned to frame out another room on Saturday, in the afternoon when they were done working on the common space.

And then there was the building itself, the old tenement. Just a pile of bricks to the City, but not to her. It told her stories. It whispered to her about immigrant lives as she brewed her coffee in the morning. Some nights it haunted her dreams. The building lived and breathed. It poured out the sorrows and the hopes of everyone it had sheltered. Yiddish, and Spanish voices echoed out from its brick walls. The building had possessed her; taken her to a place she had never been before and no, God damn it, no, she wouldn't leave, couldn't leave without a fight.

Fuck the City! Fuck Housing Preservation and Development! Fuck the cops! It was her place, her home, her life; she had built it and nobody was going to take it away from her. It wasn't fair, it was like they had found something somebody had thrown in the garbage, pulled it out and fixed it up and now the City was coming around and saying it belonged to them.

She beat her fist against the wall and a patch of plaster fell away, crumbling into a fine white dust on the blanket. She had decided. There really was no choice but to stay. Stay and fight. She could see it clearly now. Let the others all leave. She didn't care. She wouldn't abandon, couldn't abandon the old building to the wrecker's ball. There was too much life here, too much of her life here to just walk away.

She thought about how to fight, how to win. She was tired of losing battles. She had to find a way to save the building. She was up against the most powerful forces in the city. Money and real estate ruled Manhattan, she had been around long enough to know that. But there had to be a way. A petition? No there wasn't time, and they wouldn't change their mind because of a petition anyway. She wondered who else she could count on. There was Mike, always Mike, and Lisa, she wouldn't give up without a fight. Charlie the Rag Picker? He had warned them it would probably come to this, and he had been through it before. Bobby and Riff? Probably, most likely they would stick it out. But the others? She didn't know. She just didn't know.

They gathered later that afternoon in Lisa's apartment. Most of the people who lived in the buildings were there. Charlie argued that they should mobilize community support, which sounded like a good idea. The problem was that with less than twenty-four hours to go until the scheduled demolition a major organizing effort seemed futile. They barely had enough time to call their friends and people from the other squats, who they felt fairly certain they could count on.

"Direct action's the only way," said Mike. "We put our bodies between the building and the wrecking ball. We'll turn out as many people to support us as we can, but it's really gonna be up to us. I can guarantee it."

His argument seemed to make sense, though some of the less committed people were inclined to just move on and find a new place to crash, and they said so. When the discussion ended there were eight of them who agreed to chain themselves to the building's front door in an effort to stop the demolition. Charlie, Mike, Riff, Bobby and Lisa, with Jamaal in tow, headed out to talk to the other squats and see what kind of support they could drum up.

Catherine was still shaken by the mugging. Mike suggested that she to go over to Paula's to take a bath and try to relax. She rang Paula's bell and was buzzed in. She went upstairs and Paula greeted her at the door. Catherine told her what had happened in the past twenty-four hours, crying a good part of the time, and then headed for the bath tub. She relaxed in the hot water, and the tension began to leave her neck and shoulders. After twenty minutes or so of soaking in the tub she felt better. When she wrapped a towel around herself and reentered the studio's main room she found Paula seated on the futon smoking a joint.

Catherine sat down and took a hit. "Are you okay?" Paula asked.

"I'm feeling a little better. Like, it's just too much, you know what I mean? Oh, who am I fooling, I'm a mess if you really want to know. I can't get rid of this feeling like something terrible is going to happen."

"Would a massage help?"

Paula's hands worked the knots out of her neck, shoulders and back. Paula kneaded her muscles with a strong deep motion that became progressively more gentle as the knots disappeared. Catherine could not say when exactly, but at some point the massage became sensual, and despite her exhaustion, or perhaps because of it, she found herself responding to the slow gentle motions of her friend's hands. She turned over, and she and Paula kissed, tentatively at first, and then slowly, but insistently they began to make love, as they had occasionally for almost a year. Paula's caresses soothed Catherine and eventually brought her to climax, and with the climax came a kind of release. For a moment, at least, her anxiety fell away and she slept.

Catherine felt much better when she woke. Paula cooked an omelet for their dinner and after they finished eating they walked over to ABC's where they met Mike and Charlie the Rag Picker. Almost fifty people had pledged to be there in the morning to support their resistance. Catherine ordered a beer and thought about the previous day. She let out a deep sigh.

"How you doing? You all right?" Mike asked.

"Yeah, I think I'm Okay." She reached across the table and squeezed his hand. "At least I'm starting to be Okay." And it was true. She was putting her fear behind her and starting to focus on the task at hand. She finished her beer and then she and Mike went home to prepare for what the morning would bring.

Chapter 22

I had known Sam for many years from the Fraye Arbayter group. A soft spoken man, but very committed. Not a firebrand, like Mannie, but a man of principle and the highest ideals. He helped us, me and Momma, after the Palmer Raids. He came to me and offered anything we needed after Mannie was deported to Russia. And we did need help. We had to leave the apartment because it was too expensive. And also the repression of the radicals didn't stop after the **Atlantic** sailed past the Statue of Liberty. We had to lay low for a while. Some people went underground. Sam was a very committed man, but he never felt comfortable in the limelight, making speeches and such. They were less interested in someone like Sam.

As I was saying, we moved into his apartment. He gave Momma and me his room and he slept on the couch, in the front. His flat was bigger, and a little more modern, with a bathroom inside and a tub in the kitchen. I was pregnant with Abe at that time, eight months. It was hard; I couldn't work, so he took care of us. Other comrades too, we all helped each other, but it was mostly Sam. Abe was born in the bedroom of his apartment, and he helped the midwife with the delivery.

A year or so after the baby was born he came to me one night. He told me that he had liked me for a long time, found me very attractive. I was flattered, but I was in no mood for a lover. I was still mourning Mannie and I had a little baby to care for. So I told him no, let's just be friends. I was afraid he would be mad, make us leave the apartment. But he didn't, he respected me.

These were not the best of years, for me or the movement. It seemed like our moment had gone. History had passed us by. When they deported Emma and the others we lost most of our leaders. Of course anarchists don't need leaders. But they took the people who were most articulate and outspoken, the people with experience and wisdom. They left us in pretty sorry shape.

Oh, we kept things going up to a point. Sam and I, we stayed pretty busy in those days. But you had to be careful. The repression was still very bad. The Bolsheviks in Russia had the bourgeoisie all stirred up. The press fanned the flames, of course. They created a regular red scare that went on for several years. We worked underground. We met in secret. We didn't have any big public rallies. It was terrible. Out at Stelton they were scared for the children at the school.

So, between the two, the repression and the Communists, things got very bad. I wouldn't say all activity ceased, but close to it. We worked with the unions, Sam was a business agent for the I.L.G.W.U. But otherwise we kept pretty much to ourselves, hoping things would get better. Then we got the news about Sacco and Vanzetti. Their case caused quite a stir.

216

The hypocrisy of a society which could send such men to death and still claim to be civilized! Oh, their case had an impact on a whole generation. It made us realize how far we still had to go to turn our dream into a reality.

Their death brought a few new people into the movement, but not many. And for the Yiddish-speaking wing, I can see now, the end was already in sight. They shut off immigration in 1924, and those who came earlier were becoming Americans, leaving the ghetto. They moved to Brooklyn, Queens, New Jersey, and if they didn't, their children did. Oh, there was still an active movement on the Lower East Side, very active, but without young people coming in it was just a matter of time.

Things got very bad after that, economically. Sam lost his job. The whole garment industry was suffering. We were heading into the depression you know. It seemed like everyone we knew was out of work. These were very hard times. Sam got a job with his uncle, a kosher butcher, so we always had meat. This wasn't true for most of the people we knew. So every week we would cook a big brisket and invite the comrades over for dinner.

Abe was getting to be a big boy now, nine years old. I remember I was so angry at him. He came home from school one day and announced that he had become a Communist!

I couldn't believe it, but he had joined the Young Pioneers, the party youth group. I thought it was because all his friends were members, but maybe because he knew it would upset me. There was nothing I could do about it though. He had to find his own way. I always believed in freedom for the individual so how could I tell my son "no" about something like this? I tried to explain the problem to him, but he didn't want to listen to

217

me. It nearly broke my heart. After all, it was the party that killed his father. But I didn't tell him that. Maybe I was wrong; maybe I should have told him. But I didn't want to upset him. He had a strong will and a mind of his own, which I always respected.

Sam hated the butcher's job. He came home every night covered with blood. After that job he became a vegetarian. It was a long time before he ever ate meat again. So, when the chance came he left his uncle's shop. By 1932 the depression was at its worst. Roosevelt was elected and he started all kinds of programs; C.C.C., W.P.A., a regular alphabet soup. J.J. Cohen, who had left the **Fraye Arbayter Shtime,** *and some other comrades were buying land to start a co-operative farm, up in Michigan. As soon as he heard about it Sam said "That's for me, for us. That's the place to raise our son. We will return to the soil!"*

I was less enthusiastic, I was a city girl. What did I know from farming? But Sam was adamant, and Cohen and the others painted a very pretty picture; land, a co-operative, grow our own food, like that. They raised money from all of the comrades for a down payment and used the new government programs, loans and farm subsidies, to cover the rest. Each family put up $1000 to join. Sam borrowed the money from his uncle. He wanted me to go out there with him immediately. But I had my doubts. We agreed that he would go first to get established and then send for Abe and me and my Mama.

It was a good thing too. The letters started coming back, and while I admired what they were trying to do, it was not a situation for me and Abe. They had a ten thousand acre farm, but nobody really knew much about farming. They grew sugar beets, they grew peppermint, raised poultry, dairy and horses. When they got there, things were ready to harvest but there were only a few of them to do the work. So they hired farm laborers to help. They were lucky that there was a foreman there left over from the old owners. A Dutchman, Sam wrote. They became good friends and he helped them out of a real jam.

Second, there was no place to live out there. The men were housed in a dormitory or barracks. But there was very little room for families so Sam advised that it would be better if we waited a while. He stayed there through the winter, which was very hard, there and here. Momma got pneumonia and died that year. Abe got sick too, but I nursed him back.

Sam wrote twice a week, without fail. I know he missed us, but he never complained. He threw himself into the work. He was always a worker. They spent the winter fixing up the farm buildings. Cohen, meanwhile was running around the country recruiting new members. By the next year they had three hundred fifty people living there. Sam came home to the neighborhood for a week that spring. He was so skinny I hardly recognized him. He felt that maybe by the summer we could move out there. I still had my misgivings, but come June we went by train to Lansing and they came to take us out to the colony.

It was early summer 1933. He picked us up at the station in a Model T sedan. It was a very bumpy ride, the roads weren't so great. Sam finally stopped in front of an iron bridge crossing a stream. A large sign across the bridge read "Sunrise Co-operative Farm Community". The road went on and on to a cluster of white buildings way off in the distance. Maybe two miles away.

"Welcome to Sunrise, your new home," Sam told us. He drove us toward the settlement. "Everything as far as you can see is ours. Ten thousand acres, like a kingdom!" he said.

Oh, it was a far cry from the Lower East Side. We worked very hard that summer, but to tell the truth, I enjoyed it. I would hoe in the vegetable garden, breaking the manure into the soil. I had to wear a babushka on my head, the sun was so hot. But the earth I was turning was cool, it felt good. The garden was huge, at least ten acres, and there were dozens of people spread out all over. We would sing old IWW songs. We had to expand the gardens if we were going to feed everyone.

Oh,, I had never worked the soil before, but I came to love it. Birds chirped and sang in the apple orchard that bordered the garden. I was very surprised, I had never thought of myself as a farmer. The cobblestones and concrete of the Lower East Side was what I knew, though I never forgot summer visits out in Stelton. Despite my concerns, I was happy there. It was beautiful, not like in the city, and the land, rolling away as far as I could see. I could watch Abe play kick the can at the edge of the garden with the other children. He had regained his health, I was thankful for that, and because he was away from the influence of the communists.

There were all sorts of people at Sunrise, mostly anarchists, but some socialists as well; all progressives. No party members though, the central committee forbid it. Those folks thought Sunrise was petite bourgeois individualism, the same crime that Stalin was executing millions of peasants for in Russia.

Weather allowing, I spent every day out in the garden. I got very strong and brown by the sun. Sam would tease me at night when he came to our tent. "So, how is the great farmer tonight? How does your garden grow?" Besides long hours in the field, Sam spent his free time making an old chicken coop into a shack where we could live when the winter arrived.

We had huge meetings, and a farm manager who divided up the work. There was always some controversy. Do we talk to the dairy cows in Yiddish or in English? Septic tank or sewer system? Sam and I tried to stay out of the quarrels, but it was very difficult not to take sides. There was a group, a clique, who wanted to get rid of Cohen. What ever he said, they said the opposite. He said yes, they automatically said no, good-bad, right-left. Finally it came to a big vote, and we had to side with Cohen. I never cared for the man that much, personally, even when I knew him from New York. Not to speak badly of him, but he was always a little arrogant, not just at Sunrise. But he was also quite brilliant, really. When he was editor he transformed the **Fraye Arbayter Shtime**. He had an eye for talent, published all of the great Jewish writers. He gave them their first chance.

But anyway, he was somebody we knew and trusted. So we backed him up, spoke up for him. And this made us very unpopular with the others who opposed him. And if this wasn't enough to make us uncomfortable, the housing shortage still remained. To get some privacy Sam and I spent most of the summer living in a tent. We took our meals all together in a big dining hall and Abe lived in the children's house so it was all right.

Anyway, that fall we had a big argument with the school district. They said we were subversives, didn't want to take our

221

children. We took them to court and a judge in Lansing said they had to accept them. But by then, who wanted to go anyway? So we started our own school and made the district pay the cost. The neighbors had been curious at first, a few even helpful, but now they became hostile. The local paper printed editorials against us. And we heard rumors that the American Legion was going to raid us and burn the farm.

It got very cold. I was worried about Abe getting sick again. There were no antibiotics back then -- people died from a little infection. Without the gardens, my life was grim. I missed the Lower East Side and wanted to go home. I thought the community was a good idea, though still I didn't totally agree with taking money from the government. It was a good place, full of struggle of course. What worth doing isn't? But it wasn't right for me. Sam and I argued, not for the first time.

He wanted to stay and finally I agreed that we could try it for another year. That made Sam happy. He always said that it was the only time I ever gave in to him. Of course it wasn't. Any relationship that lasts has to have give and take in it. But anyway I said okay. It was possibly the biggest mistake I ever made, as it turned out. Well, maybe not the biggest, but it was a mistake.

It's true, there were parts of it I loved; the gardens, the community. A beautiful idea, a marvelous concept was Sunrise. But the fighting became worse, more bitter, over the winter and many people decided to leave. Our little shack was bad enough in the fall, but we really suffered through the cold months. And the winter lasts a long time in Michigan, not like here. All in all it was hell. And things didn't get much better when spring *came. Those who left demanded their money back and we had another big payment on the land due. It looked like we might lose the farm.*

There was another revolt against Cohen, and this time he lost. Now the incompetents took over the management and things went from bad to worse. In fact, so bad that the people demanded that Cohen come back in charge! Oh, what a mess! Finally, after a very poor harvest it was clear that it wouldn't work. So in the end we sold the farm to the government. I think that they used it for the Rural Resettlement. Cohen and a few of the others, just a handful really, bought a much smaller place in West Virginia. But not Sam and me. After Sunrise we moved back to the Lower East Side. That year and a half was the only time I didn't live here since I was a little girl.

Recorded: March 28, 1967, Transcribed: April 15, 1967
For: Columbia Oral History Project, Immigrant Voices

Chapter 23

At eight A.M. a truck-mounted crane, outfitted
with a wrecking ball, lumbered up to the front of the
squat, accompanied by five police cruisers full of New
York's finest. They were greeted by a group of about
twenty-five protesters holding banners and signs that
read "Save our Buildings!" "No Housing, No Peace --
Lower East Side Squatters", "Gentrification=Gen-
ocide" and, of course, the ubiquitous "Die Yuppie
Scum". Mike and the others had made the rounds of
the other squats the afternoon before, going door-to-
door asking for help.

Their supporters stood in a knot on the sidewalk in
front of the building, shouting slogans to raise their
spirits, and huddling together to ward of the cold.
Their frozen breath rose in a cloud, refracting the thin
morning sunlight that, as yet, had done nothing to
warm the day. Behind them, wrapped in chains that
were padlocked to the front door, sat the eight resi-

dents of the squat who had agreed to resist, including little Jamaal. The banners billowed out with a sudden gust of wind from the river, and the crowd shivered.

A police Sergeant with a bullhorn took charge of the cops. "Disperse or you will be arrested, this is an illegal assembly. This building has been condemned. Leave for your own safety."

The protesters stood their ground, chanting. "Housing for people, not for profits." The twenty cops, dressed in full riot gear with batons drawn, milled around uncomfortably in the street, shifting nervously from foot to foot, waiting for orders from their Sergeant, a big, beefy man with a red face.

"This is an illegal assembly. You have one minute to disperse or you will be arrested." His voice boomed out of the bullhorn. The protesters were quiet, but they stayed where they were, some linking arms. A minute passed, and then two. The cops glared at the protesters, but still made no move to arrest them.

The Sergeant retreated to his cruiser, and while the protesters watched, spoke into his radio. Catherine, seated cross-legged on the cold sidewalk, attached to Mike on one side and Charlie the Rag Picker on the other by a thick chain that encircled her waist, began to chant "The people united will never be defeated" and the others picked up her cry.

The Sergeant, done consulting with headquarters over his radio, walked back to the squad of officers. "At ease, men", he ordered. They put their billy clubs back into their holsters.

It was beginning to look like a stand-off, and Catherine felt herself relax a little. Not yet ready to declare victory, she had a sense that they had at least gained some time. She looked at their crowd of supporters, still standing firm on the sidewalk, and then turned as she heard shouts coming from up the block.

Raven and a half-dozen of his bleary eyed cronies were approaching the protest. They were carrying signs that read "Lower East Side Shining Path" and "Class War Now!", chanting "Death to the Pigs". The cops turned to face Raven as his group crossed the street to the building, still taunting them. The waiting police responded by drawing their batons and lowering the face shields on their helmets. They stood there while Raven and the Shining Path shouted at them. Some of the cops were pounding their batons into their open palms, glaring through their face shields at their tormentors, and the shouts became less forceful, as though a few of Raven's group were reconsidering their strategy.

The other protesters looked on, clutching their banners and placards, and barely breathing. As the cops continued staring down the Shining Path, their chants died out altogether. The block was silent except for the sound of a truck laboring down the Avenue that drifted toward them. In the midst of the silence Raven launched a beer bottle that bounced with a re-sounding clunk off of the helmet of one of the cops.

The bottle shattered on the sidewalk.

The Sergeant gave an order and the cops suddenly waded into the protesters, swinging their clubs right and left. Most of the demonstrators broke away, dropping their signs and banners, running, trying to protect themselves. But four fell to the curb. A group of cops chased after those who tried to run away, and a smaller contingent began handcuffing the four who had been beaten. A paddy wagon pulled around the corner, siren screaming, and the protesters who had been unable to get away were dragged, some by their hair, into the back of the van. Raven and the Shining Path were among the group that escaped.

Those chained to the door watched helplessly as their supporters were hauled off. Then the cops turned to Catherine, Mike and the others. Though they were sitting on the cold sidewalk and defenseless, the cops came at them with their batons held high. Catherine looked up into the angry eyes of a panting cop, and saw a club descending toward her. She covered her head with her arms, but took a glancing blow on her shoulder. She suddenly wished she was back in Scarsdale.

After a few moments of mayhem, the Sergeant called his troops off, and a cop with a bolt cutter clipped the padlock holding the chain to the door of the building. They prodded to their feet by the club wielding policemen. Catherine, tears rolling down her cheeks, tried to cling to Mike's arm, but they were pulled apart. The chain was removed from their waists and then they were herded into another paddy wagon that had arrived on the scene. Siren wailing, they were sped downtown for processing.

Chapter 24

Paula posted bail for Catherine and Mike at their arraignment later that afternoon. They were charged with criminal trespass and resisting arrest.

"What a joke!" responded Catherine when she heard the charges, rubbing her shoulder. Mike had a cut over his right eye where a cop's baton had struck him, and he had also been kicked in his already sore ribs. The three of them left the courthouse in silence, Mike grimacing with every step, Catherine nursing her shoulder, and Paula looking somber and disturbed.

"Where to now?" Paula asked. "I'd suggest dinner in Chinatown, but I emptied my account to make your bail. Can't you guys stay out of trouble for a minute? What are you, a couple of anarchists or something?" No one laughed.

"I just want to go home and sleep." Catherine's shoulder ached.

"What home? They've probably torn down the building by now," Mike remembered the wrecking ball.

"Oh, shit! You're right. All of our stuff! Mike, what are we gonna do?" Catherine was once again on the verge of tears.

"I don't know. Let's go by there and see. Maybe we can get some of our things."

They caught an M-1 bus, got off at Houston Street and walked cross-town to the squat, or at least to where the squat used to be. A lot filled with a pile of fresh rubble confronted them. They saw Lisa climbing over the pile, trying to salvage what she could of her belongings. She was having little luck. Jamaal stood in the lot watching her.

"Lisa!" Catherine called out. "Are you okay?"

"Oh Yeah! Lost my house and everything I own. I'm just fine."

"I meant, you know, with the cops. I didn't see you in the paddy wagon or at the arraignment. I was worried..."

"One of the black cops took pity on us and let me and Jamaal go. But shit, look what they did. There's nothin' left. I can't find a god-damn thing, it's all buried in here somewhere. They could've at least let us get our stuff out. What a mess!"

"What are you gonna do? Where will you go?"

"I don't know. I guess we'll go to a shelter. Jamaal can't be sleeping outside. As much as I hate it, at least a shelter put a roof over our heads for tonight. Shit, I don't fuckin' believe it! You try to build something, you try to do what's right and this is what it comes to! I been here six years. Don't those people have no hearts? Oh, Cathy, this is bad, real bad. Me and my baby ain't got no other place to go. What's gonna happen to us now? Those shelters are evil places, really evil. I'm scared."

Cathy wished that she could offer Lisa comfort. But she was confronted by the same questions. "I don't know Lisa, I don't know."

Jamaal had walked over and tugged at the sleeve of Catherine's leather jacket. "Cathy, they buried my Teddy Bear and my books and my toy from McDonalds." He looked up at her with tears forming in his eyes and she squatted down and hugged him.

"Don't worry Jamaal, it'll be all right. Your Mom will get you new toys. She'll take care of you. You know that, she wouldn't let anything bad happen." The little boy started to cry, and she squeezed him tightly to her.

They stared at the rubble. It seemed pointless to try to salvage any of their belongings, but Mike apparently spotted something, because he had scrambled onto the pile of bricks. He dug down for a moment and then his hand emerged, triumphantly waving a battered hot plate over his head.

"Forget it Mike!" Catherine yelled up to him. "Like, it's a lost cause. Come on over, we need to talk."

Mike descended the rubble pile, looking crestfallen. "I bet if we dug around we could find our stuff. We were on the top floor so it can't be buried too deep." He tried to sound optimistic, but his words had the opposite effect on Catherine.

"Give it up Mike. It's gone forever." She walked toward him with Jamaal still on her arm. "We've got to figure out where we're gonna go. Besides, it'll be dark soon. We can come back tomorrow and look, if you insist." Catherine's shoulders slumped and she let out a sigh. The pile of rubble represented almost a year of her life.

"We can go crash at Raven's, if he's out of jail yet."

"That bastard! Didn't you see what he did?"

"No, I was too busy ducking billy clubs to follow what happened real close."

"Well I saw!" Catherine's voice rose with anger. "Dude, like, he threw the bottle that started the whole thing, and then he ran! He got away too. Fuck him! You bet I want to see him, but not to crash on his floor!" Her nostrils flared.

"I assumed that you guys were coming to stay with me." Paula spoke quietly.

"Really? You sure it's okay? I mean there's two of us and your place is pretty small." Catherine's relief was tangible.

"Of course! It's not like you have a lot of stuff to move in. And it's only temporary, until you can figure something out."

"Thanks!" replied Mike. "That's great. That solves one problem. Now can we go get something to eat, a falafel or something? I'm starving."

Catherine squeezed Jamaal's hand. Lisa was still

going through the rubble in hopes of uncovering some of their belongings. "Lisa, what about you and Jamaal? We can't just leave you here."

"No, nothin' you can do now. We'll be okay, we're survivors, me and Jamaal."

"You sure? There must be something" offered Catherine.

"What the hell you gonna do? You got no place we can go. We'll take care of ourselves, been through worse than this before. We'll go stay with my mom, or something."

Catherine looked at the ground, and imagined that they had. "Look, I'll be at Paula's. Here's the number." She took a marker from the pocket of her leather jacket and wrote on a piece of scrap paper that she handed to Lisa. "Call if you need anything, if I can help, money, anything. Stay in touch, let us know where you are!"

Lisa nodded absently. "Uh huh, sure thing."

Catherine hugged Jamaal and turned to join the others heading towards Paula's apartment.

Enrique Langdon was across the street watching them. While Mike climbed the pile of rubble he was writing in his notebook. He tore out the page and handed it to Catherine when she walked by. She was startled.

"What is it?" Paula looked over her shoulder.

"I don't know, it's in Spanish, I think."

"Let me see." Paula took the page from Catherine's hands. "It's a poem. He wrote you a poem, It's about crying in the moonlight. I need a dictionary to get it all. My Spanish isn't that great."

Catherine turned to see the back of Langdon's blue helmet retreating down the block.

Chapter 25

Hoffman's apartment was small, a railroad flat, and sparsely furnished to the point of austerity. The tiny kitchen used to be a closet. The living room held an armchair, a frayed gray sofa, a coffee table and two stacks of folding chairs; the bedroom was furnished with a bed, a desk and a chair. Every wall in both rooms was lined with bookcases. Books were piled high on the coffee table, on the desk and even on the floor. Books overflowed the living space into the bathroom.

At the desk, Jack bent over an I.B.M. Selectric. He was typing with amazing speed, his fingers racing to try to keep pace with his thoughts, as though he were in an altered state of consciousness. The rest of the world had ceased to exist for him. There were only the keyboard and the paper quickly filling with words; Hoffman's words, spilling out in a fluid stream; Hoffman's words, both his gift and his curse. He had abandoned everything; friends, his architectural practice. He had left behind an ex-wife and two children, still living in the Bronx, but pushed to the periphery of his life, his ideas compelling him to the exclusion of all else.

When he was in a state like this it was as though even his own body disappeared. He forgot his aches and pains and gave himself over completely to his ideas and his words. Hoffman lived like a monk in his cell, and writing was his meditation, his spiritual exercise, though he would have blanched at that description.

He was working on an article responding to one of his critics, an Australian Deep Ecologist. The man had written a revue of *Philosophy and Ecology*. "Moron", Hoffman muttered under his breath, "Did you even read it?" He was used to responding to critics. And they were many, since he liked nothing better than slaying sacred cows, especially those of the Left. At age 68 he was on the attack, as ever.

He kept on typing, as he had been since early that morning when he got out of bed, put on slippers and a robe, quickly downed a cup of coffee and picked up the article where he left it late last night. Always driven, today he felt a particular sense of urgency. His visit reminiscing with Sonia had unnerved him. He suddenly felt old.

Hoffman got up from the desk and stared out the window toward Second Avenue. He shuffled into the tiny kitchen and poured himself a glass of seltzer, thinking about how much things had changed, and how much he still wanted to do.

He developed his thinking through a process of

negation, and he pulled no punches. His comrades discovered that if a flaw existed in their logic, or if he disagreed with their analysis, on even a minor point, Hoffman subjected them to blistering critique. As a result, conflict followed him in his odyssey from group to group and project to project.

"We can't just depend on the working class," he had argued with Dave, a C.I.O. organizer he knew from his early days. "We saw the unions in the thirties; they can only go so far, and they're becoming more and more economistic. They don't even think about ecological issues. That old Marxist crap doesn't cut it any more, we've got to get beyond it; move out from the shop floor into the community." He had a full head of hair then that he brushed back with his hand to keep it out of his eyes when the wind shook the tops of the locust trees ringing Tompkins Square.

"Ecology?" Dave had looked at Hoffman, eyes wide in surprise. "What, you're gonna organize the bourgeoisie? You're crazy, Jack. Sure, lots of luck!" Then he turned and walked away.

But Hoffman had no static theory, he adhered to no dogma. He followed his truth where it led him, and for the most part it was a lonely journey. He constantly felt betrayed, and angry at the failure of those around him to heed his message. He was cynical about what existed, but he still managed to maintain a sense of hope about what might emerge.

Hoffman's reverie was interrupted by a ringing

doorbell. He buzzed in Chico Santiago. "Jack, how are you? Good to see you. It's been a while."

"Chico! Always good to see you. What's new? How's the community center? Sit down. Can I get you a glass of seltzer?"

The younger man found a seat in the armchair. "No thanks, Jack. I'm all set. *La Cabaña* is fine, but now we got a problem with *El Jardín*."

"Rolón's housing project. Yes, I read about it. It sounds like he has some community support."

"That's the problem, Jack. He's getting over on everybody pretending it's for low income. We come out against it, he tells everybody we're against afford-able housing. And the movement is not what it used to be; there's not so much energy, people are tired after all these years of battling with the City. There are divi-sions too. Everything is fucked up."

"People always get tired, Chico. But even when it looks like things are at a low ebb, there's always poten-tial. People just need to be exposed to the possibilities. When I first moved to the neighborhood, the fifties, talk about grim? Eisenhower and Levittown. But I knew something was stirring, percolating deep down, and then it all bubbled over; civil rights, youth culture, ecology, women's liberation."

In the fifties Jack had spent hours in the coffee houses and bookstores, centers of the downtown scene, fascinated with the way the Beats used words. The neighborhood emerged from that decade as a boiling pot of rebellion. The community nurtured his creativity. He found support for his ideas and a place where he could feel at home; maybe the first place. He smiled while he sipped his glass of seltzer.

"Yeah I know. You're right; organizing, education. I just don't know how we're gonna get to them," Chico shifted his bulk in the chair as he spoke. "Rolón got people really confused."

"Look, you have to cut through Rolón's bullshit and highlight the issues. Some kind of creative direct action maybe?"

"You're old school, Jack. It's not the 60s anymore. I'm not sure we could get enough people to pull it off."

"I'm surprised to hear you this dispirited, Chico! I hate where this society has gone, but you always have to believe in potentiality. Think about it in ecological terms. Broaden your analysis; connect it up with other issues affecting the neighborhood. Bring in other groups."

Hoffman took another sip of seltzer. "Never underestimate the power of non-violent direct action! I remember my fist time, when I was with CORE. We had a sit in at the Woolworth's Lunch counter on 8th St. They were segregated through the whole South. Do you remember that place? It was disgusting. So we sat there, at the grimy formica counter waiting for the cops to come arrest us. I didn't know what to expect. In the labor movement, we fought back, we didn't just sit there to be arrested. Well, it didn't take too long before the cops from the 5th Precinct came over and dragged us out. But we made our point, we got lots of support, and, while we still haven't won the war, at least we won that battle."

In CORE, at least in their local chapter, they operated without leaders in a freewheeling style that suited Hoffman well. He found a group of people with whom he could share ideas. They rented a large loft on Fourth Street and a dozen or so of them had started living there together. The commune had no rules and no formal structure, but it worked.

"You know", Hoffman continued, "This neighborhood, has always been a magnet for people on the margins, all kinds of immigrants: Irish, Jews, Italians, Puerto Ricans... They came looking for freedom and democracy; didn't really find it, but they forced this country to move closer to its ideals. Then came the young people looking for something different; liberation from suburbia, bureaucracy. For a few years it seemed like anything was possible down here. America's youth were coming alive, challenging the American Dream, biting the hand that fed them. Some of that spirit must still exists here, you would know better than me where to find it, but you've got to tap into it"

"Maybe, Jack... We had some punk rockers at the meeting the other night. But I don't know..."

"Really?" Jack thought about Sonia's great granddaughter, raised a bushy eyebrow, and then drained his seltzer. "Chico, you're sure I can't get you anything?

Coffee, a little sandwich?" He rose, then shuffled back to the kitchen to add the empty glass to the pile of dirty dishes already filling the sink.

"It's true it's not the 60s anymore, for better or worse." Hoffman settled back into the worn grey couch. "They were more hopeful times, but we were so naïve. I like to believe that we've learned something since then. Think about all the mistakes we made. Every new struggle is a chance to move things a little further along. We've got to become more self conscious Chico, remember the past and take the lessons it offers."

"But Jack, there really isn't any movement any more, you know that. Sure, you can talk about praxis! I'm just saying there's not a lot to work with out there."

"Praxis shmaxis! It's just learning by doing -- put the ideas in action, see what happens, change the ideas based on what you learn."

"Jack, it's different times. We don't have a war."

Hoffman was a key organizer of the first mass anti-war protest in New York -- the Fifth Avenue Peace Parade. He remembered he and his group marching together under a black flag. The sky was clear and the day was sunny. In Central Park, near Columbus Circle, there was a ring of drummers, and, in their center, a young woman dancing to the beat. Other groups gathered with their placards and banners proclaiming "Peace Now" and "Bring the Troops Home." Thousands of people jammed the park.

And then, finally, the marchers headed out, across Central Park South and down 5th Avenue. Hoffman and his cohorts were only a few blocks from the rally point at the United Nations when they came to a spot where the march route was lined with hecklers, a mob shouting; "Go back to Russia!", "America, love it or leave it!", "Fuck you, you commie bastards!" Hoffman looked at their faces filled with hate, and shuddered. The angry crowd was held back by a thin line of cops.

When Hoffman's group entered the gauntlet, suddenly the cops stepped aside, and the mob rushed them. They were all over the marchers with clubs and fists. They pummeled the protesters, kicked them when they fell to the ground and splattered them with red paint.

The marchers fought back as best they could, but their attackers were all athletic young men. The cops just stood by and watched. Jack was the group's standard bearer, carrying the black flag of anarchism for all the world to see. Four of the thugs headed straight for him. He swung the two by four that served as a flagpole, but he was overwhelmed, beaten to the ground, and then they kicked him from all sides. People were screaming and bleeding all over the street. He passed out and woke up in the emergency room at Doctors' Hospital. Hoffman remembered and rubbed his shoulder, arthritic today as a result of the melee.

"Chico," Hoffman shifted on the couch, "we had plenty of problems back then too. Look at what happened to S.D.S. So much potential, until the morons took over." Depressed at the memory Hoffman rose from the couch and shuffled back toward his desk. He stopped on the way, in front of a stack of old copies of *Liberation*.

He picked up an issue. "Remember this, Chico? Summer, '67." He absently thumbed through the pages. "Newark and Detroit? You're right, they were different times."

"Oh, I remember all right, New York was like a Third World city that summer; hot, crowded, and ready to burst apart at the seams. And down here, the Lower East Side... The heat and humidity were brutal, everybody was out in the streets and the park, trying to cool down. I was still running with the gang then. That was the summer all the hippies arrived"

A huge influx of kids from all around the country had descended on the neighborhood, as they did on Haight Ashbury in San Francisco. The word was out: the Lower East Side was the place to be, a groovy, happening spot. Hoffman worked with the Diggers. They set up a soup kitchen opposite the Park in order to feed the migrants, and a "free store" where the kids could find clothing and other things to ease their way. Hoffman was amused watching the progress of these pilgrims to the promised land.

While he grew his hair long, in the style of the times, Hoffman was not a typical hippie. His day usually started with a bagel and a cup of coffee that he picked up at the Orchadia, the deli on the corner. He walked over to a bench on the south side of the Park, near the band shell. A small group of friends met there every morning to share news and gossip. "Did you see the body count today? According to MacNamara we've already killed most of the Viet Cong and the war should be over in a few weeks!" He was interpreting the lead story in that morning's Times, and a crowd had gathered to listen. He thought of the park as his agora, the gathering place in ancient Athens where Socrates met his students.

And in fact, Tompkins Square did serve as an outdoor classroom, where competing ideas battled for the hearts and minds of the counter-culture. The HariKrishnas were there, at the Western entrance, dancing and proselytizing in their flowing robes, as were the turbaned sufis, who hung out in a central area, not far from Hoffman, and, of course, the various leftist sects, leafleting and selling their newspapers on the promenade near the basketball court. The odor of patchouli oil, which always made Hoffman feel sick, mingled with the scent of sandalwood incense and the ever-present smell of marijuana.

Even then, in the middle of the confusion of the counter-culture, he was single-minded and his production was voluminous. He spent the entire afternoon at his desk, writing inflammatory articles and answering the mass of correspondence that arrived daily.

He had kept to his routine come rain or shine,

oblivious to the distractions and temptations all around him. He had felt compelled to work every day, afraid that the times might change again before he was able to have a sufficient impact.

Hoffman put down the magazine and turned back to Chico. He threw up his hands in despair. "I don't know what to tell you. You're right, it's pretty bad these days, but you've got to take a closer look. We've always got to ask ourselves; what can the given become?"

In the 60's he had felt buoyed by the young people who surrounded him. Their idealism and their energy were a tonic after the years of struggle just to keep the ideas alive. He was no longer a voice in the wilderness. He had an audience; sometimes it seemed like a whole generation, who were enthusiastic about his vision. But even then he had no desire to be a guru.

People looked to him for answers, and a part of him was afraid that he could not provide them; ideas, yes, answers, no. He tried to stimulate creativity in those around him, and to a certain extent he succeeded. Bright and talented young people came to learn from him, but they were easily distracted, partly because they were young and partly because of the way things were in flux and people were constantly in transit. And it seemed like nothing lasting could be built.

Hoffman, always intellectually generous to those he considered serious, was constantly disappointed. Eventually there were fewer and fewer people who he considered serious. He surrounded himself with a small group and concentrated his energies on educating them. They worked with him on his publications and lived with him in his loft. By the early seventies though, beyond this circle, while his myth grew ever larger, his real influence waned. His warnings had been ignored and the counter-culture began to sputter, as he feared, a victim of its own excesses. Its anti-intellectualism made it easy prey for every guru, quack and huckster who came its way. And they all eventually came to the Lower East Side.

"Yeah, the 60s," Chico nodded. "Hey, you remember that asshole Raven? He's been using his paper to attack us. This past issue he called me a sellout! Can you believe we still gotta deal with him?"

Chico's mention of Raven made Hoffman think again about his recent meeting with Sonia's great-granddaughter. "Chico, don't let him bother you. He's an ineffectual moron. No one reads that rag but the most confused characters, and even they don't take it seriously. Listen, I really think the key is to reframe the issue of *El Jardin* in ecological terms. It is not just about housing, it's about the ecology of the neighborhood; open space, culture, art, health, education, ownership and control, all interrelated. The things we always talked about."

Before most people even heard the word, Hoffman had thrown himself into trying to start an ecology movement. Most of his Leftist buddies, even the anarchists, pooh poohed the idea that ecology had anything to offer. "What possible relevance," Paul, a guy he knew from the Libertarian League had asked scornfully, "does ecology have to the proletariat, or the oppressed minorities, or victims of U.S. imperialism in the Third World?"

But Hoffman saw it all clearly back then and he began to build a radical response. Hoffman proposed revolutionary solutions to the ecological crisis. And he had developed an urban focus in his work that he used to analyze the ecology of the Lower East Side; to discover its problems, and to propose ecological solutions.

And so, Hoffman had begun again; the principle of hope he nurtured for so long, relegated by others to the dust bin of history, had reasserted itself in Loisaida.

"Remember, Chico? When we first met? You got it right away, You knew what I was talking about. You understood the ecology of the neighborhood even better than I did. Fascinating..."

"I just knew the streets Jack. I didn't know shit about ecology. I never heard the word 'till I met you."

"You're way too modest , Chico."

"Oh, bullshit! You're the one with the words."

"Maybe I had some words, but you knew the ideas my friend, and that's what matters."

"Thanks Jack, but I'm pretty much out of ideas for *El Jardin*."

"Chico, what can I tell you? Sorry I don't have any answers for you. *Illigitimi non carborundum*."

"What?"

"Latin. Don't let the bastards grind you down."

"Well, thanks Jack, I'll try. And at least you give me something to think about." Chico rose to go.

"No, thank you for stopping by. You know, actually, you should start coming to my classes again."

"Thanks Jack, I just might."

Hoffman got up and hugged the big man, then shut the door behind him when he left. He sighed, sat down at his desk, and turned back to his typewriter.

Chapter 26

"Jesus Christ! The motherfucker is really crazy. 'Remember Willy!' That's what Rolón said. 'Remember Willy!' Shit, ain't nothing to remember but some brains splattered on the sidewalk and a yellow chalk outline. If I knew it would come to this I would never got started. Crack is one thing. Damn, man's got to make a living. What am I supposed to do, wash dishes at some yuppie restaurant? But then Rolón sent me to start a fire, and then scare off some girl. I didn't want to mess with no girl, what's that got to do with crack?." Roberto turned his Yankee cap backwards on his head. The wind bit through his leather jacket as he and Julito walked toward the bodega on the corner.

"What's with Rolón and this girl? Why he want to get rid of her? It must be politics or something." Julito wasn't stupid, but he knew he was out of his league here.

"Politics, real estate, crack; man, Rolón has his fingers in a lot of pies. *Cabrón*, the son of a bitch pretty much said he would kill me if I didn't scare off the girl. Well I scared her, but what's next?" Roberto didn't know what to do. He didn't even know who he could talk to, who could give him advice. He felt overwhelmed, sick to his stomach with the waves of anxiety that were washing over him.

"I ain't no coward. Everybody on the street know I ain't no punk. I fuck up anybody who dis me. But this is something else. Rolón play by a different set of rules. The man has powerful friends." Roberto couldn't see any way out. He knew what he had to do. The street, for all its seeming chaos, had its own rules. He could see it now clearly. But he couldn't get rid of the feeling in his gut.

He thought about the girl with her purple hair and her nose ring. He had only seen her up close that one time, and it had been dark. She was pretty. He knew that she was scared that night, he saw it in her face, and he knew she was soft. It had been easy. Why was he freaking out over this? But he didn't have any choice.

"If you want to play, you got to pay." Julito told him what they had said when he was just starting out with the gang, a little kid.

But something inside Roberto rebelled. He had lived with violence, and he dealt his share, but always in defense of turf or honor. The crack earned him a good living, but now his sister was strung out, he was having doubts, and his mom wanted him to move to PR with his pops. Besides, there was no honor in what Rolón had him do. Only shame. Maybe it was time to get out. Only there was no way out.

Then he thought of Chico Santiago. Chico had come out of the gangs too. Maybe he could help. Roberto decided to talk to him tomorrow. He frowned as he turned up the collar of his jacket to ward off the cold wind blowing from the East River; it howled in his ears like a funeral dirge; long, low, and mournful. He was hit with a sudden wave of nausea and he doubled over, throwing up into the gutter.

Chapter 27

The *Avalanche* collective gathered at the office in Raven's basement that Sunday evening. "All right! How's everybody doing?" Raven swaggered through the door. They had been waiting for him for almost an hour. "Great demo the other day. I can see the headline now `Shining Path Battle Pigs: City Blasts Building!'. Who's going to write the story? How about you Cathy? You were there."

"So were you Raven," Catherine's voice was icy. "You're the one who threw the first bottle, remember?"

"I always try to take my leadership responsibilities seriously."

Catherine shook her head and rolled her eyes. "Dude, what happened then? We all got beat up and hauled downtown. Where were you?"

"I smashed a cop who was coming after me and got away. No point in getting busted. I'm a lot more effective out on the street than I am in jail. Besides, if the Pigs had gotten hold of me they probably would've tried to assassinate me. They're out to get me you know. They always target the leaders."

His glibness was disarming. Catherine wondered if he really believed his own bullshit, he mouthed it with such conviction. "Like, I saw you run away. You just threw the bottle and ran."

"Did I? I don't remember exactly what happened. The old adrenalin was pumpin' overtime." He sat at his desk, grinned and looked around the room at the unsmiling faces of the other members of the collective. It seemed to Catherine that he squirmed a little in his seat. "So what's on the agenda? What stories are we going to run this issue?" He spoke quickly.

"Well, we want to run Cathy's story on the history of *El Jardin*," offered Paula.

"No way!" Raven was emphatic. "We're not going to use my paper to glorify some reformist sell outs"

"Your paper?" Mike was angry.

"Yeah, mine! Who else's?" Raven puffed himself up to rise to the challenge. "Yours? You just doodle some cartoons, and nobody else'd publish 'em if I didn't!" Mike stood.

"Wait a minute!" Josh stepped between them. "We're a collective. We make decisions together, don't we?"

Catherine and Paula both nodded in affirmation.

"Hey!" snarled Raven. "Who pays for the fucking paper? Who bought the computers? Who lays out for the bills? Who's office space is it? Sure, we're a collective, but I've got final say. It's my money on the line, not yours!"

"Who does all the fucking work?" Catherine's voice rose.

"What, you think you're a great talent or something? Writers are a dime a dozen, I don't need you to put out the paper!"

"Hey man." Mike had calmed down. "All we're saying is we're in this together and we should all have an equal voice in what we print. That was our agreement."

"Take a look at the masthead stupid!" yelled Raven. "I'm the publisher!" He looked around the room at their angry faces. Realizing that he wasn't convincing them, he decided to take another tack.

"What's the problem? Have I ever been anything but fair? Have I ever killed a story before? We work on consensus. I'm just saying I don't think it's a good story, all right? It's a bunch of liberal horseshit. We don't need it." The expressions on the faces of the others made it clear that they remained unconvinced.

"Dude, we need democracy on the paper." Catherine was insistent. "How can we preach freedom when we don't practice it ourselves?"

"Listen, you've got more freedom on *The Avalanche* than you do anywhere else in your life. We've got a great thing going here. Don't blow it." Raven glared at her.

"Is that a threat?" asked Josh.

"Do you really think I need you?" Raven sputtered. "I can replace all of you like that!" He snapped his fingers. "Anybody who doesn't like it can leave! We'll get along fine without you. Can I make myself any clearer?"

"Oh, I guess that's pretty clear, you fucking asshole! It's as much our paper as yours, even more. Why don't you leave?" Catherine glared at him.

"Yeah, sure!" Raven laughed. Mike put his hand on Catherine's shoulder.

Paula tried again. "We just want some clear guidelines for collective decision making."

"We're supposed to be anarchists. We don't need guidelines!" Raven sneered. "Come on, we've got work to do. We've got an issue to get out. I don't have time for this bullshit! You're either with me, or you're not. It's that simple."

No one rose to leave and Raven seemed oblivious to the displeasure of the collective. "Okay, now that that's settled, let's get to work."

Chapter 28

Catherine was at the library on Tompkins Square. It was Saturday afternoon and Mike had gone to ABCs with Bobby and Riff to have a few beers. She looked up from her book as Paula approached.

"Your great-grandmother," Paula was gasping for breath.

"What about her?"

"They called me from the nursing home. Something's happened; they want you over there right away. I came to tell you," Paula panted.

"What? Is she all right?" Catherine brow furrowed.

"I'm not sure," answered Paula. "Heart attack or something. Sounds pretty serious. How old is she anyway? Isn't she really ancient?"

"Ninety three," Catherine fumbled for her leather jacket. "I've got to go. Can you tell Mike? He's over at ABC's, or I'll leave him a note. I've got to go now."

"Don't worry, I'll tell him. I'm heading over there. Are you O.K. Cathy? I mean you don't look so good yourself." The color had drained from Catherine's face.

"Yeah, sure, I'm fine. Listen, I've got to run!" Catherine bolted out of the reading room and ran down the stairs as fast as she could manage them. She burst out of the double doors, leaped down to the stoop and turned toward the East River, still running, not noticing the warm wind blowing from the south, which under other circumstances would have delighted her.

Sonia lay on her bed. There was a respirator on the stand next to her and she was wired into a monitor that showed a slow heartbeat. The doctor and nurses were amazed. They thought the first spasm of her heart would lead to cardiac arrest. She surprised them all with her resilience. When she had the heart attack they gave her oxygen. They fully expected that she would not last the night. But she had, and when she woke she asked them to contact Catherine.

Her heartbeat on the monitor was weak but regular. She was asleep when Catherine entered the room. The desk nurse told her what had happened, but still Catherine wasn't prepared for what she saw. Sonia's skin was gray and she was lying inert on her bed. So still, in fact, that Catherine thought her dead until she saw the old woman half-open her eyes. "You've come," Sonia spoke slowly, in a horse, barely audible whisper.

"Oh, Grandma!" Catherine tried to choke back the tears she felt welling up.

"I was selfish," whispered Sonia. "I wanted to see

you again. My darling, my Cathy, your visits mean so much." Sonia fell silent, gasping for breath. Catherine reached down and took her great grandmother's hand, translucent skin stretched thin over bones and blue veins. Sonia's labored breathing steadied and after a time she began again. "You're a good girl."

"Don't talk, Grandma. It's O.K."

"I tried to tell you a few things but now it's too late for me."

"Don't say that, Grandma! You'll be fine."

"Don't be ridiculous, darling. Of course I'll die. I'm ninety-three. I should die. It's nature's way." She stopped to catch her breath, and then continued. "But I'm counting on you. You must do something for me, something important." She looked up at Catherine with her clouded gray eyes. "Keep the idea alive, darling. Don't let our vision get lost, don't let our dreams die. There must be hope Cathy, always. This is what I lived my life for." Sonia fell silent again, gasping.

"Yes, Grandma, of course, I promise. I won't let you down." Catherine stroked Sonia's hand reassuringly. She took a tissue from the bedside stand and wiped a drop of spittle from the corner of the old woman's mouth. "Don't worry Grandma, relax, go to sleep."

Sonia's eyes closed and her breathing became more regular as she drifted into sleep, exhausted from the exertion of speaking. Catherine continued to sit by her, holding her hand. There was nothing she could offer except her presence. But maybe it was enough just to be there. She wondered if her parents knew. Would they come even if they did? Sonia seemed little more than an afterthought to them.

Catherine had been sitting there for a half an hour when Sonia stirred again. Her cloudy eyes opened and she seemed momentarily disoriented. Then she focused on Catherine. "Don't let the dream die, darling. I won't live to see it come true. It doesn't matter. Some day…" A spasm shook her frail body, stiffening her for a moment before she collapsed.

"Oh, Fuck! No!!!" Catherine screamed. "Grandma! No!" She pounded the wall with rage. A nurse came running. They tried to revive Sonia, but she was gone. The nurse put her arm around Catherine, to offer comfort. But Catherine pushed her away and staggered out of the room, her body wracked with sobs. She ran down the stairs and out of the nursing home, salty drops streaming down her cheeks. She had lost Sonia. The old anarchist had slipped away forever.

Chapter 29

A memorial meeting was held a few days after Sonia's death, called by the Libertarian League. It had been years since Sonia attended a meeting there, but they remembered her. The mourners met in the basement room of the Workman's Circle, on Eighth Avenue, near Twenty Ninth Street.

It was a rainy evening and Mike and Catherine tried to find a cab to take them cross-town. They wound up waiting fifteen minutes for a bus, and by the time it arrived they were both soaked and shivering. They entered the room where twenty or thirty people milled around. They were mostly old, though there was a smattering of young punk types. The only person Catherine recognized was Jack Hoffman, who she studiously avoided.

She and Mike gravitated to a folding table that held a tray of butter cookies, a jug of cider and a coffee urn. They each took a cup of coffee and stood there awkwardly, warming themselves and waiting for the memorial to begin. Catherine walked over to another table, this one full of books, pamphlets, magazines and newspapers. Several of Jack Hoffman's books were prominently displayed, but so too, she noted with pride, was the latest issue of *The Avalanche*. She picked up a copy of Hoffman's *Ecology and Ethics* and flipped through it absently, killing time until things got started.

She noticed that Hoffman was surrounded by a group of admirers, both young and old. He saw her for the first time and acknowledged her with a nod of his almost bald head. "There's Hoffman," she whispered to Mike. "That jerk I was telling you about. Like, he was her friend, so I guess he has a right to be here. But I can't stand the guy. What an asshole!"

People began to drift into the circle of folding chairs arrayed in the center of the hall. Mike and Catherine joined the gathering crowd and sat, with their backs facing the entrance to the meeting room. She was anxious for things to get underway. She wasn't sure what to expect, but she hoped for some solace, and she was touched by the fact that someone had cared enough about Sonia to call the meeting.

She was also anxious because she had to rush to work as soon as it was over. She had a fight with her boss about getting time off to attend, and he relented only after she promised to come in as soon as the ceremony ended.

An older man, in his fifties or sixties, with a full head of gray hair, wearing a tweed jacket, began. "We all knew Sonia, as a comrade, a friend, a relative," he nodded toward Catherine, "and as a true anarchist." She assumed that Hoffman had pointed her out to the speaker. "We are here not to mourn her death, but to celebrate her life; to remember her in public so that we may each privately cherish those memories. There is no structure, no formal ceremony here tonight. We sit in a circle and those who have something to say can speak when the spirit moves them. This is the way Sonia would have wanted it.

"Even though it's been several years since Sonia was able to come around, I know that her heart was always with us. I remember when I came to my first meeting here, in the early sixties." He paused "I was doing research for my dissertation and I was very nervous. But Sonia made a point of coming up and putting me at ease. She introduced me to all of the other old-timers.

"She had a wonderful way about her, caring, she really cared about people, not just humanity in the abstract but individuals, real people. She befriended me, and took an interest in my research. I couldn't have done it without her. She got me interviews with everyone I needed to talk to, and later helped me to translate some of the Yiddish pamphlets I was working with.

"And the stories she told me about her own life. I could have written a book about Sonia herself. Amazing, really; she knew everyone, and was involved with all of the significant struggles of her era. In many ways she embodied the whole history of the move-ment in New York.

"She was an extraordinary women; generous, kind, and above all, committed. She was an idealist, and she admired idealism in others. She was a remarkable per-son, truly remarkable."

After he spoke, silence engulfed the room. It was probably a minute before a woman wearing a black jumpsuit rose. She had jet-black hair and she tossed her head before speaking. With her heavy makeup it was impossible to tell her age, she might have been fifty, or she might have been seventy. Catherine real-ized that she had seen her somewhere before, but she couldn't place her.

The woman projected her voice out into the room. "When we began the theater, Sonia was a huge sup-porter. She came to all of our performances. She helped us make costumes. She was a marvelous seam-stress you know, before the arthritis crippled her. But beyond that she was a dear friend to me. She was like a mother, giving me advice, fussing over me. I feel badly that we'd been out of touch lately, first with Henri's death, and then with me touring. But I'm sure that she would forgive me. When I learned of this memorial I knew I had to come.

"If there is such a thing as an anarchist saint, she was one. In an age of cynicism she remained true to her beliefs. I will miss her greatly. We will miss her greatly. The movement will miss her greatly. There will never be another Sonia."

Catherine remembered where she had seen the woman now, on stage with the Lower East Side Puppet Theater, a political theater group that she and Mike had seen last year. Once again she found herself surprised by her Great Grandmother.

Jack Hoffman knew the woman, Rebecca Moore, well; and while she spoke he remembered the first time he had seen the Puppet Theater in action back in the 60s. It was a beautiful morning in the early summer, with high cumulus clouds giving some shade from the sunlight. There was a fresh breeze blowing from the river. Jack was sitting near the band shell in Tompkins Square Park on his usual bench, holding forth on the dialectic at his regular Sunday morning talk, "Hegel, Bagel, and Lox", he called it. He was lecturing to a rapt audience of Hippies, Yippies, Black Panthers, Young Lords and assorted hangers-on. He was sure that most of them weren't getting it, but that didn't stop him from hammering home his points.

Suddenly he stopped in mid-sentence. He heard tambourines and drums echoing across the park. He looked toward the sound with obvious annoyance. The others turned too, following his stare. Hoffman squinted his eyes, his glare turned quizzical, and then a smile broke out across his face. Stilt walking towards him and his little group was a twenty foot tall Uncle Sam, a grotesque and pig-like Uncle Sam, dressed in stars and stripes and holding a six foot long cigar. Uncle Sam was surrounded by a group of hippies dressed in white, playing kazoos and beating tambourines and drums. Several huge white birds, flapping their sixteen-foot wings brought up the rear of the procession. Three people carried each bird puppet, and the birds seemed to take flight as Hoffman watched.

The procession drew a crowd as they danced their macabre dance through the center of the park. They stopped in front of the band shell and a short man with a long beard stepped forward. He shook his tambourine and began to recite. "We come to celebrate life. Life over death; Peace over War; Love over Hate." The huge birds began to attack Uncle Sam, circling him and beating their wings. The crowd watched silently, entranced by the bizarre drama unfolding before them. The sun came out from behind a cloud, illuminating the scene with a golden glow. The birds began to call as Uncle Sam cowered in defeat. The crowd gasped and the kazoo band began to play "Amazing Grace" as the birds cawed and danced in triumph. The crowd joined them.

Hoffman rose from his bench and began to dance with the birds. He flapped his arms and spun in circles, sweeping through the sky, and soaring above the park. He cawed with the others, calling out, drawing the rest of the crowd in until there was no distinction between performers and spectators. The whole park rang with their caws and their laughter and the procession spontaneously moved out across Avenue A, stopping traffic and startling passersby, and then headed up St. Marks Place. As they danced on, people poured onto the sidewalk from the stores and restaurants. Hoffman felt delirious, caught up in the moment, cawing his battle cry to the sky with no further thought of Hegel at all. It was like a scene from a Fellini movie, one he had seen just a few weeks before at the St. Marks Theater for a dollar.

They stopped traffic at every intersection. As they proceeded down the block the drumming and the dancing became quicker, finally growing to a frenzy of whirling bodies and beating drums. And above it all, floating serenely, framed by the blue sky, were the white birds. As a measure of how times had changed, now Hoffman could hardly walk, let alone dance. Still, the memory was sweet.

Catherine was screwing up her courage to speak, gathering her thoughts. She had called her parents in Scarsdale to tell them about Sonia's death. They seemed sad, but hardly devastated. Her father, who was executor of Sonia's will, had made the arrangements for her cremation. They planned a small family gathering to spread her ashes next weekend, which Catherine had agreed to attend. That afternoon, when she learned of the memorial at the League, from a telephone call at Paula's, she called Scarsdale again. There was no one home, and, though she left a message, Catherine really hadn't expected them to come. Still, she felt disappointed.

Catherine was just about to speak into the silence when Jack Hoffman's voice boomed out. "She was an extraordinary woman, just extraordinary; a beautiful person. I probably knew her longer than anyone in this room, since the 1940s. She saw it all, she was a part of it all. Maybe she wasn't the most sophisticated theorist around, but she had common sense, and she lived her beliefs. She was a person of a sort that doesn't even exist anymore. If she believed in something she gave one hundred percent. She stayed active and involved right up to the end.

"I had an argument with her just the other day when I went to visit her at the home. She was a tough old bird. She scolded me. I used to love to argue with Sonia. She was one of the few people I could argue with and still stay friends." A wave of nervous, knowing laughter swept around the circle, and Catherine rolled her eyes at Mike.

"She was a woman of great vision and character. She possessed a depth of humanity which one rarely encounters, in fact never encounters today. She lived her whole life in a principled way. She gave everything for the cause. She never turned her back on it, not for one minute!" His voice was growing more impassioned as he spoke, and, despite her distaste for the man, Catherine felt herself drawn in.

"She stood for the life force." he rubbed his large nose, "for her dreams, for an abiding hope that humanity could discover its own potential. But she was no mere dreamer. She gave all of her energy, all of her intellect trying to make the dream a reality. She was a great woman, an inspiration to all of us who knew her.

"Books have been written about Emma Goldman, Elizabeth Gurley Flynn, and Mother Jones, but to my mind Sonia's contribution was equal to any of them. She just lacked their egos. She was a humble person, self-deprecating. But she provided an unfailing moral compass for the movement whenever it began to drift off course. She was a marvelous person.

"Sonia was no saint though; she was a living, breathing, passionate woman; a fighter who never gave up. She was born in another world, she immigrated to an America that was less than welcoming to its immigrants and positively hostile to its anarchists. But that never stopped Sonia from speaking her mind and standing up for what she believed in. She paid a high price for living by her principles. Her first husband was deported to Russia, and he died at Krondstadt.

"She and Sam, her second husband, were the mainstays of the movement in the years following the Palmer raids. They kept the idea alive, they nurtured the movement and worked constantly behind the scenes to make sure that it remained a living, vital ideal that could re-emerge when conditions allowed it. Her energy and her idealism were unflagging until the day she died. She was known and loved by all of the *compañeros*, and the fact that we can meet here today is in no small part due to her efforts.

"Sonia's life holds lessons for us all, if we're smart enough to learn them." Hoffman looked pointedly at Catherine, who returned his look with a sneer. "She understood that revolution can only be brought into being by struggle; that education is the key to that struggle; that communication is the key to education; and that real change can only occur when we exercise both our memories and our imaginations.

"She lived all ninety-three years to the fullest, and of course we should celebrate her. But I, for one, will miss her. I will miss her a great deal." Hoffman's voice cracked, and he stopped, tears in his eyes. Catherine was crying too, and as she looked around the circle she saw that she wasn't alone. Hoffman took a handkerchief from his pocket, sat down, and blew his nose.

When the sobbing subsided Catherine spoke. "I'm her great-granddaughter, but I feel like I really only got to know her in, like, the last couple months. I've been visiting her at the home, and she'd been telling me stories, about her life and the movement. She was awesome. I didn't know anything about her before, not really. I was with her when she died. She sent for me. The last thing she said was, well, like, basically, that now it was up to us to keep the dream alive. I guess the past couple months when we talked she was trying to teach me something. She did, she taught me a lot. But she also said I still had a lot to learn. I guess we all do. I don't know what else to say. Except I loved her and I'll miss her too. I really will."

No one spoke, and after a minute or so, when it became apparent that no one else was going to, the crowd began to get out of their chairs and move toward the refreshment table. Catherine gathered her things, put on her wet leather jacket and headed toward the exit with Mike. People clustered around, drinking coffee and talking. She would have liked to stay, but she felt pressured to get to work. As she was about to leave Jack Hoffman took her arm.

"Sorry about Sonia. I really am." He spoke in an uncharacteristically gentle tone.

"Yeah, sure, thanks. Me too," she was anxious to get to work.

"You know she thought the world of you."

"She thought a lot of you too."

"She asked a favor of me the other day...She asked me to teach you."

"Teach me?"

"Well, that's the way she put it." Hoffman hesitated. "'I give talks, about my work. We meet at my apartment once a week. I lecture, we do some reading together and have some discussion. She wanted you to come."

"Really?" Catherine was surprised. "And how would you feel about a `moron' like me being part of your class?"

"Maybe I was a little harsh the other day. But that Raven infuriates me. I have a whole history with him you know. But look, it's nothing to me. I promised

Sonia I would offer. It's up to you."

Mike, who had been ignored by Hoffman, had none-the-less been following their conversation with interest, and at this point he interjected. "Yeah, we think Raven's an asshole too. We're gonna kick him off the paper." Hoffman raised a bushy eyebrow.

"Michael!" Catherine elbowed him in his sore ribs. He winced with pain. "Where and when does this class meet?" she asked suspiciously.

"East Third Street, Friday nights at Seven."

"Well, maybe we'll check it out. Mike can come too, can't he?" she demanded.

"I suppose so." Hoffman, wondered what he was letting himself in for. The group was intentionally small and select. "It's not an open meeting though, it's a class. Only come if you're serious." He jotted his address on a card and handed it to her.

"Okay, I get the picture. Maybe we'll see you there. I've got to go now. I'm, like, late for work. I appreciate what you said about Sonia, though. I really do. Thanks." Then she walked out on Mike's arm into the rainy night.

Chapter 30

In the days following the memorial Catherine felt Sonia's presence everywhere that she went. When she stopped at the Gem Spa to buy a newspaper she glimpsed the back of an old woman with a thick white French braid disappear around the corner onto Second Avenue. Waiting for a cup of coffee at Leshko's one afternoon she was sure that she heard Sonia's voice in line behind her. When Mike met her after work to walk her home she felt Sonia's watchful spirit hovering above them. And Sonia inhabited her dreams as she slept on the futon that she and Mike unrolled every night on Paula's floor.

But despite the constant reminders of Sonia, life went on. Catherine made decent money at work, as the warmer weather seemed to be bringing out more customers. Mike had picked up a freelance job that kept him busy during the day. And they settled into Paula's tiny apartment.

Catherine spent an afternoon with Charlie the Rag Picker at a warehouse where they bought used clothing by the pound, putting together a new wardrobe to replace what she had lost in the squat. And she continued scouring the neighborhood for some place where they could set up a new office for the paper. She had no luck on that front, though, and was beginning to get discouraged.

"It's Friday" Mike reminded Catherine. "Are we goin' over to that old guy's tonight?"

"Oh, I don't know, like, he's such an asshole. He pisses me off."

"It was nice, what he said about your grandma the other night. He seemed like a really smart guy."

"Yeah, I guess he's smart, but he's, like, really a dickhead. I don't know." She had been looking through a copy of Hoffman's book *Ecology and the City* that she found on Paula's bookshelf. "Oh, what the fuck, his stuff is actually pretty cool. Let's check him out."

That evening at seven they rang the bell in the lobby of Jack Hoffman's building. They were buzzed up and after climbing three flights of stairs they walked into his book-lined apartment.

"Welcome. Come in, sit down. You're the first to arrive." He offered them each a folding chair from the stack leaning against one of his bookcases. "I didn't know if you would make it."

"Well, we're here." She opened the chair and shrugged off her jacket. "I've been reading one of

273

your books. I like it. I never really thought about ecology in the city before. It's, like, interesting."

"I'm so glad you find it interesting," Hoffman snorted. He was wearing worn, blue slippers with his usual khaki pants and green work shirt with a pocket full of pens. He shuffled a few steps into the kitchen, "Do you want some coffee?" He poured them each a cup from the electric percolator on the counter. The bell rang again and Hoffman pushed the buzzer. A few minutes later three intent looking young men, and a woman with long red hair walked in. They were in their early twenties, or maybe a few years older.

"Ben, Chuck, Eric and Rebecca." Hoffman, introduced them with a flourish of his hand. Catherine thought she recognized at least one of them from Sonia's memorial.

"Hello" said Eric, the dark haired guy Catherine recognized. "We live in the neighborhood. We're grad students at the New School. Ben, Chuck and Rebecca study Philosophy and I'm in the Anthro department. Chuck is writing his Doctoral dissertation about Jack."

They took chairs from the stack and arrayed themselves around the room. Catherine and Mike shifted in their seats while the others got themselves coffee. A few minutes later the bell sounded again, Hoffman buzzed, and then opened the door to let in an older woman with close- cropped gray hair, and, to Catherine's surprise, Chico Santiago.

"Hi Mary. Chico! Great to see you!" Hoffman

smiled. "I thought you'd forgotten us."

"Sorry Jack, but after talking the other day... You know. I hope it's okay."

"Of course, whenever you can make it. Here, take a seat." He pointed in the direction of the remaining folding chairs and poured the newcomers the last of the coffee. Mary introduced herself, "I teach Gender Studies at NYU."

They chatted for a few minutes as they sat in a rough circle around the book-filled living room, and then Hoffman began the meeting. "So, we're here tonight because we care about the future. Somebody has to." He chuckled and looked around the room. "We're here to educate ourselves, to learn what we can in order to become more effective politically. But, we define politics in a different way. We're not a political party. We're part of a social movement. At least we're trying to help start a social movement."

Eric and Chuck smirked at each other, and Hoffman glared at them. "What, you think that's funny? You think education is just to get your degree so you can become a Professor, a big *macher*? You kids are unbelievable." he snorted, shook his head, and took a deep breath. "We have to educate ourselves. We need to learn to think, it's that basic. You have no idea the extent that this society has eaten away our ability to look at it critically; the erosion of reason; the hype, the mysticism! More of America believes in angels and UFOs than in evolution! We're in bad shape if people are going to sit around waiting for angels or aliens from another planet to solve our problems, believe me. And the Academy is no better; the crap they're teaching in the Universities?" He looked over at the New School students. "There it's all Post-Modernism; relativism and obfuscation, or, worse yet, cost/benefit analysis! Unbelievable! What ever happened to ethics, and rationality?

"Yes, we need to learn how to think, and we need to learn from the experiences of others. We need to explore anthropology, history, and philosophy to understand the lessons that they offer, and always we need to critique everything we study, even my work," a thin grin crossed his face, "understand its limitations and its strengths. We need to think dialectically, to understand potentiality and transcend the given. You young people are so limited."

"Here we go," Catherine muttered to Mike "a rant."

"Once you learn to think, you can start to do what you call `outreach'." He laughed. "We need to learn how to talk with people; to have a real critical discussion of how things are, and how they could be. So we understand education, real education, not just classroom learning", Hoffman glared again at Eric and Chuck, "as the way to achieve our goals.

"And you know our concerns are not just environmental, but ecological in the fullest sense. Ecology is all about interrelationships. Like the relationship between environmental issues, peace, social justice, and democracy. The relationship between the global and the local." Hoffman used his hands as punctuation. "But this can't be just some kind of stupid, mindless localism. Are the corporations just local? Does capitalism confine itself to one neighborhood? Of course not! It will take an international movement to really change things, a confederation, but it has to be locally based. It has to start where we live.

"My agenda is to develop theory in order to apply it in action, see how it works out, and then revise it based on our experiences. I know it may sound silly to some of you, but we're trying to build a foundation for real social change." Catherine was twirling a strand of hair while he spoke.

Hoffman looked pointedly at her and Mike. "We have a commitment to work together. We take it seriously. If you're not serious, don't waste my time. Real change won't come out of a spray paint can; it's the result of sustained work; thinking and acting. That's what we're trying to develop here. We try to get at the roots of the present crisis. We don't just complain about Capitalism, which we certainly condemn. But we also try to understand the sources of Capitalism in hierarchy and domination.

"We want to take that knowledge," his voice was rising, "and use it to help people build non-hierarchical relationships and democratic institutions in their own communities. Only then can we solve the ecological crisis; it's really a social crisis. The attempt to dominate nature grows out of the ways we dominate each other; whites over people of color, rich over poor, men over women, straight people over gays. Only when we challenge all of that, the whole schmeer, can we achieve social justice; only then will there be real peace; and only then will we have true democracy."

"Shit, this guy can really talk." Mike whispered to Catherine, who, still playing with her hair, looked skeptical as she considered Hoffman's words.

She turned to Mike. "Yeah, but, like, it's all about him. Another old guy who thinks he knows it all."

Jack didn't notice. "We have redefined politics in a way that goes beyond how it's used now. It isn't statecraft, or the management and manipulation of public opinion. Not that cynical spin game they're playing down in D.C.. Real politics is the relationships built between people where they live, in their neighborhoods and communities, to take control over the decisions that affect their lives. It's a process for rationally weighing alternatives and making informed choices through direct democracy."

Catherine tilted her head, listening more closely. He was saying things she had always thought; things she had wanted to say in discussions with the *Avalanche* collective, but had not been able to put into words.

Hoffman was on his feet now, shuffling back and forth within the circle of chairs, gesturing broadly with his hands and arms, his voice rising with passion. "Our movement must always keep in mind a vision of a new society. Not a blueprint, not some flakey fantasy land, but a set of principles. Ethical principles that can serve as inspiration and ideals to help us make sure our everyday actions are moving us towards real change and not just reform of the existing system. We need to operate on at least two levels at the same time, the visionary or utopian, and the more mundane, concerned with the here and now; that way we can try to make sure that the little steps we take are really leading us towards a new society, not some nightmare.

"I know it's daunting, I know to some of you it sounds impossible, but the ecological situation leaves us little choice. Our current system is threatening the biological integrity of the planet. We run the risk of unraveling three and a half billion years of evolution. The dangers that we face are frightening, but there are alternatives. We have to take the slogan of the French student uprising in 1968 to heart. `Be realistic, do the impossible.' If we don't do the impossible, we face the unthinkable." Hoffman sat down. The circle fell silent for a moment.

Mike spoke up. "Yea, that all sounds good, but what do we actually do, how do we get there?"

Hoffman snorted. "We've got to build a majoritarian movement; one that can get beyond people's single issues and change the larger structures of society that are the underlying cause of the ecological and social crisis. Community control, decentralization, confederation, non-violence, direct democracy a moral economy...that's what we do, and how we get from here to there. We can't afford to have contradictions between our ends and the means we use to achieve them. So our movement must be ecological; anti-racist and feminist; non-hierarchical, rooted in unity and diversity, mutualism, spontaneity and homeostasis, all hallmarks of a healthy ecosystem. Failing that, we might as well give up now.

"Is it possible? I believe it is, but in the words of Erico Malatesta, 'Everything depends on what people are capable of wanting!' What do you want? It's easy to shout about what we don't want, it's a lot harder to talk about what we do want; our vision, our dreams.

"Sure, we've got to protest, we've got to say no! But we can't let it stop there. We've got to offer an alternative too. An alternative that we can make real, not some cloud cuckoo land, but a better world; one that goes beyond what's given, but grows out of it; one that draws on possibilities already here; utopian, but not utopistic."

"Sounds like a pretty tall order." said Mike.

"Yes, of course it's a 'tall order'!" Hoffman voice rose. "What is wrong with you kids? If not you, then who?" He challenged. "Who will do this work? All great social changes begin with small groups of principled people. Work together with people to stimulate your collective creativity; to build community and learn your way out of this mess.

"Don't fool yourselves, it's not going to happen overnight. If you're not in it for the long haul you might as well leave now. The ideas are going to have to percolate for a while, soak into the culture. How long? I can't tell you. Back in the Enlightenment it took a hundred years before their ideas made a revolution. Shouldn't take us that long, not with the media and information technology we have access to. But who knows? All you can do is try, and keep on trying until things change.

"We have to see beyond what is to what could be. I know all of this has fallen out of fashion with the post-modernists, but if we abandon reason what do we have left? Mysticism and relativism will never get us out of this. It's going to take a lot of hard work and clear thinking, not just instrumental rationality, but real reason.

"Are you up to the task? I'm not sure. You've got a lot to learn, and you're going to be tested.. ridiculed, persecuted, jailed, maybe even murdered before it's all over. That's the way it's always been with people who work for real change. Are you ready to make that kind of commitment?" He surveyed the circle with a harsh glare.

Yes, thought Catherine, I am ready. She could hardly believe what she was hearing. Despite her dislike for Hoffman, it made sense, it was like something she had always known but never been able to articulate. Still, she had questions.

She looked at Hoffman intently. "So, it sounds like

you have all the answers. What makes you so sure?"

"Look, I'm an old man. I grew up in the Bronx when the Grand Concourse was still grand. I've seen a lot. It's just that I remember and there are only a few of us left who are still active from the old days. And the old days weren't so great anyway, I'll tell you that. To be honest, they stunk. We started with the highest ideals and we ended up with Stalin. So we didn't know where to go, as smart as we thought we were. But I've figured out a few things.

"You think these ideas are new. But they're not new. You're just ignorant, your whole generation. Nobody remembers; nobody cares. You think history began with the Beatles. But you're wrong. You're really wrong. The things I talk about are old. The ideas have been around as long as people have dreamed about freedom, about a better world.

"You think communes are something new? We had communes in the twenties and thirties, and in the 19th century too, and before. Ever hear of the Gnostics? You think you invented free love? You think you're the first generation to ever protest? I remember these things, that's all. I'm an old man with a good memory.

"But don't make too much of what I say. I don't have answers for you. Memory doesn't provide answers, just insights. The answers are here and now; up to your imaginations. Dreams always depend on memories, but they don't end there. And you have to have your own dreams. You've got to find your way

282

yourselves out of this mess. There aren't any road maps. I can't teach you any magic chants or mantras you can repeat. And even if I could, I wouldn't. You're on your own."

"I don't want answers, and I'm not ignorant! Why do you think you can teach people by insulting them?" Catherine fumed.

"If I offended you, I'm sorry." He shrugged his shoulders. "But I'm surrounded by morons, present company excluded, and I'm not as patient as I used to be."

This was typical of Hoffman. He would sometimes make a point of ordering a hamburger at a table full of vegetarians. He enjoyed swimming against the current. It was where he felt most comfortable, and he wasn't about to stop now.

The class took a short break. Catherine brewed a fresh pot of coffee. Chico walked over for a cup.

"I didn't expect to see you here," he said. "Most of you squatters are more street-action types."

"Like, we're not stupid you know. This is pretty cool. Mike and I will be back. I was kind of surprised to see you here, though."

"Why, because I'm Puerto Rican?" Chico shook his head. "I've known Jack since the sixties. We've worked together a lot over the years. I haven't made it over here for a while, I've been really busy. But it seemed important to come again. I need all the ideas I can get, and there's always plenty around here."

"I got the feeling the other night that you didn't care much for anarchists."

"I don't care much for people who think all it takes to be an anarchist is an A in a circle. Besides, I'm not interested in labels, I'm interested in ideas."

He remembered the ideas he found the day he first read one of Hoffman's books. Chico had knocked on his door that same evening and he left five hours later. By the end of their discussion they had formed a strong connection.

As Chico began to define his own work in ecological terms, Hoffman had become more and more fascinated by his projects. Jack watched as Chico's ideas broadened and deepened. He was also impressed by Chico's understanding of the city and the neighborhood, as well as the young man's organizing abilities. Hoffman began to harbor great hopes for the Lower East Side.

"Since you've known him so long, can you tell me what he's so angry about?"

"Jack? I guess he's angry since he feels like nobody listened to him. He's been on the outside throwing stones his whole life."

"Well, like, maybe nobody listened 'cause he's so nasty. I mean, like, he has some really good ideas, but he's always attacking somebody. And, it's like watching a dinosaur or something."

"What do you mean?"

"Like, when he lectures, it's like one of those old

movies, like he's up on a soapbox or something."

"Yeah, well, Jack is really old school. He started out on a soapbox."

Catherine, Chico and the others took their seats and the class began again. The rest of the time Hoffman lectured about the role of local politics as part of a broad strategy for change, something Catherine had never thought about before. But she sat there listening with interest, both attracted and repelled, and she asked a few questions. He went on until after eleven. Her head swimming in new ideas, she and Mike left to meet Paula and Josh at ABC's for a beer.

Chapter 31

Catherine continued to search for a new office for the *Avalanche*. As she walked the streets she noted traces of the world Sonia had described; faded Hebrew lettering in gold leaf on the plate glass window of a bodega; a boutique on Avenue A housed behind an ornate facade that had "Congregation Beth Shalom" etched over the entry. She savored the yiddishisms of Dave the counterman at the B and H Dairy Restaurant on Second Avenue and one day stopped by Yonah Schimmel's for a potato knish. There was a thread running from Sonia's life to her own, and she felt it tugging at her sometimes in the most unlikely ways.

The tenements that lined the blocks echoed with the sounds of pushcarts and horse drawn wagons; it was as if she carried Sonia's memories inside her. She walked past the spot where Max Birnbaum had been clubbed to death by the mounted police and thought she saw a faint bloodstain on the sidewalk. Whenever she passed through Union Square she had visions of

Mannie, in suit and bow tie, addressing the crowd at the May Day Rally. She found herself paying attention in a way she never had before to the old Jewish men and women she saw buying bialys on Essex Street. She savored the sound of their voices, the sing-song trace of Yiddish that reminded her of her great grand-mother.

She missed Sonia with an intensity that was surprising; she hadn't expected it, but the old women's voice came to her as she walked the streets or lay in her bed. Not haunting her, but reminding her, "Don't forget! Keep the dream alive!" The voice, rather than receding with time, became more insistent.

Catherine thought that the spreading of Sonia's ashes out in Scarsdale might lay the voice to rest, but it continued. Her parents told stories and Catherine talked about her visits with Sonia. They cried together as they scattered her ashes under a row of lilac trees, bare under a threatening sky, but promising scented blooms in the coming spring. She took the train back to the city that evening with a shopping bag full of clothes her mother had urged on her, and a matchbox full of Sonia's ashes that she planned to spread in Tompkins Square.

Sitting on the train she thought about what Sonia had told her about her father. It was hard for her to imagine that he had taken the time to record Sonia's story, or for her to envision him as an organizer. He was so uptight now, so proper. But as she sat there she began to remember incidents from her childhood; the book about Sojourner Truth he read her at bedtime, and how they had both cried over the way children were separated from their parents and sold down river, and his outrage over the Contras in Nicaragua. Maybe he wasn't so bad. But what had happened to him, to make him change? And she realized that, of course, she was what had happened. It was a sense of responsibility, wanting to take care of her, that had led her parents to move out of the city to Scarsdale. They had tried to protect her and shelter her, like most parents do. Maybe Mike was right. She was too hard on them, they were only trying to help, but they didn't know how.

She decided to write them a letter, try to explain to them what she was doing with her life, why it was so important to be on the Lower East Side. Maybe they could understand. She sniffled, dug a tissue out of her leather jacket and blew her nose. At that moment she missed them, wished for an instant that she could go back to the familiar house on the big corner lot and spend the afternoon in the kitchen, like she had when she was a kid, making chocolate chip cookies with her mother.

On one of her expeditions around the neighborhood she saw a hand drawn poster announcing a follow-up meeting at *La Cabaña*. In the excitement of the last week she had almost forgotten about it. When she returned to Paula's apartment she phoned around until she found somebody to fill in at work that night and reminded Mike about the meeting. Paula decided to come too.

They walked into the cavernous lobby of the old school at around seven, and headed to the basement auditorium. The musty smell reminded her of the last meeting, but this time there were only a few people there, scattered in knots throughout the hall. Chico Santiago stood at the front. His shoulders sagged and he was tapping a pencil on the podium. He looked anxious, Catherine thought, nervous and tired. After a few minutes he began to speak.

"We were hoping for more people tonight. But I guess this is it. Why doesn't everybody come down to the front, so we can hear each other without shouting?" People began to move down, everyone except Enrique Langdon. *"El Árbol que Habla"* sat off in a corner, by himself.

"That's better." Chico smiled. "Now I can see you." There were no more than twenty-five people in the room. "Well, we did some more research, and like I said last time, you need to know what's going on. It's not a pretty picture, but it turns out that Rolón was right. It's all legal, and the whole deal is pretty much signed, sealed and delivered. All they need is Community Board approval. Rolón and Action for Housing will own the buildings. They got to rent some of the units to low and middle income folks, which means people who make up to seventy five thousand dollars a year, the rest can go to anybody, but that's just for the first eight years. After that, out go the poor folks, and it's what ever they can get for all the apartments."

Chico surveyed the crowd, which had started to grumble while he made his report. As he expected, they were down to the hard-core; Maria Lopez, wearing a red sweater, huddled with some other housing organizers whose names he didn't know in the first row; Pedro was there, and his usual smile was replaced by a grim look when Chico laid out the situation; Angie sat next to him, serenely knitting a pink sweater for her niece. The girl with purple hair he had met at Hoffman's the other night was back with her boyfriend and they had brought someone else with them. About a half dozen of the young bloods who worked with them in the after-school program had come. Liz Johnson, from the Green Guerrillas, was down in front with a handful of others from her group. Chico knew he could count on the gardeners. Overall, though, it didn't look good.

"It may be legal." Angie stopped knitting. "But that don't make it right! It still sounds like a scam to me. What we gonna do about it?"

"We can fight it at the Community Board!" offered one of the young bloods in the first row wearing a t-shirt with a Puerto Rican flag printed on the front.

"Yes, we can," responded Chico. "But let's be real. We only got a few days before the Board meeting, and Rolón controls the board. He appointed them."

"Let's get up a petition!" The speaker was a woman

who Chico knew to be an experienced housing organizer.

"Sure." Chico addressed her. "Good idea, but how many names can we get in a couple days? And how we going to get the word out to let people know what's really going on? Rolón has been big news, talking about how great this project will be for the neighborhood. How do we get out our side? He's making it look like anybody against Garden Towers is against low-income housing."

"Seventy five thousand ain't low-income!" Someone yelled from the left of the auditorium.

"I know," said Chico. "But that's what they call it, low and middle income. They call that middle income."

"Bullshit!" The young man was in the first row. "That's rich. How many people here make that kind of money?" No one raised a hand. "See, I told you that's rich. Nobody in this neighborhood makes that but the yuppies." The others laughed.

"True." Chico was tapping his pencil. "But that doesn't help us now. How can we let people know what's really going on? How can we stop the bulldozers? We can't give up without a fight." He paused. "I guess Rolón convinced a lot of people at the last meeting, 'cause they're not back here tonight. But the people who are here mean something. We can make a difference."

Catherine had been sitting in the second row. "Sure, we've got to go to the Community Board. But like Chico said, don't get your hopes up too high. It's time for direct action, you know, civil disobedience; that might work."

"What? Like rocks and bottles?" Maria, the woman in the red sweater spoke derisively. "You people have already screwed things up for us. If you hadn't taken over *El Jardin* we wouldn't be in this mess now!"

There was a low grumble from others in the room. Catherine scanned the crowd quickly, looking for someone to come to her defense. She felt her stomach tighten at the hostile stares that returned her gaze.

"Hold on Maria." Chico took the floor. "Can't be fighting among ourselves here. We isolated enough already. Need all the help we can get."

"Her kind is the reason we're isolated!" insisted Maria, with her nostrils flaring. "All those people know how to do is tear things down and make a mess! We don't need the cops coming in and busting heads!" She glared at Catherine. "You know that's going to happen if those people are involved!" Those around her nodded their assent.

"No! Non-violent direct action." Catherine had an edge of panic in her voice.

"Since when are you people non-violent?" Maria was angry.

Catherine swallowed the lump in her throat. "Look, I know that there are some violent people out there, but … I mean, like, there's no way we can win in a battle with the cops. We've got to make our point to the people, and some kind of civil disobedience is the way to do it. Like in the anti-nuclear movement, or civil rights."

"It would only work if we could turn out a lot bigger crowd than this." Chico's tone was skeptical.

"Of course," argued Catherine. "We turn out hundreds, surround *El Jardin* with bodies."

"You're talking a lot of people."

"We have a press!" Catherine, suddenly made the connection. "We can print posters, flyers; we'll plaster the whole neighborhood."

Chico's eyes narrowed as he thought about the idea. "Well, it's worth a try. It's not like we've got a whole lot of other choices. What do you all think?"

The crowd offered its support with varying degrees of enthusiasm, but it was clear that however reluctant people were, they had to do something dramatic if they wanted to save *El Jardin*. Even Maria agreed eventually. They spent the rest of the meeting talking about how to organize the action. Chico had his doubts, but he knew that he was backed into a corner. They formed committees, and by the end of the meeting Chico was feeling a bit more optimistic. As he walked toward the rear of the auditorium Catherine broke away from a group in the aisle.

"Chico, can I talk to you for a minute?"

He stopped as he neared the exit. "Sure, 'sup? Cathy, right?"

"Yeah, it's Cathy. Thanks for your help."

"Well, you had a good idea tonight. Who knows if it will work, at least it's worth a try."

"Oh, it will work." She spoke with a confidence she didn't really feel. She hesitated for a moment and then looked him in the eye. "Listen, you know that press I mentioned? Well, like, we need some place to put it, to set up an office and our whole publishing operation. You know of any where? Do you have any room here in the school?" She twirled a strand of hair between her fingers.

He took a moment to think over her request. "Yeah, we might have some space over here. How much do you need?"

"Oh, not much, just enough for a couple of desks and the press, plus a little storage. Like, a corner of one of these old classrooms would work fine. Could you really help us? That would be great!"

"You kick in some money for maintenance, say two hundred dollars a month, and we can probably work something out."

"Listen, maybe we can do some printing for you in exchange for rent. We're kind of broke right now. We can probably come up with some cash in a month or two." She was almost pleading.

Chico thought about it for a minute, furrowing his brow. "Okay," he finally replied. "You can move into 204. The paint is peeling and it needs a little cleaning up, but it's not too bad. You fix it up, paint it, we call that first month's rent. You want to get a look at it?"

"Oh, definitely! Great! Mike! Paula!" She called over to her friends. "Guys, come here. Let's go with Chico and check out some office space!" There was a ring of triumph in her voice and a broad smile on her face.

Chico, looking at her purple hair, wondered if he had just made a mistake.

They walked up the stairwell, with its low ceiling almost brushing the top of the large man's head, and emerged on the second floor. Halfway down the deserted corridor was room 204. The walls were covered with an institutional-green paint that was half peeled off. There was a pile of dirt in the middle of the room, which was furnished with broken desks, scaled for school children. The blackboard at the front was painted over with graffiti, but there was a row of large windows looking out over Ninth Street that promised air and light. Definitely a step up from Raven's basement, thought Catherine as she surveyed the room. She looked at Mike and Paula and they nodded.

"It's perfect! Just great! We'll move in next week."

"All right, but no lease or anything. We'll just go month to month, see how it works out, okay?" He was hedging his bet.

"Sure, no problem." Catherine agreed quickly. This was just what she had been looking for. She couldn't believe her luck. Maybe things were finally starting to go their way.

"Come see me tomorrow. I'll make you a key for the front door." Chico turned off the lights and shut the door behind them.

They walked down the stairs together and out the

lobby. Chico turned to lock the building. Catherine had not noticed Roberto, who had remained in the shadows at the rear of the auditorium during the meeting. Now he was watching them from the entry of the building across the street. He wore his Yankees cap backwards on his head and followed them from a distance as they walked to the corner.

"Where are you going?" Chico turned downtown.

"Over to Fifth Street."

"I'll walk with you."

Chapter 32

At Hoffman's that Friday night Chico broke the news. "We're organizing a civil disobedience for *El Jardin*. We want to get a couple hundred people to sit in and stop the bulldozers."

"Strictly non-violent," added Catherine. "Like, we need help organizing and we need people to turn out for the action. Nobody knows exactly when they'll come, but we got to be ready."

"Are you really prepared for something like that?" asked Hoffman.

"What do you mean"? Mike was angry. "You want us to just sit around and talk theory?"

"I've seen too many promising projects destroyed by focusing on action for the sake of action."

"But we've got to do something!" Catherine's voice rose in frustration. "Like, we can't just let them grab *El Jardin*!"

"I'm not saying don't do it. But think about what

you're really trying to accomplish," the old man pleaded, "not just the single issue. How does your action connect with your long range goals? How will it advance you organizationally? Can it help educate people and draw them into the larger struggle? Is it structured in a way that reflects your ideals? Is it just a protest or does it also have a reconstructive component?

"Make sure," he was on his feet now, shuffling around the small book-lined living room, "that you build an action that draws on people's highest aspirations, not a lowest common denominator. How many of these single-issue battles have you fought over the years, Chico? And why isn't there a more coherent analysis of the real sources of these individual problems? The movement will continue to go nowhere unless you can break out of these old patterns."

"What are you, like, an armchair activist? We're gonna take it to the street!" Catherine's nostrils flared.

The next afternoon at the community center, where the collective had been cleaning and painting their new office in preparation for the move, there was real warmth in Chico's greeting, something Catherine had never noticed before.

She woke at 7AM on Sunday, and made sure that her bustling around the stove to make coffee roused Mike and Paula. Catherine was anxious to get the day underway. They had decided that the best time to move the office was early morning. Raven and his minions rarely got out of bed before 1PM or so. They had borrowed an old Ford van from a guy Josh knew and Catherine had picked up a key to the front door of *La Cabaña* from Chico earlier in the week. Things seemed to be falling into place, but she was still nervous, unable to eat even a bite of the bialy that popped up from the toaster.

By the time the coffee was brewed Mike and Paula were up and dressed. She phoned Josh and told him to meet them at Raven's with the van. It was a beautiful morning with more than a hint of spring in the air. The blue sky and bright sun seemed like an omen, and there was a freshening in the southern breeze that bore the promise of new life.

The streets of the neighborhood were deserted, except for an occasional jogger or dog walker headed for the Park and a couple of stoned-looking revelers stumbling home from an after-hours club.

They walked west and saw the rusty van parked directly in front of the entrance to the basement office. Catherine looked at the empty space behind the van's front seat and calculated that they should be able to fit everything in one trip. She hoped so, anyway.

The previous Friday Paula had emptied the collective's bank account, apparently undetected. If they could transfer the equipment this morning without Raven waking up, Catherine figured that they would be home free. She held her breath as Mike turned the key in the lock and pushed the door open, half-expecting to see Raven there with his boots up on his desk. But the office was empty. Dust danced in the shaft of early morning sunlight that poured through the open door.

They worked quickly and quietly, first loading the folding tables into the waiting van. They removed the bulging file drawers from the cabinet and carried the files to the truck, followed by the case, the computer, the laser printer, jugs of ink, and bales of left-over papers. Raven was right upstairs, not ten feet above them, and they all stepped lightly and spoke in whispers. Catherine had goose bumps and beads of sweat stood out on her upper lip.

The van was not as large as she had thought, so they decided to leave the desks. The press itself, an ancient photo offset that Josh constantly massaged to keep in good running order, was the hardest item to move. It was a cast iron relic and it took all four of them just to pick it up.

"This is it," Mike grunted as he lifted the weight, "the last of it."

When they started up the stairs Catherine lost her grip, and the press began to slip out of her hands.

"Steady!" Mike hissed.

"I can't hold it!" Catherine had a vision of the press crashing to the floor, followed by an enraged Raven blocking their path to the van. Mike, holding his corner with one hand, extended his arm and took the weight from Catherine. Their end of the press tilted toward the floor. Catherine grimaced and found purchase on the slipping corner just before it hit.

Panting, they rested the press at the top of the basement steps, "We should have brought a hand truck." Mike said, while he wiped the sweat from his forehead. Then they hoisted their load again and carried it to the van. With the last piece in place Mike slammed the rear doors shut.

"All right!" Catherine cried. "We'll meet you over at the new office!" Mike and Josh drove the van and she and Paula walked back across Tompkins Square. Five minutes later they met in front of *La Cabaña*.

They unloaded the equipment at a leisurely pace. Catherine basked in the sunshine between trips up the stairs, and watched the neighborhood come to life as the morning progressed. Except for a lunch break they worked steadily until they had re-assembled the office in room 204. They found a pile of old teacher's desks in one of the classrooms and Chico said they could use them. By early afternoon they were settled in. They padlocked the classroom door and headed back to Paula's.

When they arrived at the flat Mike hit the flashing red light on the answering machine. Raven's voice screamed out "Listen you little motherfuckers! If I don't have all my shit back by tonight I'll kill you all!"

"We knew he'd be mad. But what's he going to do about it?" Catherine tried to sound confident. "Go to the cops? I doubt it. Fuck him."

"He says he'll kill us!" Paula was scared.

"He's full of shit," offered Mike. "Let him scream.

He won't do anything."

"I think we should talk to him," said Josh. "Explain it to him. Maybe he'll learn something. Maybe he'll change."

"Raven, change?" Catherine laughed. "Like, no way. But if you want to meet with him go ahead. Only count me out. I don't want to have anything to do with the guy."

"You know, Josh is right. I think we should all go meet with him. Settle it once and for all. I don't want to have to watch my back for the rest of my life. What's he going to do, really? He's a bullshit artist and a bully. We'll face him down now, and then he'll back off. I'll call him."

"Mike, why do you always have to be so macho?' Catherine implored.

"Fuck you! Why do you always try to run away from your problems?"

Catherine looked away and then sighed. "All right, go ahead and call him. Let's get this over with."

They set up a meeting for later that afternoon at ABC's. When they arrived they found Raven seated at a booth flanked by two of his dime bag dealers. The bar was fairly empty, it was still early.

"You fuckin' shit heads! Rip me off, huh?" Raven snarled when Catherine and the others approached the table. "I want my shit back and I want it now!" His eyes were narrow slits.

"It's not yours," Mike's voice was calm. "It's the

collectives, and we decided we want a new publisher. You had your chance and you blew us off. You made everything real clear the other night. We're going to publish the paper ourselves. You never did any work anyway. We're sick of it. We operate democratically. We took a vote, and you're out! That's all. Too bad you weren't willing to work with us."

"Fuck you!" Raven's bloodshot eyes almost popped out of his head. "Where'd you stash it? I want it back, now! You're not gonna get away with this!"

The four stood their ground silently. Suddenly Raven was on his feet and out from behind the table. He lunged at Mike, swinging his fists wildly. Mike moved quickly, stepping aside to avoid Raven's charge. Then he threw a hard right to Raven's middle. Raven clutched his stomach and doubled over, stumbling back into a chair. His companions stood there dumbfounded, and when Mike took a step towards them they cowered.

"Look, don't ever try to fuck with us again!" Mike stared at Raven, who was still hunched down in the chair and gasping for breath. "Not any of us. Understand?" They turned and left the bar with Raven cursing at them through his pain, a look of pure hatred in his eyes.

Chapter 33

The day after the fight with Raven, Catherine walked up the stairs and removed the padlock from the door of the new office. It still smelled of fresh paint, and the recently washed windows flooded the space with sunlight. Humming to herself, she turned on a computer and went to work. She and Chico had drafted a pamphlet earlier in the week that called on the community to save *El Jardín*. She entered the text both in English and in the Spanish translation Angie had provided. They chose an old drawing of Mike's that showed the willow trees and the amphitheater in the garden for a graphic. She laid everything out on the desktop publishing system and by the time she left for the restaurant that evening Josh had run 5,000 copies on the old press.

But time was almost up, and Catherine felt the pressure. The Community Planning Board would consider Rolón's proposal for *El Jardín* in two days. And it was only a matter of weeks before April, the time the bulldozers were scheduled to roll.

They had another strategy session at *La Cabaña* to prepare for the Community Board meeting. There were a few more people in the musty auditorium this time.

"I preached a sermon on Sunday asking my parishioners to get involved." Father Bob was enthusiastic. "I was surprised by how many people came up to me after mass."

"I been talking it up all over the neighborhood," Chico sounded upbeat, "wherever anybody would listen. More of the community groups are coming around and I think I got some gang kids interested. I've got a meeting scheduled with that kid Roberto. Says he wants out of the crack business, wants to do something for the community. We'll see."

Pedro reported that a city-wide gardening coalition had come out against Rolón's project. The group liked the flyer that Catherine and Chico produced.

"How many people can we turn out for the Community Board meeting?" Maria Lopez was hopeful.

"I don't know," said Chico, "maybe a couple dozen."

"It doesn't matter," Catherine interjected, "it's a lost cause, Rolón's got the board in his pocket. Let's concentrate on our action."

"Hey," said Chico, "they can't completely ignore us. We got to give it a shot."

Catherine would have to find someone to sub for her at work, but she didn't expect that to be a problem. Though she remained skeptical about the Community Board, there was no way she was going to miss the meeting, even if it meant losing her job.

The Board met on Tuesday night at the Library on Second Avenue. Catherine, Chico, and about twenty others entered the room ten minutes before the meeting began, and claimed the first two rows of folding chairs. There was an expectant buzz in the room as the board members arrived and took their seats at the conference table in front.

Just as things were about to get underway Raven burst in with a crew of four street kids. They held signs that said "LOWER EAST SIDE SHINING PATH" and "DIE YUPPIE SCUM". He glared, at Catherine, Mike and the others, and gave them the finger, as he walked in and took a seat in the fourth row. But when the Board Chair called the meeting to order Raven stood up, shouting "Save the Garden, All Power to the Shining Path." The crew who had entered with him took up his cry.

The Board Chair banged on the table with a water glass. "Order! Order! I want quiet or I'll clear the room!"

"Shut up you asshole!" Catherine shouted at Raven.

Chico shook his head in disgust, and pulled Mike back into his chair after he rose muttering something about killing Raven. The shouting continued for about five minutes. Four cops arrived, and, using their batons, prodded Raven and his buddies out the door and onto the street.

306

The Board Chair spoke again, "I declare this an executive session. We will not tolerate any further disturbance."

"You can't do that! This is a public meeting!" insisted Chico.

But the Board Chair, a balding middle-aged guy who owned a clothing store on St. Marks Place didn't listen. "We can't hold a meeting with you people here disrupting it. I want you out!" The cops complied with his wishes, ushering Chico, Catherine and the others out onto the sidewalk with threats of arrest and drawn billy clubs. There they waited, angry and frustrated, while the Board made its decision behind closed doors.

As they stood there Chico noticed Rolón's Mercedes parked in front of a hydrant on Second Avenue, though he had not seen the Councilman in the meeting room. After about a half an hour, while the crowd milled around on the sidewalk grumbling, Rolón stepped through the Library's double doors, onto the stairway. He had a smile on his face. "Fellow citizens!" The crowd booed and hissed. "You'll be happy to know that your Community Board has unanimously endorsed Garden Towers. We've got the go-ahead, and it signifies a new era of progress for the Lower East Side!" The crowd on the sidewalk began to shout with anger as Rolón strutted through them on his way to his car.

Chico wasn't surprised, but he felt betrayed anyway. Catherine was flooded with disappointment. She thought that they would at least get a hearing. She wanted to strangle Raven. He couldn't have done more harm if he had been working for Rolón.

At least their choice was clear. Now they had to prepare for the real struggle, the action to save *El Jardin*.

Chapter 34

Two days after the Community Board debacle the collective met at the office to talk about the upcoming issue of the paper.

"The name… I don't know", Catherine shook her head. "*The Avalanche*, kind of violent, destructive."

Paula agreed, "Raven came up with it."

"So, what should we call it, *Sunshine*?" Josh snorted.

"Actually, I was thinking of *Harbinger*", offered Catherine.

"What the fuck does that mean?"

"Don't be such an asshole, Josh!" Paula glared at him. "A harbinger is a messenger; something that announces change. I think it's a great name."

"Me too," said Mike. "I like it. Besides, we need a new identity, now that Raven's out."

Over the next week the premier issue of *Harbinger* took shape. They decided to feature Catherine's article about the history of *El Jardin*. She also transcribed an interview that she taped with Chico, which they ran as a sidebar. Paula spent hours working on an exposé of Rolón and the disaster at the Community Board meeting, and they reprinted the leaflet that Catherine and Chico had written about saving *El Jardin*.

Mike dropped out of sight for a few days and surfaced with a whimsical drawing of gardens, windmills, parks and buildings, the future Lower East Side, that they ran as a centerfold. They published a review Paula had written of Jack Hoffman's *Ecology and the City*. Most importantly, with a heroic effort on Paula and Angie's part, all of the articles were translated, and the paper was laid out to contain complete editions in both Spanish and English, something new for them. They were exhausted by the time the first copies came off of the press.

The following Friday night Catherine and Mike brought a stack to the class at Hoffman's. Catherine tugged on a strand of her hair while Hoffman looked it over.

"Not bad... *Harbinger*, eh? You know that's what Emerson named the magazine they published at Brook Farm. You've got quite a tradition to live up to."

"Like, we're gonna use it as an organizing tool for the garden. We're gonna win!"

"Don't think in terms of victory or defeat around *El Jardin*. Keep the larger picture in mind!"

Catherine grimaced. Why was he always so negative?

Hoffman's life was full of disappointments. He

thought back to another group of young people he had nurtured. The commune where Hoffman lived was one of the first. But others soon joined it with the coming of the Hippies. Hoffman was convinced that a high degree of self-consciousness was necessary to sustain any movement for real change. And the Hippies were, for the most part, unconscious. He remembered the Human Be-In.

The day got off to a promising start. There was still coffee in the pot when he woke up and he found a half a bagel left in the toaster. But the others were already gathered in the center of the loft, busy making banners and painting slogans. The world was going to change that day; they all knew it. It was all a question of attitude. Be here now. Love one another. It was simple. Why couldn't Hoffman see it?

Despite his misgivings Hoffman had allowed himself to be drawn into it. He brought a stack of pamphlets to hand out. It was going to be a beautiful day and Central Park in the spring was gorgeous. He refused to wear the beads they offered him, however. The others had laughed, but he was twenty-five years their senior. He had grown his hair long, and a mustache, but he had to draw the line somewhere.

A Human Be-In, Hoffman liked the concept; an anarchic happening, a gathering, a celebration, though the name grated on him. He watched the others dress in flowing robes and long skirts, bright tie-dyes and fringed and beaded buckskin. He wore his usual khaki pants and green shirt with a pocket protector full of pens and pencils. He was just going to check it out, take the pulse, read the zeitgeist.

He felt his mood lift as they approached the Sheep Meadow. Trickles of brightly dressed kids arriving from all directions turned into steady streams that fed into the broad grassy field and overflowed into the surrounding hills and woods. Banners flew overhead and the air smelled of burning incense and marijuana.

Drums, guitars and tambourines mixed with sounds of laughter and chanting Hari Krishnas. He shook his head as he walked by a circle of them dancing with smiles of mindless ecstasy plastered on their faces. He followed his housemates to a flat spot on top of a hill overlooking the whole scene. They lay down the blankets they carried with them and raised a huge black flag.

He looked around the crowd and realized with a shock that he was the oldest person in sight by far. He took a certain satisfaction from that fact, and began to poke through the bag of sandwiches they had brought. He withdrew a corned beef on rye, and unwrapped it eagerly. But then he was suddenly deflated. "No Pickles?" he groaned. "How the hell do you expect to make a revolution if you can't even remember the pickles?" Someone placed a daisy chain on his head.

He tasted defeat. They were playing. It was more about appearance than substance-attitude, not real change.

"It's going to take a huge organizing effort, but I've just got this feeling that we're gonna do it." Catherine's comments snapped Hoffman back to the present.

Catherine left class that night with her head spinning. She had never thought of herself as an intellectual, but she was intoxicated by the ideas she encountered there. Things were starting to make sense to her. These were not just words; they were connected to the world, and her life. Despite Hoffman's sardonic comments, she was amazed at her own excitement. It made her want to read more, to expand her background in order to enter into the discussions at a higher level. It was thrilling for her to discover this side of herself, a side she had always denied and ignored. Her experiences in school had been deadening. Now she found herself drawn to books and ideas that just a few months ago she would have dismissed as useless.

She did not, however, have much time for study or reflection over the next several weeks. She was too busy organizing the resistance at *El Jardin*.

Chapter 35

Jamaal left the encampment early that morning, to beat the others to the dumpsters. He and Lisa had a regular route that they followed. He headed over to Avenue A first; there was a market there, slim pickings lately, but he might find something. It was barely dawn, but he saw two others already pawing through the garbage. He looked around carefully, but he didn't see any cops, so he joined them.

He found a case of partly rotting lettuce among the empty boxes and began to stuff the best heads into the cloth bag he had concealed under his coat. One of the other foragers saw him, a tall man with an acne scarred face.

"Give it over here kid!" the man demanded. "I was here first, this is my spot!"

"No way!" said Jamaal.

The man walked toward Jamaal, snarling as he came, "You little shit! I said give it over!" Jamaal backed away from him, but stumbled over an empty box. The man pulled a kitchen knife from under his jacket. "I guess it's mine now!" Jamaal regained his feet and scampered away, abandoning the crate and his cloth bag.

He walked out on the Avenue towards Tompkins Square. Suddenly he felt a hand on his shoulder. He stiffened and turned around.

"Jamaal?" Catherine hugged him, "Jamaal, what are you doing here, where's Lisa? Are you all right?"

"We're down in the camp, under the bridge, just for a little while, Mom says." There was a catch in his throat. "I don't like it there Cathy."

"I don't blame you. Poor baby." Catherine squeezed him. "Like, what happened?"

"First we stayed with my Grandma, but she really didn't have room for us. Then we tried a shelter, but they stole Mom's purse, so we left. Mom built us a cabin under the bridge"

"Are you getting enough to eat down there, sweetie?"

"Not really. Mom's sick, we didn't eat much yesterday, that's why I'm here."

"Does your Mom know where you are?"

"No."

"Jamaal! We've got to get you home! Lisa must be freaking out." She took his hand. "Let's go. And we'll stop at the Korean Grocery too. I'll get you something to eat and then we'll go see your mom. Me and Mike have been worried about you. You should have let us know where you were. Maybe we could have helped."

"Well, you know Mom," Jamaal said, staring at the sidewalk. "She don't like to ask for help from nobody. I guess she figured there was nothing you could do. I mean, maybe you can give us some food today, but you can't find us a place to live, can you?" A note of hope crept into his voice.

Catherine looked at him and didn't answer. A cop who had been standing on the corner started in their direction. "Come on," Catherine took his hand and they walked toward a Korean fruit store where she had been heading, after working all night in the new *Harbinger* office. With Jamaal's guidance she filled a basket with groceries.

They walked past Houston St., down to Delancy. Catherine was amazed that Jamaal had come so far by himself. They found Lisa asleep under an old sleeping bag in a makeshift shack built of scrap plywood and sheet metal, part of an encampment of homeless people tucked under the abutment of the Williamsburg Bridge. The architecture was a hodgepodge of cardboard boxes, abandoned cars, plywood, and sheet metal shacks, canvas tents, and an improbable looking Indian style teepee, all stretched out with the bridge soaring above them.

Lisa woke with a start when they entered the shack. "Cathy? What the fuck! What you doin' here?"

"Lisa! Are you OK? I found Jamaal wandering around up on Avenue A, he said you were sick"

"Damn, Jamaal! I told you to stick close! What the hell you doin' over there?" Jamaal began to cry. "You know how lucky you are you ran into Cathy? Scare me half to death if I woke up and you was gone!" Lisa reached out and hugged the little boy. "Thank you Cathy! Thank you."

"Jamaal said you were sick, and you might be hungry. We brought some groceries."

"Yeah, I been running a little fever the past few days, but I'm feelin' a lot better this morning. Couldn't get out to get nothin' to eat yesterday."

Catherine opened a can of soup she had bought and heated it in a dented saucepan over a sterno stove, the only visible source of heat in the shack.

"Thanks." said Lisa. Catherine sat awkwardly watching as Lisa and Jamaal shoveled down the warm meal.

"We'll be all right now." Lisa finished the soup. "Fever broke, I'll be out and about today."

"Lisa, what can I do to help?" Catherine looked around the tiny shack. Their former squat was a palace in comparison.

"Nothin', nothin' you can do. We're gonna be just fine, this is only temporary. I appreciate your concern, and thanks for bringin' my baby home. But we'll be fine. Been takin' care of myself and Jamaal a long time now. Don't need no help."

"I didn't mean you couldn't take care of yourself, I just… I mean I'm your friend, and Jamaal…"

"I know," Lisa cut her off, "and like I said, I appreciate it, but we'll work this out ourselves. How you doin' yourself, girl?"

"All right Lisa, sorry." Catherine shivered. "I'm still over at Paula's. Things are OK; me and Mike are getting along better. We're working with Chico Santiago and that group to save the Garden. We put out a new paper, *Harbinger*. Dude, check it out!" She pulled a copy of the paper out of her bag. "We got rid of Raven and it's like, going pretty good. I was just working over there, I couldn't believe it when I saw Jamaal. I was heading home from the office after an all-nighter. I'm exhausted."

"Yeah," Lisa said, "That's rough. Don't let me keep you."

"You're not keeping me, I'm just saying I'm tired."

"No, no; we're okay now, just fine. You go on home. Thanks again for bringin' Jamaal back."

"All right, I'll go, but I'm so glad I got to see you. Listen, please stay in touch, Let me know if I can help with anything…I don't mean help…anyway, you know. OK? Here's my number again." She wrote Paula's phone number on the copy of Harbinger. "I'll go now. Bye, Jamaal!" She stooped down and hugged him. "Stay out of trouble. Listen to your Mommy." Catherine turned and left, with tears streaming from her eyes.

That night as Lisa lay dreaming, a smile played across her usually somber features. In her dream Lisa climbed the steps of a tower until she reached the top. A feeling of calm washed over her. A windmill turned slowly in a light breeze blowing off the river, its blades floating through the air making a dull thud with every revolution. The neighborhood lay beneath her, and Lisa looked down over a tapestry created by the blocks below, a patchwork of buildings and lush, green rectangles of vegetation.

People strolled, or rode bicycles down tree-lined walkways paved with brick, passing fountains and pools connected by narrow raceways of running water.

Downtown one of the blocks had a stream running through its center, meandering toward the banks of the river that lay to the East, freed from a conduit and tons of paving stone and asphalt that had buried it for centuries. There were long grasses growing along its banks.

The buildings themselves were the tenement houses that she knew so well, but opened up to allow fresh air and light into their rebuilt interiors. The restored facades and the detailing of the antique ironwork of their banisters, fire escapes and balconies gave them each a unique flavor.

The windmill on the tower was not alone. Other units dotted rooftops throughout the neighborhood, adding variety to the cityscape. Lisa could see solar panels facing south on other rooftops, and, on the river, some kind of generating plant bobbing on the surface. When she looked north, the shining mirror of a solar foundry caught the bright sun. She turned in her sleep and sighed with contentment, washed over by images from the centerfold in the copy of *Harbinger* Catherine had left.

In her dream she watched as the limousines of the one-per-centers filed out of the city in a convoy, abandoning their enclaves. She and others from the neighborhood mined the canyons of Wall Street and the towers of the Upper East Side. They tore down the Stock Exchange and carried a seemingly inexhaustible supply of steel, glass, brick, marble, granite, copper, aluminum, and brass to a neighborhood recycling center.

In Loisaida the streets and sidewalks had been replaced by the paths paved with recycled brick that Lisa had seen spreading like a spider web throughout the neighborhood. Gardens, pools and fountains surrounded the paths full of people strolling and biking.

She walked toward the river and picked a ripe apple from an overhanging branch. Below the tree, blackberries grew. The whole neighborhood was a garden. Trellises framed the doorways she walked by, heavy with grapes and currents. Vines climbed the walls of buildings. She glanced up at the rooftops she passed to see greenhouses overflowing with avocado, citrus, mango and guava.

Lisa paused to watch water splashing down from a greenhouse through pools hung like steps on the side of a building. It was filtered through a series of waterfalls and fountains, returned to ponds and raceways full of silver fish that lined the path, and then pumped back up to the greenhouses. The sounds and sights of the sparkling water cascading down from the rooftops were hypnotic.

When she reached the river it was dotted with the colorful sails of small boats. The Brooklyn skyline shimmered on the opposite shore. She stripped off her clothes. The sun felt wonderful on her naked body and she soaked in its warmth for a moment before she dove in from the pier.

Lisa felt the bite of the clear cold water and then swam toward a raft moored offshore. She pulled herself out and stared back towards Corlear's Hook from her seat on the float. Her eye was drawn to a mud flat and a marsh beyond it. A flight of seagulls rose into the blue sky and she could hear them calling.

She felt part of a whole; bigger than himself, bigger than the neighborhood, bigger even than humanity. But, rather than humbling her, the feeling emboldened her. As she watched the gulls she did not abandon her humanity in an amorphous oneness. She felt it above all else; her ability to reason, to create, to become aware of the rest of nature and its connections to her. This was what made her different. And, as in all things, difference was celebrated. In her dream she dove from the float into the sky and joined the seagulls in flight over the blossoming cityscape.

Chapter 36

"Look", said Chico. "We got to figure out a way to save *El Jardín*, but there's more at stake here than that. This is really about who owns and controls the neighborhood. Do we let the developers do whatever they want down here?"

"Stick to the issue!" responded Maria, the housing organizer. "You just gonna confuse people. It's about *El Jardín*, don't bring in this other stuff. You'll turn people off. It sounds too radical."

"Sure Maria. We got a real battle on our hands here, and we better not lose sight of *El Jardín*. But we got to make sure people understand how the issues connect." Most of the group nodded in agreement.

They called themselves "Friends of *El Jardín*" and they went to block association meetings, church functions, gardening clubs, housing organizations, anywhere there was anyone who would listen. All of Chico's contacts in the neighborhood were put to good use, though not everyone was sympathetic. Rolón's public relations blitz had worked, and the community was split. There were still people who saw Garden Towers as the neighborhood's last hope for affordable housing.

The "Friends" countered Rolón's campaign as best they could. They used the latest issue of *Harbinger* as an organizing tool, dropping stacks off for free distribution at strategic locations around the neighborhood. Chico and Catherine were interviewed on W.B.A.I., the alternative radio station. They plastered the neighborhood with posters. And they set up a table in Tompkins Square Park where they distributed literature and circulated a petition to save *El Jardín*.

More and more people came to their planning meetings and the list of names on their petition got longer daily. New groups joined their coalition. Mike's friends, Bobby and Riff, organized a benefit that featured their band at *La Cabaña* and brought in a few hundred dollars. Pedro arranged for the Poet's Cafe to host an evening devoted to *El Jardín*. And the Lower East Side Puppet Theater staged a performance that told the story of the garden with giant puppets and colorful banners.

Catherine knew the tide was turning against Rolón when she went into the bathroom at Leshko's one morning and saw "Save *El Jardín*" written on the stall. Their biggest break came when *The Village Voice* ran a cover story detailing the controversy and spelling out

Rolón's role.

Mike worked with the War Resisters League to develop a non-violence training committee. Affinity groups organized the action. They planned to surround *El Jardin* with a human chain and sit down in front of the bulldozers. They would not resist arrest, but they would not cooperate either. The protestors would have to be dragged away, and, hopefully, each time someone was dragged off somebody else would take their place. It went against all of Mike's instincts to sit limply and be arrested, especially when he thought about what happened at the squat. But he figured at least it was worth a try.

"What about Raven?" asked Catherine.

"Fuck Raven! I'm not gonna let that slimy son-of-a-bitch screw this up for us. If he tries anything I'll fuckin' kill him!" Mike sat with his fists clenched.

"Great idea Dude!" Catherine shook her head. "Like, maybe we can arrange live coverage on the five o'clock news."

"Well, if you're so fucking smart what do you suggest?"

"Non-violent direct action, remember Mike?

"Oh yea? How does non-violent direct action help us deal with an asshole who's got a brick in his hand?"

"Look." Chico sat on the edge of a desk. "I'm with you Mike. I'd like to kill the guy too, but Cathy's right. If he shows up, we got to neutralize him or we'll have a police riot on our hands. We need an affinity group that's trained to deal with his kind of shit. As soon as we see him, they surround him, isolate him, and don't let him pull any crap. Keep him from throwing anything."

"Can I break his arm?" Mike was only half joking.

"Michael, stop! You're part of the problem. He's still really pissed at us about the paper, who knows what he'll do. You better stay as far away from him as possible!" Catherine shook her head. "Pedro, maybe you could work with a group. What do you think?"

"Sure," Pedro replied. "Why not? I got nothing personal against the guy. I think that would work out all right. I'll read him some of my poems. Poetry hath the power to soothe the savage breast." They all laughed.

The "Friends of *El Jardín*" didn't know exactly when the bulldozers would roll. They planned to keep a twenty-four-hour-a-day watch over the garden from *La Cabaña*, so as not to be caught off guard, and they set up a telephone tree to quickly spread the news, figuring that they could turn out two hundred people or so from the surrounding blocks within ten or fifteen minutes. After that word would travel through the neighborhood quickly enough.

They redoubled their organizing efforts, going building-to-building, stuffing leaflets under doors. Catherine and Chico went with Father Bob to the ragtag settlement of homeless people under the Williamsburg Bridge. She saw Lisa and Jamaal emerge from their shack toward the end of a row. "Lisa!" she called out, "Hey, how you doing, feeling better?" They hugged.

"I'm all better, thanks again for helping out the

other day. Things are all right, at least me and Jamaal got a roof over our heads, sort of, and the weather's gettin' warmer. It ain't so bad, better than the shelter. I got some neighbors here I can count on. We watch each other's backs. Jamaal, he likes it. Thinks we're camping out or something! Right Baby?" She laughed.

Jamaal looked at the ground. "It's not so bad." Then he looked at Catherine with eyes wide. "Me and Momma are gonna get a house soon! A real house where we can cook on a stove and everything!" He hugged Catherine when she knelt and stroked his hair.

"So you're into this crazy shit with *El Jardin*? Didn't they hit you hard enough on the head the last time, girl?" Lisa laughed.

"You'll be there, won't you?" There was a hint of pleading in Catherine's voice.

"Sure, I'll be there, Jamaal too. What have we got to lose?"

The "Friends" went to City Hall. Fifty of them marched into the huge marble lobby carrying a banner that had "Save *El Jardin*" printed on it in bold red letters. "We want to see the Commissioner of Housing Preservation and Development!" demanded Chico. "To deliver our petitions; we've got almost three thousand names."

"The Commissioner is not here and I don't expect him in today." The receptionist was a middle aged woman with a Queens accent. They left the petitions and marched out to City Hall Park to hold a silent

326

vigil. They watched themselves, clustered around their banner on the six-o'clock news that evening. Chico's interview with the reporter was reduced to a five second sound bite, but Catherine thought they came off looking pretty good anyway.

They spent a day cleaning *El Jardin* and repairing the benches and amphitheater. A Spring Festival was scheduled for the March Equinox. It featured Pedro and other Nuyorican poets, Bomba y Plena dancing, a performance by the Puppet Theater, and Bobby and Riff's band. As she stood listening to the band with several hundred others, Catherine had to admit they were getting better. It was a mixed audience of Latinos, punkers, and other neighborhood folks. The crowd grew steadily during the day and Catherine left feeling like they just might have a chance.

The "Friends" kept watch around-the-clock beginning on April first, expecting Rolón to make his move within a few days. But days turned into weeks. Life went on; Catherine went to work, She and Mike started looking for a new place to squat. Another one of the crack dealers from 9th St. was murdered, the kid named Roberto, who Chico said he was going to talk to about *El Jardin*. The weather began to warm, the grass in the garden was green and lush; the willow trees in the park in full leaf, and the daffodils planted around the chain link fence that surrounded *El Jardin* had blossomed and gone. Still they waited.

Chapter 37

The warm weather brought *El Jardín* to life. The last time Catherine walked by she saw some kids playing ball in the grassy area, three young mothers with strollers sitting together on a bench in the shade of one of the willow trees and a group of *congeros* jamming in front of the amphitheater. The "Friends" planned a rally there on Earth Day. Every wall in a ten-block radius held one of their posters, and they had left stacks of brochures in shops and restaurants all around the neighborhood. They hoped that they could provide a strong enough showing of community support to force Rolón to hold off. But they never had the opportunity to find out.

The morning of Earth Day, April twenty third, at seven thirty, a flat bed trailer hauling a yellow D-9 Caterpillar bulldozer rolled up in front of *El Jardín*. The sun shone brightly in the morning sky and a gentle spring breeze blew in off of the river. A blue bus marked NYPD pulled in front of the truck transporting the dozer, and about forty cops wearing helmets and carrying Plexiglas shields got off the bus and deployed around the truck. The department's armored personnel carrier, a small tank, soon joined them, prowling the block.

Pedro had been watching from *La Cabaña* and as soon as he saw the bulldozer arrive he put the telephone tree in motion. Within minutes a small but angry crowd gathered at the trailer's tailgate. They were held back by a phalanx of cops as they jostled to block the main entrance to *El Jardín*. More people were arriving every moment, some still pulling on their jackets as they ran toward the corner. When Catherine, Mike and Paula got there at least sixty others were already in place in front of the truck.

There was a heated discussion in progress between the truck driver and the demolition crew. The cops, looking like aliens in their full riot gear, were holding back the crowd. They formed a solid line, five officers deep between the protesters and the bulldozer. As more people arrived the affinity groups began to form up and take positions around *El Jardín*. There weren't yet enough of them to totally surround it, but they covered all the entrances and stopped easy access from the street.

The demolition crew had lowered the loading ramp on the trailer and the bulldozer belched black diesel smoke when its engine roared to life. Some of the affinity groups, about fifty people, had already maneuvered themselves between the dozer and *El Jardín*. As the bulldozer inched forward, the cops, in riot shields and helmets, with drawn batons, formed a wedge in front of it and began to push into the massed protesters, who initially yielded to the pressure, falling back across the sidewalk to the main gate.

The line of cops moved forward, one step at a time, shoving the protesters before them. "Sit down!" Pedro shouted and the protesters stopped moving and sat. The cops kept coming, kicking, and prodding the limp bodies on the ground in front of them with their batons. Mike was in this first group. He clenched his fists, and winced at the memory of his last confrontation as the cops approached.

The cops began shouting orders and trying to push the sitting bodies out of the way to gain the 'dozer access to the lot. The protesters held their ground and things seemed to be getting more chaotic by the moment. The cop who was in charge of the operation shouted through a bullhorn. "This is an illegal assembly. You have one minute to disperse, or you will be subject to arrest." His force was waiting for instructions to attack, and Mike began to have serious doubts about the power of non-violence. He grew more nervous when he saw that most of the cops had covered their badge numbers with rubber bands and black ribbons. He took that as a bad sign, and he was soon proven right as they pushed into the front rank of the protesters, kicking and hitting people and then, one cop on each arm, dragging them away to clear a path.

The arrival of a Channel 5 News Team forced the commander to revise his strategy. It wouldn't do to have the cameras showing non-violent protesters being abused. He reformed his ranks. The arrests continued, with the protesters dragged off one by one, but nobody got kicked or hit. Then those who had been arrested were carried to the bus parked on the avenue waiting to haul them to the Tombs.

People kept arriving on the scene, but for the most part when they saw the cops they stopped and watched. It looked like war, with the tank prowling the street, a helicopter hovering overhead, and a SWAT team that Catherine had just noticed scouring the rooftops for snipers. The plan to surround *El Jardín* with protesters had to be changed when it became clear that there were just not enough bodies to carry it off. By now over thirty people had been arrested and another seventy or so were waiting to replace them. The banners with which the "Friends" had lined the chain link fence that surrounded *El Jardín* were flapping in a light breeze. Catherine held back to join the second wave, as had Chico. Mike had already been hauled off to the bus serving as a paddy wagon that the cops had parked around the corner.

Catherine sat down, taking her place among the protesters. She looked around at the earnest faces of her companions with a growing awareness that it was just a matter of time before the last of them was hauled off and the bulldozer went to work. She was

331

seated in the crowd near a young Puerto Rican man. He looked vaguely familiar to her and he nodded at her in greeting. Where was everyone? She wondered. Had all of their organizing been for nothing? Was it really going to end like this? She was on the verge of despair when she looked down the block toward the sound of cymbals and drums. The cops turned away too, momentarily distracted.

Marching toward them was an army of protesters; squatters, community folks, a group of homeless people and Father Bob. They were led by the puppet theater with puppets of huge white birds that flapped their wings in the breeze and a funky marching band that had been beating their drums and cymbals. They carried banners and were chanting "Save *El Jardín*". A contingent of cops detached itself from the main body and moved forward to meet them, in formation behind the tank. The group of marchers halted. A girl with dark hair, one of the puppeteers dressed in white walked toward the armored personnel carrier holding a flower. The crowd grew silent. The tank held its ground. Catherine watched, as did the cops, who were no longer dragging off protesters, waiting to see the outcome of the confrontation. The girl placed the flower in the barrel of the cannon mounted on the APC. The protesters burst into cheers.

Father Bob stepped out and confronted the cop in charge. He was waving his arms but it was impossible to hear what he was saying. Chico stood up and walked toward Father Bob and the commander, who were now surrounded by a ring of cops and a group of bystanders. The streets were filling up. The neighborhood had come alive, and people, emboldened by the appearance of this new contingent, were pouring in towards *El Jardin* from all directions. The crowd was swelling and more and more people were joining the protesters sitting down. The cops were standing around, uncertain about what to do.

Chico joined the conversation between the priest and the cop. It was now almost an hour since the first alarm was sounded. The block was clogged with people and it was hard to tell the resisters from the merely curious. People surrounded the cops on all sides. The parley between Chico, the priest and the cop continued.

The scene in the street grew louder with the arrival of Raven and a shouting group of followers carrying black flags and their banners that read "Lower East Side Shining Path" and "Die Yuppie Scum". Catherine saw him and her stomach did a flip-flop. All it would take would be one thrown brick or bottle to set off a riot. But an affinity group, which included Pedro and Angie surrounded them completely.

As the affinity group closed ranks around him, Raven snarled like a cornered dog. "What the fuck do you think you're doing?"

"We're just trying to keep you out of trouble, brother," said Pedro. "Here to keep the peace. This is a non-violent demonstration, but we know how the cops have you targeted, man. We're here to protect you."

Raven was at a loss; he and the others with him were encircled by twenty protesters. The half-dozen or so street kids he had recruited to the Shining Path shrank back. "Move the fuck out of our way!" He shouted. "We want to get to the garden!" He shoved Pedro.

"Hold on brother," Pedro calmly stared at Raven. "Hold on. We'll go with you over there, but here's the deal; we don't want any problems. The cops are on edge enough. We're here to make a point, not to fight with them. So we'll all go over to *El Jardín* together. This is about non-violent civil disobedience, so we're going to sit down and link arms. Nobody throws any bottles or bricks, or punches. You got it?" Then Pedro turned to the kids carrying the Shining Path placards. "You guys are going to learn something today. We've got to be very disciplined about this or a lot of people will get hurt. We're not going to let anybody screw it up. Now you're welcome to join us, but you play by our rules. Understand?"

Raven was fuming. "Don't let these fuckin' P.R.'s tell you what to do! What about the Shining Path?" He lowered his sign to the ground "Bunch of fuckin' bitches! All power to the Shining Path! You can't do this to me, I've got a right to protest!" He tried to bull his way through the group. Pedro and three others stepped up into his path. Raven shoved Pedro again, and his gang of kids started pushing against the encircling affinity group, who pushed back. Raven was sputtering "Get the fuck out of my way!"

A group of cops spotted the melee and, detaching themselves from the main group, trotted toward the confrontation. Raven saw them coming. When he shouted "Cops!", the Shining Path kids stopped pushing and bolted. Raven turned away from Pedro and, screaming threats over his shoulder, made his way quickly through the crowd, heading back to try to rally his troops. His shouts were lost among the chants of the other protesters.

Reinforcements for the beleaguered cops were being deployed, a troop of mounted police, who used their sweating horses to try to push the crowd back onto the sidewalk. Though the tension in the air was building the scene began to take on an almost festive feeling, with banners flying, and the colorful murals that lined *El Jardin* serving as a backdrop. The wings of the puppeteer's birds fluttered in the wind from the river and an ice cream truck parked on Avenue C began enticing customers by blasting a macabre version of "The Dance of the Sugar Plum Fairies" over its loudspeakers.

Chico, Father Bob and the chief cop were still deep in conversation, and the pause in arrests continued. The phalanx of cops who had been methodically dragging off protesters half an hour ago looked nervously around at a crowd that Catherine figured to be well over a thousand people. It was clear that the cops had underestimated the situation, and even the troop of horsemen was not enough to control the crowd if things got out of hand.

Apparently some resolution was reached because the cop who had been talking to Chico and Father Bob walked back to his main troop with the contingent who had split off to confront the homeless people. Chico, Father Bob and the group of protesters started toward *El Jardin*. The cops began to pull back and the crowd of protesters burst into applause.

"Dude, what's happening?" Catherine asked Chico, as he rejoined her at the gate.

"They're going to let us have our Earth Day Celebration! They're backing off!" The bulldozer was being reloaded on its transporter, the tank rumbled off, and the cops were withdrawing from *El Jardin*. "I guess the higher-ups didn't like the way it was going."

"You mean we won?" Catherine was amazed.

"We'll see." Chico sighed. "At least they're not tearing anything down today."

"Unbelievable!" Just then Catherine noticed a tall figure making his way through the crowd. "Mike!" She waved her arms. He joined them. "I thought you were arrested."

"I was, but they issued citations and let us go, didn't even ask for I.D., so I gave a phony name. I thought I'd come back and get arrested again. But this is great! They've pulled out! We saved *El Jardin*!"

With the departure of the cops the crowd heaved a collective sigh of relief. A few people left, but over a thousand still remained. The Friends of *El Jardin* went ahead with the Earth Day program they had planned.

For Catherine the highlight was Enrique Langdon, "*El Árbol que Habla*", who had been sitting to block the 'dozer a row or two behind Catherine. She had noticed him writing in a dog-eared notebook. He got up and read a poem. Angie translated for her.

Today a tree is planted here,
Like a palm I placed in the warm earth,
near my farm in Carite,
The palm has grown tall,

When the south wind blows through her branches,
The coconuts speak,
Sing me a song remind me
to nourish my dreams on her sweet milk

That is the way of trees
They take root
Here today, our tree
digging deep beneath the concrete
the roots, ancient, gnarled
but still able to grow,
put forth shoots and bear fruit
to nourish our dreams in our garden.

She listened to his words, was swept up by their rhythm and carried along by his voice, ringing out across *El Jardin*, up the gray streets and across to the river. When he was done she went up to him and embraced him.

They celebrated well past dark, lighting a fire of scrap wood gathered from a nearby vacant lot to ward off the night's chill. The flames danced into the night and they went home with the glow of satisfaction that comes with victory.

They knew the bulldozers would return, and they established another watch. Two weeks went by, and the threat seemed to recede. Charlie the Rag Picker, who was on guard, brought along a bottle of wine to help him through the long night. He drank it and fell asleep.

The bulldozer returned at four A.M., and began the destruction of *El Jardin*, without anyone there to witness it. By the time the alarm was sounded the chain link fence had been flattened, the willow trees uprooted, and the amphitheater lay in ruins.

Catherine, Mike, Chico, and a dozen others arrived in time to watch the moon set over the rubble strewn lot as the truck hauling the bulldozer rattled around the corner onto Avenue C.

Catherine wrote an editorial for *Harbinger* that summed things up in its last paragraph. "Sometimes it is hard to separate victory from defeat. We fight and lose, fight and lose, fight and lose, until some day when we will win. *El Jardin* is dead. Long live *El Jardin*! Memory and imagination are the only forces that can bring about real change. Remember and imagine!"

Fomite
Burlington, Vermont

Fomite is a literary press whose authors and artists explore the human condition -- political, cultural, personal and historical -- in poetry and prose. A fomite is a medium capable of transmitting infectious organisms from one individual to another.

ta ta ta

Loisaida by Dan Chodorkoff

Catherine, a young anarchist estranged from her parents and squatting in an abandoned building on New York's Lower East Side is fighting with her boyfriend and conflicted about her work on an underground newspaper. After learning of a developer's plans to demolish a community garden, Catherine builds an alliance with a group of Puerto Rican community activists. Together they confront the confluence of politics, money, and real estate that rule Manhattan. All the while she learns important lessons from her great-grandmother's life in the Yiddish anarchist movement that flourished on the Lower East Side at the turn of the century.

In this coming of age story, family saga, and tale of urban politics, Dan Chodorkoff explores the "principle of hope", and examines how memory and imagination inform social change.

ta ta ta

The Co-Conspirator's Tale by Ron Jacobs

There's a place where love and mistrust are never at peace; where duplicity and deceit are the universal currency. *The Co-Conspirator's Tale* takes place within this nebulous firmament. There are crimes committed by the police in the name of the law. Excess in the name of revolution. The combination leaves death in its wake and the survivors struggling to find justice in a San Francisco Bay Area noir by the author of the underground classic *The Way the Wind Blew:A History of the Weather Underground* and the novel *Short Order Frame Up.*

ta ta ta

Kasper Planet: Comix and Tragix by Peter Schumann

Kasper from Persian **G**hendsh-Bar carrier of **treasures** What treasures Treasures of junk Degrader of the Pre**ciou**sness system Also from India Vidushaka Also medieval subversive thrown out **of** cathedral into marketplace A midget speaking swazzel language which **cops** don't speak

Fomite
Burlington, Vermont

❧ ❧ ❧

View Cost Extra by L.E. Smith
Views that inspire, that calm, or that terrify – all come at some cost to the viewer. In *Views Cost Extra* you will find a New Jersey high school preppy who wants to inhabit the "perfect" cowboy movie, a rural mailman disgusted with the residents of his town who wants to live with the penguins, an ailing screen writer who strikes a deal with Johnny Cash to reverse an old man's failures, an old man who ponders a young man's suicide attempt, a one-armed blind blues singer who wants to reunite with the car that took her arm on the assembly line -- and more. These stories suggest that we must pay something to live even ordinary lives.

❧ ❧ ❧

The Empty Notebook Interrogates Itself by Susan Thomas
   The Empty Notebook began its life as a very literal metaphor for a few weeks of what the author thought was writer's block, but was really the struggle of an eccentric persona to take over her working life. It won. And for the next three years everything she wrote came to her in the voice of the Empty Notebook, who, as the notebook began to fill itself, became rather opinionated, changed gender, alternately acted as bully and victim, had many bizarre adventures in exotic locales and developed a somewhat politically-incorrect attitude. It then began to steal the voices and forms of other poets and tried to immortalize itself in various poetry reviews. It is now thrilled to collect itself in one slim volume

❧ ❧ ❧

My God, What Have We Done? by Susan Weiss
In the summer before she is to be married, Pauline Black moves in with her boyfriend, Clifford, to test the treacherous waters of co-habitation. In the spring of 1942, Robert Oppenheimer and the Manhattan Project move into a former boys' school in Los Alamos, New Mexico to continue work on the atomic bomb. The newly-weds visit that historic site on their honeymoon, fifty years after the making of the bomb, compelled by Pauline's fascination with Oppenheimer, the soulful scientist.

The two emerging stories—of Pauline's marriage and of the development of the bomb-- reverberate back and forth, both fraught with the tensions brought on by loneliness, ambition, and secrecy. Finally the years of frantic research on the bomb culminate in a stun-

Fomite
Burlington, Vermont

ning test explosion that echoes a rupture in the couple's marriage. Against the backdrop of a civilization that's out of control, Pauline begins to understand the importance of persevering in her relationship with Clifford.

My God, What Have We Done? pokes among the ruins left by the bomb in search of a more worthy human achievement.

❧ ❧ ❧

"The activity of art is based on the capacity of people to be infected by the feelings of others." Tolstoy, *What is Art?*

CPSIA information can be obtained at www.ICGtesting.com
Printed in the USA
LVOW08s1059040514

384364LV00001B/9/P